THE GRAY CHAPTER

A COLLECTION OF SHORT FICTION FROM THE LAND AND SEA

Published in Canada by Engen Books, Chapel Arm, NL.

A CIP catalogue record for this book is available from Library and Archives Canada.

Print ISBN-13: 978-1-77478-153-1
eBook ISBN-13: 978-1-77478-154-8

Distributed by:
Engen Books
www.engenbooks.com
submissions@engenbooks.com

First mass market paperback printing: January 2024

Cover Design: Graham Blair

THE GRAY CHAPTER

A COLLECTION OF SHORT FICTION FROM *THE LAND AND SEA*

PAUL CARBERRY

ENGEN
BOOKS

For Dana and Rick

Because your fingerprints
are all over these stories.

TABLE OF CONTENTS

All that we see or seem
Is but a dream within a dream.

Edgar Allen Poe,
"A Dream Within a Dream" (1849)

THE OLD HAG

A violent boom shook the entire foundation of the house. Daniel jolted awake as the floorboards shuddered, short of breath and chilled to the bone. His breath was visible in the air. Despite the frigid cold, his clothes clung to his body with sweat. The bed sheets were drawn tight around him as he balled his fingers into a fist, grasping the sheets. The muscles all over his body strained as if held in place by some unexplained force. A red glow from the alarm clock by the side of the bed displayed the time as 3:15 A.M. Darkness appeared to spew from the sky outside his bedroom window. The horizon was a pitch-black gap devoid of any stars or moon. Except for the blustering wind, it was as if the outside world had vanished into oblivion. Something about the noises outside wasn't right. The tree branches scrapped off the window like fingernails sinking into flesh. The wind was a howling racket. Daniel's jaw dropped open with a hollow scream, terror contorting his face and twisting his lips.

Tink--tink-Scree-Scraa

Clawing noises rose from just outside his room. They sounded like nails slashing at the gyprock, spraying dust over the floor. An invisible entity crept down the hallway towards Daniel's room, the scraping sounds accompanied by a phlegmy cackle. A shrill chorus of tormented voices chanted horrible hymns.

Then the bedroom door creaked open. The hinges groaned as an unseen poltergeist forced itself into Daniel's room. Appearing out of thin air, an orange glow flickered and danced through the doorway and spilled into the room like a spreading flame. Deeper in the hallway, the sinister blaze glowed blood red. The edges flickered bright yellow, casting ominous shadows that spread out from the heart of the flames over the bedsheet. Decrepit hands reached over the sheets, seeking to grab Daniel with their gnarled fingers. Once again, he tried to shriek, but no matter how hard he tried, the clamour died inside his larynx. A fetid stench wafted into the room. A mixture of smouldering flesh and the sickly odour of sulphur flooded into his nostrils. Every breath became laboured. There was a moment of silence before the sounds crept closer, further distinguished now, followed by the clatter of nails across the floor disturbingly distinct. Before Daniel could react, the shadow intensified, taking on a demonic form while drifting silently with evil intentions. A resounding crash at the foot of the bed rocked the room, the dull thud of a body echoed all around. The bedroom fell hushed. Outside, the wind vanished.

Scratch-Tink-Clunk-Thump

At the foot of the bed, the smouldering flames flickered and withered. A crackling sound swelled and wilted away as the light died to a dull ember. A dreadful darkness shrouded the room. Only the haggard, gargled breathing of the Hag remained. A low croak groaned in the desolation.

From beneath the bed, a mangled clawed hand reached up and snatched a handful of the sheets. Abruptly, the bedsheets pulled tight before something worked to wrench them off the bed. Daniel's arm muscles pulled taut, straining against the unknown to reach out and hold on to the sheets. Without resistance, they slipped towards the foot of the bed, exposing goose-fleshed legs. For a moment, the blanket caught on his toes as the Hag tugged at them. It lingered for what seemed like an eternity before the sheet ripped away. Falling to the floor without a sound, it settled over the light, and Daniel found himself entombed in darkness with the old Hag. His jaw swung open, his voice caught in a hushed scream.

The Hag crawled onto the bed with him on her hands and feet. The bed shifted back and forth as she crept towards him agonizingly slow. Jagged nails tore at the flesh of his legs as the Hag inched closer. The springs groaned in protest. His heart raced faster inside his chest until he couldn't distinguish the beats anymore. Daniel prayed his heart would explode with fear. He couldn't bear to suffer her. A clawed hand dug into the flesh of his thigh as the Hag settled into his lap. Her warm, rancid breath poured over Daniel's face. The Hag's hoarse breath seemed to hiss his name with every exhalation. Her nails tore into the delicate flesh of his abdomen, burrowing deeper as she writhed her fingers. Daniel's muffled scream nearly suffocated him as the Hag pushed, pinning him down with such dreadful force it pushed the air from his lungs in a silent whisper. A hungry growl emanated from the Hag's stomach.

Then the room exploded to life, cast into vivid detail by a fiery orange flash that engulfed the walls. A pair of malevolent red eyes scowled at Daniel. Clouds of darkness swirled in her lifeless eyes. Black, dishevelled hair tumbled over the old Hag's pale skin, her flesh plagued by festering, draining wounds. Tattered rags clung to her frail frame, the soiled fabric so rotten it was forged into her pale flesh. Her mouth yawned open, revealing a terrifying abyss. The most horrible screech called Daniel's name in a thousand savage voices. Filed, yellow teeth rimmed the grim chasm that expanded. She let out a belch; the putrid fumes billowed past her cracked lips in a ghastly vapour. A high-pitched scream shattered the windows of the house. Daniel tried to force his eyes shut, but her gnarled claws held his eyelids open, the nails shredding away the flesh. Her deathly cold eyes pierced into his soul as she inhaled, her cracked lips resting over his mouth. He felt himself draining away as she enveloped him into the bowels of hell for the rest of eternity.

In the vacant room, the alarm clock flipped to display 3:16 A.M.

HALLOWEEN MUMMERS

The slow stream of trick-or-treaters had stopped hours ago. Jessie snuggled her head into Alex's lap, covering her legs with a blanket. Alex sat in the corner, and Jessie made herself comfortable on the rest of the couch. They were watching a TV that hung above the fireplace. The curling flames swayed and flickered, casting long shadows across the hardwood floor. The wood fire sent its warm light throughout the living room. Two mugs of coffee sat on the coffee table in front of the mantle. Outside, the wind howled, making the seams of the house creek as the rain pattered off the windows. A dull orange glow from the hanging pumpkin lights in the window caught in Jessie's platinum blonde hair. Alex stared at the television intently, paying close attention to the horror movie he was watching.

"What an awful night for trick or treating," Jessie said to try and start a conversation so she wouldn't have to listen to the dreadful noises on the TV. She didn't like scary movies. After a few awkward moments of silence, she looked at Alex's scruffy face. His black-rimmed glasses rested on his crooked nose, which had been broken in a fight outside of the bar last night. The skin around his eye had turned black and was nearly swollen shut, but he kept track of everything that was happening in his movie. "I said it's an awful night." Jessie's voice had shown her frustration more than she had meant it to.

Alex turned his head to study the bowl of treats next to the door. "Well, that depends."

"Depends on what?"

Alex turned his head back to continue watching his movie. "Depends on how you look at things, I guess."

Jessie knew he wanted to prove a point with his vague statement. If she wasn't so bored, she would have left it alone, but she had nothing better to do, so she played along. "Well, it's wet and cold out. That to me seems like a terrible night to be outside going door to door looking for candy."

"Exactly."

"Exactly? Are you agreeing with me, or do you have a point to make?" Jessie made no effort to hide her frustration now.

"Consider the bowl and tell me what you see." A smirk on his face made a wave of wrinkles under his eyes.

"A bowl full of candies and chocolate bars." Jessie wondered where he was going with this.

"Exactly."

"Exactly what?" Jessie groaned.

"Think about it. If every kid's parents bought treats to hand out like we did, then the kid got to stay home tonight, watch a scary movie, and eat those treats without having to put in any of the work." Alex stretched out for his coffee but was unable to reach it with Jessie resting on him. Jessie propped herself up enough to get Alex his coffee. "Since you're already up, you mind grabbing me some of those candy bars." Alex laughed.

Jessie gave Alex a playful punch in the stomach. "You jerk." She pushed the blanket aside and put her feet on the hardwood floor. The fire hadn't been burning long enough yet to warm the floorboards, and a chill ran up her backside. She made her way over to the bowl and looked down at all the treats. "What do you want?"

"Just bring it all over," Alex called out from the couch. "I'm sure we aren't getting anyone else."

Jessie looked over to find he had pulled the blanket over himself. She grabbed the bowl, and just as she turned to walk back, a loud knock on the door startled her. "Looks like you will have to share," she teased.

Jessie opened the door, startled by a squall that forced the door all the way open. Three people stood on the porch dressed up like mummers from Christmas time. The first one was a rather tall man wearing a flowered dress with a pair of polka-dotted men's boxers hauled on over the dress. His hairy legs ran into a pair of yellow rubber boots. A white sheet with triangle eye holes and a frown drawn with red lipstick covered the face and was tucked into his dress. The second person was much shorter and wore a black and blue plaid jacket over jean coveralls with the pant legs tucked into green rubber boots. They wore a pillow case with ragged eye holes and a frown drawn in black marker to cover their face. The last mummer stood in the back wearing a lacy red nightgown over a black sweater with a white hood covering their face as well. They had painted large black circles around the eye holes with an innocent smile painted in red where the face should have been.

"Any mummers ' loud in?" one of them said.

Jessie laughed. "Wrong holiday guys, but I love the costumes." None of the mummers had bags for trick or treating. "Maybe you should take those bags off your head so you can collect some candy." Jessie held out the candy dish.

"No one will let us in?" one mummer piped up. "You'll regret that."

"What did you say?" Jessie asked. "Alex, come over here."

"Let's see if the neighbours are any nicer." The mummers turned to leave just as Alex got to the door.

"What's wrong, dear?" Alex asked. "What the fuck are they wearing?" he said as he regarded their bizarre attire.

"One of them said you'll regret that." Jessie's hand trembled.

"Regret what?" Alex reached out and took the bowl of candy from Jessie's hand. "Get out of here, you assholes."

"Don't be a jerk, Alex. What if they had tried to force their way inside?" Jessie was glad they were gone, but the whole encounter still had creeped her out. Alex said nothing. He just shrugged his shoulders. "Thanks, dear, I feel so much safer," she said and pushed her way past Alex and headed back to the couch. Alex unplugged the pumpkin lights in the window and drew the curtains closed before sitting back down next to Jessie. "I can't watch this," she said. "Fuck this, I'm changing the channel." Alex objected silently but must have seen the frightened expression in Jessie's eye and just nodded in agreement. Jessie knew she would not get to sleep soon without one of her sleeping pills. "Please get me one of my bedtime pills?"

"Sure, whatever," Alex muttered as he headed upstairs while Jessie surfed the channels for anything that wasn't Halloween-related. Everything had a Halloween theme tonight, so she settled for one of the comedies airing their kooky holiday special. Alex returned with a pill and sat back down on the couch. Jessie tilted her head back and threw the pill down her throat. All she wanted to do was fall asleep and get this night over with.

"You shouldn't need those fucking pills," he said.

"So, I should just drink myself into a drunken mess every night?" Jessie snapped back. She tried to sit up, but Alex had a firm grasp on her.

"I'm just saying there's nothing to stress out about." Alex slid his hand up Jessie's shirt, his calloused hands scraping over her soft belly.

Jessie reached out and grabbed Alex by the wrist. "Not in the mood after what just happened." She stared into his eyes and laid her head on his chest. "Just hold me." Alex didn't say anything, but Jessie noticed his heart beating faster, in tune with his flaring temper. Her eyelids grew heavy as the pill took over. Alex's hand continued their business as she drifted into a restless sleep.

A loud knock on the door startled Jessie out of her sleep and she nearly jumped to her feet. "What was that?"

"It's probably the neighbour's coming to apologize for the loud screaming." Alex pushed his way off the couch and headed towards the door. Jessie rubbed her temples, her brain muddled, still groggy from her pill.

The door creaked open. "Can I help you?" Alex asked.

An eerie voice came from outside. "I'm looking for my friend. Have you seen him?"

"It's a little late to be trick or treating, even for some-one your age," Alex barked back.

"Who is it, Alex?" Jessie asked.

"We didn't let your fucking friend in earlier and I'm not letting you in either." Alex slammed the door and locked it.

"Who is it?" Jessie could feel her nerves fraying, send-ing erratic impulses throughout her body. She wanted to run to the phone, but she couldn't move or control her body from shaking.

"One of those people dressed up like a mummer." Al-ex's voice was brimming with anger. Rage was surfacing in him once again, the same temper that had gotten him the black eye at the bar. He stormed over to the window and opened the curtains. "What the hell is she doing?" Alex raced over to the door and put his shoes on.

"Alex, don't leave me here alone," Jessie pleaded, dread growing deep inside.

Alex threw the door open without listening to her pleas. "Call the cops." He slammed the door shut behind him.

Jessie jumped up and ran over to lock the door. She walked into the kitchen to get the phone, but it wasn't on the charger. Jessie cursed Alex. He probably left it lying around somewhere. She scoured the kitchen table and countertops for the phone, but it was nowhere in sight. She headed back into the living room to get her cell phone. "Where did I leave it?" She couldn't think straight, the effects of the drugs still clouding her thoughts. She looked over the coffee table and the bookcase to no avail. Alex was cursing at someone outside. Fear gripped her heart and made her want to hide under the blanket, but she needed to see what Alex was screaming about. She put her hand on the curtains and started to drag them, terror hindering her motor skills. Outside was pitch black except for the dull yellow glow of the street lights. The doorknob jingled as someone tried to turn it, then a loud knock threatened to break the door down. "Alex?" Jessie ran over to the door to let him in. She threw the door open and was nearly toppled over backwards.

"Have you seen my friend yet?" The mummer with the smile stood on the porch.

"Get out of here!" Jessie screamed, unable to summon the courage to move. Only a few feet separated the two.

"Are you sure you haven't seen him? He said he would meet me here." The mysterious voice made Jessie's skin crawl. The mummer moved towards Jessie methodically, her hands by her side. Jessie noticed dark red specks over the mummer's neck and nightgown. The mummer inched closer now, slowly raising her hands towards Jessie. The intruder was close enough now that Jessie could see her green eyes staring back at her.

"Get out of here!" Alex grabbed the prowler by the shoulders and hurtled her off the porch and onto the wet lawn. He slammed the door shut behind him. "Have you called the cops?"

"I can't find the fucking phone." Jessie was in tears. Alex raced into the kitchen, and she could overhear him rummaging through magazines on the kitchen table and cursing under his breath. "What's going on?" Alex rushed back into the living room and headed straight for the couch with a panicked expression on his face. He started ripping the cushions off the couch and looking underneath it as well. "Alex?"

"My cell phone's dead. Where's yours?" Alex flipped over the last cushion.

"I don't know." Jessie shuddered, her heart palpitating.

"You drugged-up bitch." Alex darted upstairs to look for the phone. In the silence, Jessie could hear something tapping against the window. She turned away from the window, praying that the sound would go away. She stared into the fire and her heart jumped into her throat. A small scream escaped her mouth as she saw her phone melting on top of the burning ashes in the fireplace.

A pair of hands grabbed Jessie from behind and spun her around. "Why is the bedroom window left open?" Alex shook Jessie back and forth, trying to bring her back to her senses, but all that escaped her lips were silent gasps. He turned to look at the deliberate tapping at the window. He headed straight for the curtains. Jessie reached out to stop him, but her legs wouldn't budge. Alex tossed open the curtains, revealing the mummer with the smile standing there, tapping a pair of keys against the glass. "Get out of here," Alex yelled furiously.

The mummer stopped tapping the glass and pointed her finger at Jessie. Alex craned his neck and followed the aim of her finger. "Jessie!"

Spinning around, Jessie jumped back as the mummer with the red lipstick frown stood in the kitchen. Alex pushed his way past her and met the assailant head-on, never seeing the kitchen knife in his hand. But Jessie witnessed the end of the blade tear through Alex's back. A torrent of blood cascaded down his stomach and pooled on the floor. Alex turned his head towards Jessie. "Run." Blood gurgled in his throat as he fell to the ground. A wet slap echoed in the moment of silence as Alex's intestines slipped from his fingers and dropped to the floor. Looking down in disbelief, he tried to put his organ back into the wound, but the slippery lining wouldn't allow him to get a grip. Alex stared blankly at Jessie before collapsing face-first into the mess.

Jessie's instincts finally took over, and she rushed towards the front door, but the knob was turning. She heard the lock opening, so she shifted directions and dashed up the stairs. She looked behind her as the front door opened. and just as she reached the top, she received a forceful blow to the side of the face, sending her plummeting down the stairs. The world spun around as she toppled head over heels, a volley of pain exploding from every nerve ending as she descended the stairwell. Jessie crashed into the feet of the smiling mummer, who reached down and pinned her to the floor. Jessie thrashed around, trying to break her assailant's grasp, but the man's grip never faltered. She had broken her ankle during her fall, the bone jutting through the skin. The stairs creaked as the other intruder made his way down, dragging a sledgehammer behind him. The violent metal head thumping emphatically off each step.

"Why are you doing this?" Jessie pleaded to the three mummers. The mummer with the black frown pulled off his hood. She did not know who he was or what he wanted. He just smiled at her for a moment. "Please let me go?" The hoodless mummer raised the sledgehammer above his head and held it there, staring down at her. "What do you want?"

"You should have just let us in."

Drops of blood fell from the sledgehammer as the mummer took aim, shards of smashed flesh smeared over the iron head. Jessie closed her eyes and waited for the nightmare to be over. There was a sickening thud followed by tremendous pressure as her eye popped out of the socket. Her entire body convulsed from the blow. And as the footsteps faded, she felt her life slip slowly away.

NEVER WHISTLE AT NIGHT

Richard and Dan traipsed along the archaic forest path—the trail a beaten down path through the overgrown pasture. A disco ball of sunlight burst through the canopy of leaves overhead. In the distance, an ensemble of birds chirped in tune with the wind as it blew through the trees. Gushing water babbled through the forest, the sound rising from below the bank that snaked through the woods along the path.

The fresh scent of pine was eroded by the damp aroma of mud after a morning shower. Elongated puddles along the path forced the boys to jump from one heap of dry land to the next. The soles of their rubber boots landed with a squelch in the fresh muck.

With a fishing rod slung over his shoulder, Richard looked like a soldier marching off to war. Tall and lean, with shaggy brown hair, he looked like a fresh recruit before his buzz cut. His little brother Dan, younger by just about three years, weighed the same as his older brother but was nowhere near as tall. His stripped shirt worked against him, emphasizing his expanding midsection. Dan carried the tackle box in his left hand, the contents rattling back and forth inside as they made their way to the mouth of the river. As the tree line thinned, the glossy surface of the lake came into view. Tiny white caps carried along the swell of the tide, leaving behind foam on the craggy shore as the waves receded.

Dan swatted at a stout as it buzzed around his head. "Get out of here," he grumbled.

"Don't pay any attention to them and they'll leave you alone," Richard said. He paused for a moment, weighing the next words in his mouth before saying them. "That's what Dad always said."

"Dad's not here."

Richard sighed, wishing he hadn't mentioned their father. "We can go back home. But if you want to catch a lot of fish, after the rain is the best time."

"Is that something else Dad always said?"

Not wanting to start another fight, Richard ignored his brother and made his way to the giant rock that jutted out from the bank. Overlooking the river, the ledge offered an ideal fishing platform.

"Come on," Richard called out over his shoulder as he made his way up the stone. "I'll let you have the first cast.

Despite his legs pumping fast, Dan seemed to only inch towards his brother. The contents of the tackle box rattled boisterously, metal hooks and lures clanging together inside. His shoes skidded on the rock and lost what little momentum he gained. With an outstretched hand, Dan reached out for Richard, his eyes wide with fear.

Richard stretched out for his brother's hand, grasped him around the wrist, and yanked him to the top in one powerful motion. "You alright?"

Out of breath, Dan sprawled on all fours on the rock, his chest heaving as he gasped for breath. He sputtered something incoherent, rolled over onto his backside, and stared up at Richard, his face flushed red.

With a chuckle, Richard said, "You need to get off your PlayStation and exercise more, little brother."

With a final strangled gasp, Dan sat up and stared between his legs. Ashamed, he refused to look in his brother's direction. A wave of guilt washed over Richard.

"Here, hold the rod while I put a worm on the hook." Richard held out the rod for Dan. When his brother grasped the rod, Richard slid the tackle box over the bumpy rock face and opened it. The plastic lid clacked off the rock with a hollow sound. Tucked away beneath a plastic shelf, an Eversweet Margarine container filled with dirt and worms for the day waited. Richard pulled the lid off with a loud snap. Just beneath the surface, the slimy pink bodies wriggled and writhed through the black soil. He pinched a worm between his fingers and pulled it out before sealing the lid once more.

As Richard arranged a worm on the hook, his brother asked, "Do they feel pain?"

"No," Richard lied.

The worm writhed at the end of the hook. Dan swung the line over the rock and dropped the line straight down into the rushing water. The current carried the line out into the lake. A red and white bobber floated along the rough surface, bobbing up and down as it was carried out into the deeper water.

"Let out a little more line," Richard said.

"I know how to do this," Dan complained. "Dad taught me, too." Without saying another word, Dan let out another length of line and then snapped the brake into place.

Richard nodded his head. "Good job, Dan, Dad taught you well."

"I'm a good learner," Dan replied with a giant smile that bared his front teeth.

"Dad always said that," Richard conceded.

The brothers sat in silence, the current rushing into the lake the only sound. The bob dunked into the water, and Dan jerked the rod straight back over his shoulder. "I think I got one," he exclaimed.

"Good job," Richard said, jumping to his feet. "You need my help?"

"I can do it," Dan shouted with a flare of anger and contempt. He released the brake and let the fish take the line out.

"Alright," Richard said, holding his hands up by his face in mock defeat.

Dan flipped the brake back on and swung the rod hard to the left before reeling the line back in. When the fish on the other end put up a fight, Dan put the brake back on, jerked the rod to the left, and reeled the line in. Richard watched in awe as Dan replicated their father's strategy to perfection.

"That's a big one," Dan shouted with glee as the trout breached the surface, landing back into the water with an unceremonious splash. The veins on his forehead throbbed as he strained with all of his might, pulling straight back, and forcing the trout back to the surface.

Richard cheered on his brother. "You almost got him!"

With one final furious effort, Dan reeled in the line. His forearms were taut with strain as the trout hovered over the river, its body twisting and flopping to free itself from the hook.

Both boys giggled with joy as Dan swung the rod over the rock. Richard reached out and grabbed the line, holding the trout off the ground as his brother reeled in the remaining line. Jubilant, Richard said, "You did it! Dad would be so proud."

Dan laughed. "And jealous."

"What's up, Dick?" A familiar voice interrupted the brothers as they celebrated.

Richard turned toward his friend and called out. "Hey,

Collin, come on over."

Short but laden with muscle, Collin looked much older than Richard, the first scraggly signs of a beard grew in patches all over his face. He wore a baggy black Element sweater that hung down to his mid-thigh. He strutted over to the rock, standing at the edge of the bank, and hacked up a wad of phlegm, spitting a yellowish-brown wad into the river below.

Collin lumbered up the side of the rock. With every step, Richard thought his friend would fall backwards. But awkwardly, Collin made it up with no help. "How's the fishing?"

In answer to the question, Dan held up his catch with a wide grin. The trout's powerful movements had tapered off to a slight, dying flutter. Sunlight danced on the trout's rainbow underbelly, the scales reflecting the light.

With a chuckle, Collin said, "That's huge."

"That's what she said." Richard slapped his knee and buckled over. All three boys erupted with laughter.

"That's what your mom said," Collin replied after catching his breath. They all lost it again, and Dan actually wheezed.

"When did you guys get here?" Collin asked.

"We just got here a few minutes ago," Richard said, then added, "first cast."

"Do you mind if I join you guys?"

Richard glanced over at his brother, not saying anything but studying his facial expression; he could read his brother like a book. "Sure, we don't mind, do we, Dan?"

Dan nodded his head in agreement, too occupied with retrieving the hook from the trout's mouth. He lifted the plastic shelf and laid the trout on the bottom of the tackle box. The tail twisted back towards the trout's head, too long to lay flat in the giant red box. He opened the Eversweet container and hauled out a worm. "Do you think we need to change lures?"

"Not yet," Richard answered.

Collin dug his hands into the front pouch on his sweater, his arms disappearing all the way to the elbows in the oversized pocket. When he pulled his hand out, he had a red and white cardboard box in his hand. He flipped the top open, revealing the yellow tips of the cigarettes inside. With practiced ease, he tapped his wrist just below his palm. Two of the cancer sticks popped up from the rest. Collin held out the pack towards Richard. "Want one?" he asked with a smile.

Richard stared down at the pack then back at his brother. "No, I'd better not."

"And you shouldn't either," Dan added as he placed another worm on the hook.

"Don't be a bunch of wimps," Collin said as he shook the pack at Richard. "Come on, try one."

Richard shook his head and turned his attention back to his brother. Behind him, Collin lit the cigarette. The stale aroma of smoke wafted through the air. Richard fanned his right hand in front of his face and scrunched up his nose. "Can you take that somewhere else? If our mom catches a whiff of that on Dan, I'll never see the light of day again."

"Whatever," Collin said, jumping down from the rock. "But I want a turn."

"You can have one when you're done smoking," Richard stated.

"Here you go," Dan held out the rod for Richard, "it's ready for you."

"You have another turn," Richard said.

The boys spent the rest of the afternoon casting their line into the river. They caught several trout and discussed how good they were going to taste fried up in the pan. Jokes were told and, much to Dan's chagrin, they described girls in the vivid detail only pubescent boys could. They were having the kind of summer day you remember for years despite nothing of importance happening, so they lost track of time, and the sun dipped lower against the horizon without them realizing it.

The sun reflected off the lake as it fell beneath the horizon, leaving an orange hue in the approaching clouds. Richard scratched at the back of his neck, his nails scrapping over a series of bumpy fly bites. Dan cast the line out into the middle of the current, the lure landing with a heavy plunk. Leaning against the rock, Collin puffed on another cigarette, attempting to blow circles with the smoke.

"I think we fished it dry, Dan," Richard said, irritation heavy in his tone, weighing his words down.

"Maybe I should change lures?" Dan asked with no conviction.

"We already tried that," Richard replied. "I think that it's time to go home."

With a regretful sigh, Dan reeled the line in, taking his time in hopes of one more bite. The reel clacked with a methodical rhythm as the line spooled in. The bobber rose out of the water and the hook swayed with the gentle breeze as Dan locked the brake. "Alright, let's get going."

Richard ran his hands through Dan's matted hair, sticky with sweat after a long day. "You did fantastic today. Mom will be cooking trout for days," he said as he reached out for the tackle box. He picked it up, and strained his facial expression, pretending that it weighed way more than it did.

Collin held out his hand, helping Dan down from the rock as Richard slid halfway down on his bum before letting himself fall the rest of the way. "It sure is getting dark," Collin said, pointing towards a cluster of storm clouds approaching. "Looks like it's going to rain. What way are you guys going?"

"I figured we'd take the trail back," Richard said. "That's the easiest way."

Collin placed a cigarette in the corner of his mouth and said, "We could take the shortcut through the bog."

Glancing over at his brother, Richard watched Dan's eyes grow wide with fear. "I think we'll stick to the path," He said and watched the relief flood over his brother's face, softening his features.

"Aren't you guys late for supper? Your mom's going to be pissed."

"I don't think she'll care once we show her all the fish we caught," Dan said with a smile. Richard ruffled his brother's hair and nodded his approval. The boys turned towards the trail, Richard carrying the tackle box and Dan with the rod slung over his shoulder.

Collin cupped his hand over the cigarette and lit it with his Zippo, inhaling in a quick gasp. The tip flared bright orange with every breath. A thick haze of smoke hovered around his face. "Don't be chicken shit," Collin insisted. "It's the quickest way for everyone. Besides, I have something to show you."

Intrigued, Richard stopped dead in his tracks. Dan took a few more steps before he noticed his brother had paused. "What do you have to show me?" Richard asked.

"I ain't telling you," Collin said, exhaling a puff of smoke. "You'll just have to see for yourself. If you're not too chicken to go through the bog this late at night."

"Come on, Richard," Dan pleaded, his voice high and nasally. "Let's just go." Dan grabbed Richard's sleeve and tugged. "Please."

"I'm not sticking around all day for you two girls to decide what you're going to do." Collin flicked his cigarette to the ground and stomped it out with the heel of his black work boots. "I'm out of here."

"Wait," Richard called out. He turned towards his brother, wearing his warmest smile. "Come on, Dan, it won't be so bad. There's nothing to fear."

"That's not what Dad said."

"Dad never said to be afraid of the bog," Richard sighed. "Dad said, 'Never whistle at night.'"

"But he never ever took us there. Not even in the daytime. He always took us down the trail. No matter what."

"Whatever, Dan," Richard snapped. Regret twisted his stomach as Dan recoiled from his outburst. "I'm going with Collin. I'll see you when you get home, I guess." Without waiting, Richard turned and walked alongside Collin. The boys walked along in silence, only the sound of their boots squelching over the damp soil to accompany them. Just as Richard was about to turn around and call out to Dan, he heard his brother's footsteps racing towards them.

"Wait up," Dan called out.

Richard paused and waited for his brother to catch up, staring up at the sky as a deep blue flooded into the horizon. The approaching storm clouds blotted out the stars, tearing a hole out of the night sky and leaving a dismal black abyss overhead. They started towards the clearing in the trees ahead, leaving the main path and pushing into the depths of the forest. Soon, they reached the edge of the tree line, and they all stopped dead in their tracks as if on cue.

"It's so dark in there," Dan pointed out, taking a step backwards and twisting his neck to look back towards the main path.

"There's nothing to be afraid of," Richard said, his voice unsteady; he didn't believe his own words. In his imagination, he conjured up dozens of reasons to turn around and run. "Come on, let's go."

"If it will make you feel better," Collin said, "I'll watch your back."

"What if something jumps out of the bush?" Dan asked.

Richard and Collin burst out laughing, the sound cutting through the tension that lingered over the woods.

Dan shook his head and sighed. "Let me guess, that's what she said?"

The boys continued guffawing, snorts and clucks escaping them. After they caught their breath, Richard led the way into the forest. He brushed the low-dropping branches aside, holding them for Dan so they didn't snap back and smack him in the face. It got darker as they pushed further into the forest. The trees grew taller here, taller than anywhere else around, thicker too. Overhead, the canopy of branches blotted out the remaining daylight, concealing the stars and obscuring the silvery light of the moon.

After walking through the encroaching blackness for a few minutes, the sound of Collin's Zippo cut through the air with a sharp click, making Richard jump. Angry, he spun around, ready to snap at Lincoln, not sure why the anger got to him. Instead, he bumped into his brother, who had been walking with his head down the entire way.

"Are you okay, Dan?" Richard asked, confused and disoriented in the claustrophobic surroundings.

"Yeah, I'm fine," Dan answered without conviction. Richard could hear the pain behind every word.

Collin stood in the darkness, the orange glow of his cigarette brilliant against the deep shadows of the forest. He raised the filter to his face and inhaled, the burning tip illuminating his face in an eerie glow. The shadows cast his eyes deep into the sockets, giving him a hollow appearance. His hands twitched and his entire body rattled with a slight shudder.

Dan backed away from Collin, pressing into Richard's chest. "Let's go. I don't want to be here anymore."

Richard watched Collin for a moment then whispered to his brother, "Don't mind him. He won't hurt us; he just looks scary. Probably too many cigarettes, that's all."

Richard turned back towards the trail and felt his brother reach out and take his hand. He squeezed back, and they continued down the path. Collin followed, his footsteps heavy, keeping a methodical pace behind the brothers. His breath was harsh and raspy, coughing up wads of phlegm and spitting them on the ground.

A faint ethereal glow ahead silhouetted the trees, giving them sharp definition. The branches took on the quality of limbs and twisted diabolically as the wind blew. Dan stopped in his tracks.

Richard tugged on his brother's arm. "There's nothing to be afraid of."

"Then why do you sound so afraid?"

Richard's heart thundered in his chest with anticipation. To calm himself, he took a deep breath, held it, and released it slowly; it didn't work. The trees' shadows swelled large as the light behind them danced around. He could hear his brother's shallow breaths.

"Let's turn back," Dan pleaded, yanking on Richard's arm.

"Okay," Richard agreed, turning to head back. "Let's go, Collin. I won't be able to find Dan's puffer in the dark, and he's going to have an episode if we don't turn back."

"Remember I wanted to show you something?" Collin said, his voice harsh and coarse, as if speaking through a throat full of sand. "It's just over there—the light. I need to show you the light."

Richard turned his head to match Collin's gaze, but he didn't see any light. "No," Richard snapped, "we're going back." He laid his hand on Dan's shoulder and felt his entire body trembling.

Dan pulled Richard down so they were level and whispered in his brother's ear. "There's something wrong with Collin. Let's get out of here."

"We will, little brother," Richard replied. "Just walk around him."

Dan sidestepped Collin, trying to go around the older boy, but Collin's arm snapped out straight. Collin's head tilted to the side, casting a sideways glance at Dan. "I said," his grip tightened on Dan's shirt, crumpling his sweater, "there's something I want to show you over there." Collin pointed off into the shadows.

"Hey," Richard snapped, "what's wrong with you?"

Dan strained against Collin's grip, unable to free himself from the bigger boy's grip. With his collar scrunched up over his neck, Dan appeared to be a scorned child in the older boy's vice-grip. "I don't see anything," Dan said repeatedly.

With a leering smile on his face, Collin raised his hand to his face, stuck two fingers in his mouth, and blew. A shrill whistle pierced the chilled air. "How about now?" he asked, laughing.

A faint light frittered amongst the trees, shooting back and forth between the branches, changing direction with frantic abandon. Shadows formed in the trees, eerie figures that morphed shapes, growing larger and fiercer as they neared. Surrounded now by multiple flickering

lights and dancing shadows, Dan sobbed uncontrollably, his shoulders hitching, gasping for breath. Richard
reached out and grabbed Dan, hauling him from Collin's
grasp. The two brothers stumbled backward. Dan buried
his face in Richard's chest, unable to face the horrors closing in on them.

Collin tilted his head back and opened his mouth, his
chin pinned against his Adam's apple. A guttural, war-
bling wail escaped from his stomach. Gloom cascaded
from his lips in a swirling vapour. Tendrils of blackened
ooze snaked over Collin's chin and his clothes.

"Collin, what is wrong with you?" Richard pleaded,
squeezing his brother for comfort.

"Just like I promised you," Collin called out. "Two
souls to replace my own. Now, do we have a deal?"

"We will torment your family until their dying breath,"
a hoarse voice rasped from somewhere deep inside the
forest. Wicked winds tore through the trees, knocking the
branches together.

"Please," Collin cried out, clasping his hands together
below his chin in mock prayer. "Leave us alone."

All around them, the lights and shadows crisscrossed,
whirling around them, edging closer and gaining speed.
The shadowed figures took human form. Long and lanky
arms reached out for them. With slender knives and sharp
axes grasped in their fists, they lashed out, cutting through
the pine.

Collin rushed Richard and Dan. The unexpected blow
knocked the brothers to the ground. Collin threw his body
weight on top of them, pinning them to the ground in a
cluster of struggling arms and thrashing legs.

"I'll make them whistle," Collin screamed. He reached
his hands out, wrapping them around Dan's neck. "You
better whistle, Richard."

Dan gasped and coughed, sucking in minuscule

breaths of air into his lungs as his face turned an alarming shade of crimson. From beneath the pile of twisted bodies, Richard lashed out at Collin. His fist connected with the older boy's ribs, the dull meaty thuds drowned out by the raging winds.

"Whistle, you bastard," Collin snarled, doubling his efforts.

Determined, Richard growled, "Let my brother go." Mustering all of his strength, he jerked his body sideways as his brother dug his nails into Collin's wrist.

Collin fell face first into a tree trunk, the rough edges tearing away the flesh from his forehead. Streaks of scarlet covered his face. Richard grabbed his brother, hauling him to his feet as Dan gasped for breath. With no other options, Richard tugged at Dan's collar, guiding him back towards the trail. "Don't look," Richard yelled, urging his brother to close his eyes as they ran towards the eerie light. As they raced through the tightening circle of light and shadows, strange voices whispered in their ears and the tree branches reached out for them, urging them to stay.

Behind them, Collin shrieked as the whispers morphed into a deafening symphony of cruel voices. The brothers didn't dare peek over their shoulders. Once they hit the trail, they ran all the way home, never daring to look back. Out of breath, standing on their front lawn, the welcoming light of home filtered through the living room window. Basked in its comforting light, Dan opened his eyes. "Richard?"

"What is it, little brother?"

"They wanted me to whistle." Dan hesitated, searching his memory. "The voices in the shadows."

"I know," Richard said. "But you can't invite the spirits in. You never whistle at night."

BIRTH OF THE CRUEL

As I step outside into the chilled morning air, I hug myself, rubbing each arm with the opposite hand to ward off the chill. I run through the freshly fallen snow towards my Civic. The door groans incisively in the still quiet. Before I jump into the car, my gaze wanders upwards towards a pitch-black sky, not a single star or sign of the moon in sight. I land in the seat with a heavy thud to worse coldness awaiting me inside the car. The engine turns over with a choked grumble. A blast of cold air assaults me from the vents, attacking me from every angle.

"Goddamnit," I mumble through chattering teeth.

All I can do is wait for the air to turn hot, so I bundle into a tight ball and rock myself back and forth in my seat to generate some warmth. It takes the car far too long to warm up; ice covered the windshield in a thick layer of frost. But it's too frigid outside the car to bother scraping. The car slowly melts the ice, forming orbs on either side of the front window as the cab warms.

The boisterous air blowing through the vents drowns out the radio. I don't turn the volume up. Instead, I keep my hands nestled in the folds of my jacket to preserve as much heat as possible. One final trembling shiver rocks my shoulders before the first signs of heat are building up in the cab.

I take out my cell phone and unlock it. The harsh glare

hurts my eyes in the night's extreme darkness. There's one unread message from Janie; it only takes me a few seconds to read.

I hope you can pull through for Alexander. For once in his life.

Each word is a crafted strike to my self-esteem, sent to elicit a sense of inadequacy. Angry, I toss the phone into the cup holder. It clatters against the cold plastic. "I wish I had pulled out!" I scream at my phone, regretting it. Despite my failures, Alexander is the best thing in my life, and he loves me unconditionally. I want to do better for him—need to.

Hunched over the steering wheel, I peer through the expanding holes as I ease the car out of the driveway. Once I'm out of the driveway and heading down Pine Street, I flick on my headlights. Glittering in the snow, the LED lights give a midday lustre to the city as I drive. The windows are all black as I drive past a ghost town, but I know everyone is snug in their beds, dreaming sweet fantasies as I make my way towards the mall for Black Friday. My gaze wanders to the dash. "5 am," I gasp. "I'm going to be late."

As the car turns off Pine and merges into the major arterial route, I embrace the warmth flooding through the vents and turn the dial down until the roar of the air becomes a gentle breeze. An ad for the big Black Friday sale rises above the rattle of the car engine, informing me I have two hours before the stores open early. There is more traffic on the highway than I'd hoped for. But there's nothing I can do about that now. All I can do is try to make up for lost time. I drive past the Tim Horton's drive-thru and second-guess myself for not stopping. Maybe the warmth would make standing in line for the next two hours bearable.

"No," I say to myself, "you shouldn't have slept in.

Janie is going to be pissed if I don't get Alexander that PlayStation he's been asking for. And you can't afford it at full price. Focus, Edward."

My phone buzzes, drawing my attention to the bright flash of light. Another message from Janie. "Christ, doesn't she have to get ready for work or something?" I mutter to myself.

Peter is going to buy one today. If you don't get one for Alexander, he will.

"Who the fuck is Peter?" I growl at my phone. Our breakup is still too fresh for Janie to be with someone long enough to be introduced to Alexander. As I reach out to send a message back, a cherry red truck pulls out and passes me, the back end of the cab swerving in the slick snow. A set of balls dangle from the hitch, knocking back and forth. "Goddamn dick head," I yell. It takes a moment before I realize I made a great joke, wishing he could hear how clever it is. But knowing he can't hear me affords me the benefit of acting brave.

His taillights flash red as he slams on the brakes. In slow motion, I slam on the brakes and ream the wheel towards the curb. The tires slide across the icy shoulder of the road, and the front right tire digs into the curb. As the car slams into the snowbank, I jerk forward in my seat. The seatbelt pulls tight against my chest and compresses my chest, driving the wind from me.

"Asshole," I scream as the Dodge Ram drives on, leaving me in the snowbank.

White knuckled, I realize my fingers ache. I force myself to release the steering wheel and sink back into the seat, breathing heavily. Headlights drive past me in a steady stream. I curse under my breath at each one. Startled by a humming buzz, the sound drew my eyes to my cell phone.

Are you in line yet? Or did you sleep in?

"Get off my case," I answer out loud. But I don't respond to her message. Instead, I put the car in reverse, ease back into the lane and get back on track. Headlights snake up the off-ramp towards the mall. At the sight of the long line, my stomach floods with despair and failure.

Without thinking about the consequences, I dart across the highway and drive the wrong way onto the off-ramp. My heart thunders in my chest, thrashing off my rib cage. Luckily for me, there's no traffic leaving the mall at this hour. The lane is bare, and I bypass the long line of traffic. Car horns blare at me as I dash past in the wrong lane. The sound is amplified in the frigid morning air, startling me and forcing me to exhale a breath I didn't realize I'd been holding. I drive over the curb into the parking lot, and the car lurches to the right and halts. Momentarily stuck in the snow bank, I press the peddle to the floor. The tires spin in the snow, kicking up a trail of white behind the car as the rubber searches for traction on the ground beneath.

Suddenly, the car lurches forward and I'm driving through the parking lot. I pick a spot far away from the crowd and turn off the car. My breath is rapid, and my hands tremble with the flood of adrenalin. Euphoria washes over me as my system continues to pump the adrenalin into my bloodstream. I turn off the engine and throw open the door; a blast of chilled air greets me. As I walk away from the car, I can still hear the engine knocking.

The lineup to get inside snakes around the front of the building. Engines rumble as more cars pile into the parking lot. A pair of headlights follow me down the road, the heavy tires crunching snow as the vehicle rolls towards me.

A gruff voice snaps at me. "Hey, asshole!"

I turn around, momentarily blinded by the bright light. I raise my forearm to shield my eyes. The truck rolls alongside me, cherry red. With his window rolled down, the man leans over towards me, his elbow propped on the center console. There's a coffee in his hand, but he thrusts his finger towards me as he resumes. "I saw your little stunt back there. And if you think you're getting in line before me, you got another thing coming." He barks at me, not a human voice, but an animalistic growl. All the veins stand out prominently over his bald head. His scruff is thick and black, growing patchy over his neck, blending into the faux fur collar of a camouflage jacket.

"Fuck off," I snap back. A flare of anger at the sight of the truck boils my blood. I don't dare meet his furious gaze. Instead, I keep my head tilted down and focus on the snow-covered pavement in front of me.

"This isn't over, you little shit," the man barks before driving away. The tires screech over the slick pavement, kicking up clumps of soiled snow. As he drives away, I can see the balls on the back of the hitch swaying.

"What the fuck is that guy's problem?"

I pick up the pace, almost jogging to the back of the line to make sure we don't end up standing anywhere close to each other in the lineup. An older couple see me racing towards the line and quicken their pace to beat me there. Out of breath, I stand behind the elderly couple and suck freezing air into my lungs; it stings.

More people join the line behind me and the steady stream of traffic in the parking lot increases. The blare of car horns and grumble of engines drown out the sound of chatter in the lineup. A man wearing a black jacket crosses the parking lot and heads straight for the door, keys dangling from a hook on his belt loop. As he opens the door, I can see the word "SECURITY" in block letters across the back of his jacket. Angry voices shout at him as he opens the door to let them in. Without a word, he slips through the opening and slams the doors shut. A loud clunk echoes amongst the chaotic clamour. I don't envy the mall staff today.

"Hey, asshole!" a familiar gruff voice barks at me.

I turn around and watch as the line disperses, avoiding me as if I carried a lethal disease. The man from the truck is stomping towards me, his hands balled into fists. Despite the frigid morning chill, his face is red hot. "You think I'm going to let you cut the line like that and get away with it?"

I back away from him, my eyes scanning the crowd for help. Everyone avoids eye contact with me. "Listen, mister, calm down," I say as I back away.

"You could've killed somebody back there with that stunt you pulled." A trail of vapour rises from his mouth and spittle flies from his lips, reminding me of a pit bull.

"Just stay away from me." My voice cracks with fear. "What's done can't be undone."

"What's it all for, asshole?" the man demands.

"I need to get my son a PlayStation," I answer, not understanding why I even acknowledge the man before me. "You wouldn't understand, man. Just leave me the fuck alone, got it?"

I watch the next sequence of events in slow motion. His body twists and compresses before uncoiling. His right first follows a wide arc before connecting with my orbital bone. Stars dance in my vision and red-hot pain fills my skull. My vision turns white, and the earth spins as I lose control of my senses. For a moment, I feel nothing at all. When I come to, I'm on my back, staring up at my attacker, a wicked snarl on his face.

Whispers and concerned gasps fill my eardrums as the crowd gets over the initial shock of what just transpired. The man pounces on me, pinning my arms to the ground with his knees. He's built solid. His leg muscles ripple against my side. I try to shake him off with everything I have left; he doesn't budge.

"Please help," I call out, my voice weak and tiny as the man raises a clubbed fist above his head before driving it down into my face.

A pounding pain radiates from my temple as I regain consciousness. Even the dull glow of the buzzing light above bores into my skull as my eyes flutter open. My face is swollen, the lump so large I can feel it stretching my skin. There's a bitter, coppery taste in my mouth. I roll over onto my side and spit out a wad of brownish-yellow that lands on the cold floor with a loud slap.

"Hello?" I call out, my voice echoes back in the emptiness. "Is there anyone here?"

Silence.

The details of the room make themselves known, emerging from the shadows. I don't know where I am, but I know it's not a hospital room, which is where I need to be. Metal shelving lines the three walls around me, boxes and containers stuffed into every inch of space. Copper pipes and wires race across the ceiling and vanish into a gray box at the edge of the room. A dull yellow bulb dangles from an orange chord above my head.

I swing my legs out over the edge of the counter they have discarded me on. As I sit up, my vision blurs and a cloud of confusion settles over me. The urge to vomit rises in my stomach, bitter bile rising into the back of my throat. I lower my head, using my right hand to probe the damage. Even without a mirror to see, I can tell someone disfigured my face. The tip of my nose is bent flat against my cheek. It's wet and pulpy.

Behind me, a door opens, sending a wave of bright light and a dancing shadow across the storage shelves. Despite the pain, I twist around to see who is in the room with me. My heart flutters. My assailant's angry smile flashes in my mind.

Almost unrecognizable, my frightened voice squeaks through my swollen lips. "Who are you?" Without a word, the door closes behind the stranger with a soft click. "Please don't hurt me."

"Calm down, sir," an angelic voice answers. A female security guard strides in front of me, a two-way radio clipped to her shoulder. She tilts her head so that her chin is touching the mouthpiece clasped to her collar. "He's awake now."

"Thank you for saving me," I say, my voice trembling as a tear streaks down my cheek, stinging the swollen flesh as it goes.

"Rodger," a muffled voice responds from the receiver. "We're ready for him. Bring him to the red bay door."

"This way, sir."

"Have you seen my jacket?"

The woman doesn't wait for me. Instead, she has already made her way through the door and out of sight, forcing me to scurry to catch up. The bright light in the hallway forces me to squint and shield my eyes with my hand as I stumble to keep stride with the security guard. A pair of handcuffs dangle from her belt, the metal chain clanging against the holster resting against her hip.

"Because my phone was in there," I call out as struggle to keep pace with her.

"All of your belongings are waiting for you," she answers, her voice robotic.

We are in a long hallway, the walls lined with soiled white brick in desperate need of a fresh coat of paint. The cement floor is worn and littered with dark stains and trash. Unmarked metal doors break up the hallway, each one painted a different colour. At the end of the hallway on the right-hand side, a door painted deep red waits for us.

"Thanks for calling an ambulance for me," I say, trying to break the ice. Under different circumstances, I would have tried to get her number. She doesn't respond, and her pace hastens. My sneakers scuff along the cement as I try to keep up with her on wobbly legs. I don't know how much longer I can keep this pace.

Before I realize it, the woman is holding the door open for me, her baton grasped tightly in her free hand. "This way," she demands, tapping the baton against the brick wall.

I stumble past her. The brisk night air soothes my swollen face. A pair of brilliant glowing white eyes stare at me, casting the paramedics standing beside the ambulance in a manufactured shroud of darkness. I turn to thank the security guard again. But she's gone, the door clicking shut behind her. A dull thunk echoes in the vehicle bay as a deadbolt slips into place.

"Friendly," I mutter sarcastically, hoping that the paramedics overhead. I stumble forward, using my hands to shield against headlights. As the darkness disperses from the figures, an alarm inside my head goes off before I can piece it all together. The shadowy figures are not paramedics, and they aren't here to help.

The vehicle's lights turn off and the driver's side door creaks open. The vehicle isn't an ambulance. Instead, it's a white van with blackened windows that hide the interior. I think I can see a shadow occupying the passenger seat, but I can't be sure. A man wearing blue coveralls steps towards me. I backpeddle until I reach the exit. My hand fumbles with the knob, forgetting that the guard locked it behind me.

"Listen, man," I say, my voice riddled with panic. "I can pay you." My hand pats my jeans' pockets, feeling each blow against my thigh. "Fuck," I shout as I realize my wallet is stolen.

"All of this for a PlayStation?" the stranger asks. A cruel fit of laughter punctuates his tone. In the light, I can see the man is younger, early twenties. His hazel eyes match his auburn hair, which is slicked to the right, every strand meticulously placed. This man is no stranger to the spotlight, making his mechanic coveralls and scuffed-up work boots seem out of place. I want to make a joke about him being the model for an automotive magazine, but there's something not right about him, and I don't want to push my luck.

Still not believing my luck, I turn my pockets inside out, as if I could have tucked my wallet into some hidden crevice. "Listen," I begin, raising my hand, "I've had the shittiest night. Please, just let me go home."

"Well," the man pauses, a wide grin snakes across his face, "tonight is your lucky night." The man waits for me to answer. When I don't, he continues his monologue. "You're going to have the chance of a lifetime tonight, my friend. I'm going to give you a chance to walk out of here with your very own PlayStation."

"Listen, man," I say, unable to contain the venom in my tone. "I lost my wallet and I can't pay you." I turn and face the door, jiggling the handle to show that it's locked. "Just let me out of here so I can head to the hospital and get this fixed up. The security guard mentioned you have my jacket. If you could give me that, I'd appreciate it. Then I could get out of your hair, and you won't have to worry about me."

Ignoring me, the man waves his hand, beckoning some hidden figure to join him from the shadows. In the back of the vehicle bay, a door slams shut, drawing my attention. A man wearing identical coveralls strides along the side of the van, a PlayStation 5 box clutched against his bulging stomach. He places it on the van's hood, one hand resting on the top of the box just in case I get the urge to make a break for it.

"I want to give this to you."

" Quit messing around, man," I interrupt, growing impatient. " I don't have any way to pay you. All I'm asking for is my phone. "

Wrinkles crease the man's brow as he furrows his brow and shakes his head. "Money isn't everything." He waggles his finger back and forth. The passenger door opens and a fourth man wearing coveralls steps into view. He's holding an expensive camera in his hands. He scuffles his feet across the floor as he makes his way beside his friend. "There are other methods of payment accepted here."

I shake my head in protest. "No fucking way." Anger replaces the fear in my belly, and my heartbeat quickens as I get ready to fight. "I'm not sucking your dick, not even for a free PlayStation. Why don't you and your freak friends go find somebody else? Because there's no chance in hell."

Laughter erupts from the four men. The man who's been doing all the talking buckles over and holds his stomach. "Hey, Charlie," he says in between gasping breaths, "can you believe this guy?"

Embarrassed, I shout, "Shut up!" at the top of my lungs.

The man reaches into his pocket and takes out a wallet—my wallet. He flings it open with a snap of his wrist, thumbing out my ID.

"Edward Buckle?" he asks knowingly as he stares at my photo from three years ago. The only difference is the scruff of facial hair on my chin has filled in. "My clients aren't interested in that..." He hesitates. "Well, at least that isn't what they are paying for here. I don't know, maybe a few of them could be into that sort of thing. Charlie, ask around and see if there's any money in that sort of thing."

"Right, boss," the man holding his hand on the Play-Station responds obediently.

The ring leader introduces himself. "My name is Franklin, and these are my colleagues. You don't need to know who they are. All that matters is what I'm about to say next. Are you listening?"

I glare at him, but I don't respond. I nod my head in agreement.

"This is a win-win scenario for you." Franklin turns towards one of his companions and whispers into his ear. The man turns and leaves the group without another word. "All you have to do to get your PlayStation is let us film you getting your revenge."

Franklin snaps his fingers, turning his head back towards the van. "What's taking so damn long? You're ruining everything."

Led by one man in blue coveralls, they escort my assailant towards the front of the van. With his hands tied behind his back and a rag stuffed into his mouth, he stumbles forward until they force him to his knees with a quick kick at the back of the knee. He falls hard against the cold cement, and a muffled whimper dies in his throat. Frightened, his eyes lock onto mine, a plea for help locked deep within his terrified gaze.

Franklin reaches into a deep pocket on his thigh, hauling out a thick lead pipe. He thumps it against the palm of his hand several times, the heavy pounding sound amplified by the hollow space. " We'll cover up the mess afterwards. What do you say?"

"This is fucking crazy." The words fall out of my mouth before I think about it. "No way, I'm out."

A wave of relief washes over my attacker's face. His lungs deflate, letting out a held breath.

Franklin sighs. "I'm trying to make this easy for you. I don't know what it is, but there's just something about you. Something deep inside that I can relate to." He stretches out his arm, offering the lead pipe to me. "Come on, take it and this will all be over before you know it. Then you can leave with all of your stuff and the PlayStation. Hell, you can use the extra money you save from not having to buy that damn gaming system to get away for a few nights."

I reach out and take the pipe in my hand, feeling the weight of it as Franklin lets go, which catches me off guard. I almost drop it. Deep, hitching sobs escape my attacker's throat, his head tilted up at me so that I can't avoid his petrified eyes. His entire body trembles. Slowly, I bring the iron pipe towards my face, close enough to see every imperfection, every dent, on the rough surface. There are deep stains embedded in the iron that I don't want to think about.

"That's better," Franklin says. "Get that camera rolling. Our clients won't want to miss this."

I raise the pipe above my head, lining it up with my attacker's skull. Euphoria washes over me, riddled with a wave of conflicting emotions. Fear, vengefulness, regret, guilt, anger, excitement, and even joy. But I know I can't do this. I toss the pipe to the side. It clanks off the cement floor with a deafening clatter. "Just let us go," I say, my voice just above a whisper.

"Alright," Franklin announces. "Get the ropes off this man's hand."

They yank my assailant to his feet. The caps of his boots scrape off the floor as one man grabs a fistful of his hair and forces his head down while the other man unties the ropes. When his hands are free, he pulls the rag from his mouth. "Thank you, thank you," he repeats as he stumbles towards me, his arms outstretched. He grips me tight, pulling me into a bear hug.

"Don't mention it," I answer, pulling away from the strange embrace.

"Christmas miracle," Franklin grunts. "I didn't think we'd have any problems getting you to bash this asshole's skull in."

"You're a sick fuck," I say, spitting on the cement at Franklin's feet. "Let's get out of here."

"Hold on just a second," Franklin says, holding up his hand. "We aren't done here."

"We are done," the man beside me answers for both of us. "No way we are playing your game."

I nod my head in agreement. When we get out of here, I have a feeling the man I just saved will buy me that PlayStation 5, anyway.

"Edward, do you even know who this man is?"

"It doesn't matter," I answer.

"Does the name Peter ring a bell?"

I think about it for a moment before saying, "I don't know anyone named Peter."

"But Peter knows you," Franklin says to me, then turns to Peter. "Don't you?"

Peter doesn't respond, but his body language says it all. He takes a tentative step away from me, lowering his gaze to the floor. After a moment of awkward silence, Peter responds, "I only met him tonight." He turns towards me, making sure I'm paying attention to him, not Franklin. "I swear on my mother's life that is the truth."

"He's not lying," Franklin draws out the last word, making it last far too long before continuing. "Technically, he's telling you the truth. However, there's something he's keeping from you. It's not a coincidence you both ran into each other here."

"What's this got to do with anything?" I interrupt. "I don't fucking care about any of this. Just let us leave."

Peter reaches out, placing his meaty hand on my shoulder; the weight of it nearly topples me over. "I'll explain everything once we leave this place. Beers are on me. What do you say?"

"Sure," I smile, "that sounds way better than whatever bullshit this is."

"Isn't that fucking sweet, boys?" Franklin asks sarcastically, twisting at the hips to face his friends on both sides of him. "Maybe you can bring your new girlfriend, Peter? What's her name again?" He pauses, letting the worried expression settle in over Peter's face. "Is it Janie?"

"Listen, Edward," Peter begins before one of Franklin's companions drives his fist into Peter's gut. The wind escapes his lungs in a harsh rasp, the blow buckling him in half. He coughs into a clenched fist, staggering forward until his attacker steadies him.

"What the hell is going on?" I demand, unsure if I directed my question at Franklin or Peter.

Franklin shuffles over to the driver's side door, almost dancing as he makes his way. "This is where it gets fun." He throws open the door with reckless abandon; the hinges scream in protest. He leans into the vehicle, his upper body vanishing inside the cab. Behind me, Peter's heavy breathing steadies. The man holding the camera raises it to his face and flips the switch. A single red light blinks.

"Here it is," Franklin announces. When he emerges from the van, he has a hand gripped in his right fist. He taps the barrel off his forehead several times, then slaps the side of the door. "Now I remember. Peter is fucking your ex, Edward. And he came to the mall to buy your son a PlayStation, so that he could take your place as Alexander's father."

The text from Janie earlier scrolls across my mind's eye. My blood boils with rage and my heart flutters in my chest. I coil my fingers into the palm of my hands, my nails digging at the flesh.

"Listen, man, I just wanted Alexander to have a great Christmas. Ever since you and his mother split, he's been having a shitty time." Peter is talking so fast his words blend together. "I'm not trying to replace you. I never could."

"Shut up," I growl. "I don't want to hear it." I take a step towards Peter, my muscles tighten with anticipation, and I cock my arm back, ready to swing.

Before I can throw the first punch, Peter lunges at me, wrapping me up in a bear hug. "Calm down," he whispers into my ear, his breath hot on the side of my neck. "Don't let him get to you. That's what he wants." He shoves me away from him, holding out one arm to fend off any attack I might make. He's far too strong for me, and he's already proved that earlier tonight when this whole ordeal started.

Franklin cackles, enjoying himself. "Now that we got that out in the open, I think we should lay out the ground rules here." He waves the gun back and forth, urging us to separate. "I'll make this short and sweet because I'm running out of patience with you two. Edward, if you want that PlayStation, you need to kill Peter. Or you can walk out of here, let him buy your son that gaming system, and replace you as his father and he can fuck your ex-girlfriend in your bed. So, what's it going to be?"

Franklin pulls a keyring out of his pocket, jingling them as he waits for my answer.

"I'll buy that PlayStation and let you give it to Alexander for Christmas," Peter says, then adds, "He never needs to know."

"All I want is to get Alexander that PlayStation for Christmas," I say, holding out my hand for the keys.

"You disappointed me, Edward," Franklin sighs.

He hurls the keys at my chest. They jingle off my sternum, and I pin them against my stomach before they can fall to the ground. "Keep that camera rolling," I say, pointing a defiant finger at the cameraman. "People enjoy Christmas miracles this time of year."

"I owe you," Peter says with a sigh of relief. He turns towards me with his arms open wide as he shuffles towards me.

"Think nothing of it," I say as Peter leans in. I grasp the keys between my fist and drive the ragged tip into Peter's throat just before he rests his head on my shoulder. A warm gush of blood explodes from his wound in a dense, hot gush. Vital fluids gargle in his neck as he cries out in shock. With a heavy thud, he drops to his knees, his hands clutched over his throat. "All I want is that PlayStation," I say.

Bouncing on his heels, Franklin claps his hands and twists to face the camera. "I knew he had it in him." He points a triumphant finger at the camera. What did I tell you? A man will do whatever it takes to provide for his family."

When the camera turns off, Franklin comes over and gives me a firm handshake, placing something in my hand. When I glance down, a cheap business card is left crumpled in the palm of my hand.

Franklin guides me towards the door, rapping his knuckles off the metal door. It opens with a groaning creak. The female security guard is admiring her nails, waiting for me. As I leave, I hear Franklin call out my name. I turn to face him, and he has his hand mimicking a phone held to his ear.

"Call me if you want to have a little fun some night." Franklin points towards the card gripped in my fist. "I'll make it worth your while."

Mariah Carey's "All I Want for Christmas" blares through the speaker, the static adding a shrill note to the already annoying pitch of her voice. A small fire crackles in the fireplace. Not because it's Christmas tradition; I couldn't afford the heating bill this month, and I'm saving the oil for the colder months ahead. I sit in my worn recliner, watching Alexander open his Christmas presents. The scent of roasted turkey lingers from our Swanson's microwavable supper. A dull twinkle of green and red light falls against the window from the pathetic strip of light hanging from the eve. It's nothing close to the Christmases I remember growing up, and I feel a sense of shame. But the smile on Alexander's face as I watch him open his PlayStation makes it all worthwhile.

"Dad," Alexander says, turning towards me with the biggest grin I've seen on his face since the divorce, "what's this?" His finger is pointing towards a bloodstain that makes the image of the game appear faded, lacking the polished lustre of the rest of the box.

"That's coffee," I lie.

I can see his mind spinning behind his big blue eyes, processing what I just told him. He's a smart kid, and deep down inside, he realizes I'm lying to him. But he's been asking for this gift since the first time he saw the commercial, so he pushes the truth aside. I help him take the gaming system out of the packaging, set it up on the television, and let him play the first game all by himself. While he's occupied, I discard the packaging in the fireplace, burning away the guilt.

I take out a business card covered in the same substance, eying the phone number. "Hey Alexander," I say, remembering Franklin's offer to return. "Would you like an Xbox for your birthday?"

Alexander claps his hands and smiles with glee. I send Franklin a text and wait for the location to meet him. There's nothing I wouldn't do to make my son happy.

MARKER TWENTY

A smouldering red blaze, fading into the horizon, appeared to fall from the sky like a drifting flanker headed for the Pacific Ocean. In the daylight, the crystal blue water reflected the sunlight in a thousand glaring sparkles. But now, as the daylight was dying, the clear water blackened into a deep purplish blue. A growing chill entered the day's warm breeze, churning the crest of each wave into white caps.

"How much further?" Sandy asked, her voice laden with exhaustion.

Dave squinted against the blister sunset. "There." He pointed towards a flashing white light. "That's Marker Twenty. I can tell by its pattern," he announced with pride. "The beach is just past that buoy."

"It's not that much further," Amy said. She glanced over her shoulder at her younger sister, who appeared ready to quit; her leg quivered, and her lower lip was curled into a pout. Amy knew her sister was ready to throw a tantrum. Deep down, she wanted to scream at Sandy for asking to come. Dave's infatuation with her sister had ruined their date. She fixed her focus back on Dave's broad backside. His muscles rippled as he paddled through the water, his board cutting the choppy waves with ease. The breeze blew his swim shorts tight to his muscular thighs.

"I want to go home," Sandy cried, her voice shrill and

whiney.

Amy drew in a deep breath, filling her lungs with the fresh sea air. The aromatic air tickled the hairs on the back of her nose. "We're almost there," she called out, not bothering to look back at Sandy, realizing the sight of her sister's spoiled face would disrupt her calm.

"My arms are tired," Sandy declared. "And my feet are sore."

A loud splash drew Amy's attention. When she turned around, she found Sandy sitting on her board. Her paddle was only a few feet away, but the current already claimed it, drawing it out to sea. With her head tucked between her knees, Sandy let out a series of hitching sobs. Amy stopped paddling and tried to change directions. Not considering the rolling waves, she lost her balance. Her feet kicked the board from beneath her, and she plunged into the chilly water. Her muscles constricted, the body's effort to self-regulate its temperature, and she drew in the briny water as her instinct to breathe kicked in. When she surfaced, she heard Sandy's childish laughter, and it infuriated her.

"Shut up," Amy screamed, spitting out a mouthful of salt water. The bitter taste in her mouth forced her to gag. She tried to say something else but couldn't catch her breath long enough to speak. With the paddle still gripped in her fist, she slashed at the water, trying to splash her sister.

"You alright, Amy?" Dave asked, a hint of laughter concealed in his tone. He paddled alongside her and bent down to one knee, offering his hand to pull her up. "It'll be fine." He slid off his board as he pulled her up.

The dying sunlight kissed her backside, and she enjoyed its warm embrace. Despite the warmth, Amy shivered. Dave swam towards Amy's board, immune to the water's frigid temperature, and pulled himself up with ease. Rivulets of water cascaded down his back, following its contours towards the small of his back. It didn't take long for Dave to retrieve Sandy's paddle. Amy smiled as she watched Dave bend over to retrieve it.

Out of the corner of her eye, she realized Sandy was checking Dave out as well. Her cheeks flushed red with rage. It was everything she could do to suppress a scream. Sandy was gawking at Dave as he stood before her, his chiselled abs glistening with the sunlight's reflection. He said something that made Sandy laugh, and a wave of jealousy washed over Amy. With Dave's help, Sandy stood up and started paddling towards Amy. All Amy wanted to do was wipe that smirk off her sister's face.

"You okay, Sis?" Sandy asked. Her cheerful voice enraged Amy even more than that shit-eating grin.

"Peachy," Amy snarled. "Just great."

"It's not my fault you fell off your board," Sandy said.

Before Amy screamed at her sister, Dave interrupted their building quarrel. "Hey, check it out," he shouted, his voice filled with excitement.

It didn't take long to see what got him so wound up. A pack of seals swam towards them, bobbing and weaving through the water as they approached. Their bodies appeared a slate grey blur beneath the surface and darkened every time they dived deeper. After a moment of awe, Amy realized the pack was swarming through the waves straight for them. Her heart froze in her chest, and her mouth felt dry. The seals passed beneath them, breaking the surface all around them. Puffs of water sprayed over Amy, and she let out a terrified scream as the last seal bumped her board.

Sandy burst out laughing at her sister. When Amy looked over, it infuriated her to find her sister pointing at her. Even worse, Dave was cracking up at her, too. Fueled by hatred, Amy took a swing at her sister and missed. Thrown off balance, Amy felt the front of the board dip into the water, and the backside lifted into the air. Unable to regain her balance, she plunged into the Pacific again. This time, she fell face first, almost diving. The frigid water was disorienting. If the water was chilly before, this time, she found it frigid. All she saw was darkness in every direction, her legs cramping up with the cold, constricting her lungs. Air bubbles danced across her face as she screamed, and she knew enough to follow them to the surface.

"Goddamnit," Amy screamed as she broke the surface. She slashed at the water with her palms, slapping at it to get out her frustration. At least she didn't get another mouthful of the salt brine.

Once again, Dave was beside her. But this time, his teeth chattered together, and his shoulders were hunched together as he shivered. "Jesus, it's like someone just turned on the cold water," Dave said, his teeth chattering together, making his words choppy.

Drained by the cold water, she struggled even with Dave's help to get back on the board. With her body out of the water, the dying daylight struggled to comfort her. Dave swam back to his board, but Amy wasn't interested in watching him pull himself out of the water again. All she wanted was to get warm.

"Come on," Sandy called out. "Last one to the marker is a rotten egg."

Whenever Sandy spoke like that, it would remind Amy just how childish her sister was. She didn't grow up without a mother. Amy filled that role until their father remarried. Maybe she was partially to blame for her sister's immaturity. But sometimes, she hated her for it all the same.

The marker bobbed up and down with the current, the white caps washing over the rusty red paint. Barnacles had grown over its rough surface, giving it an abandoned appearance. A seagull perched on top, cawing its ocean tune, joined by a flock of birds circling overhead. The light grew brighter in the approaching darkness, the pattern a rapid series of repeating flashes.

Something bumped the bottom of Amy's board. Her leg muscles tensed, but she somehow maintained her balance. A grey blur streaked past her vision, racing towards Marker Twenty, not wanting to be the proverbial rotten egg. The seal dived out of view for a moment, then reappeared, racing for the surface. It thumped into Sandy's board, flinging her into the air. Her startled scream was cut abruptly short as her face smashed into Marker Twenty with a resounding thud. Scarlet smears streaked Sandy's blonde hair, and she sank into the Pacific. Dave and Amy both called out, but there was no response as Sandy slipped beneath the surface.

"Help her," Amy cried. Visions of their childhood raced through her mind. If something happened to her baby sister, it would be her fault. She should have told her she couldn't come with them. That it was too dangerous. Dave dived from his board, his arms and legs propelling him through the choppy water.

After the initial shock wore off, Amy knew she needed to get over there. She plunged her paddle into the water, and it bounced back at her as the blade struck something solid beside her. "Fucking seals," Amy cursed.

When she looked down, her heart jumped into the back of her throat. A two-foot fin sliced through the water, leaving behind a wake as it rushed past her like a freight train. The tail slashed through the water, churning up the sea as it sped past. The ominous bluish-grey body pro-pelled forward. It moved with unbridled speed and grace, closing the gap between her board and Sandy with ease. Her jaw hung open in a silent scream, a warning cry stuck in her throat. Before the fin reached Dave, it slid beneath the surface. He didn't notice its sweeping tail churning up the water below him until it was in front of him. He changed directions in an instant, heading towards the shore.

"Dave," Amy screamed, "get Sandy before she drowns." Without saying a word, Dave swam towards the shore, his arms and legs pumping, churning the water beneath him. "Get back here, you coward," Sandy yelled. Her protective instincts took over, and she paddled to-wards her sister faster, her shoulders burning with the strain. Her board bounced over the waves, the bottom slapping off the surface as she made her way towards her sinking sister.

Out of nowhere, the fin cut through the surface be-hind Dave, instantly closing the gap. Dave managed a single, shrill scream before the shark yanked him beneath the surface. Overhead, the gull's shrill cawing increased. Dave burst through the surface, wailing in agony. A gar-gled, choking scream drowned out the call of the seagulls as Dave spat out the brine, thickened by blood. His arms thrashed against the surface, drawing Amy's attention towards the horrific scene. Blood spurt from his severed wrist, his mangled stump a gnarled mess, creating a bloodstain all around him. The shark's fin sliced through the water, making a whistling sound as it cut through the waves.

Amy dragged herself away from the gruesome sight. She was close enough to Marker Twenty now that she saw globs of blood smattered over the rusted surface of the buoy. Still visible, Amy watched Sandy's outstretched arms sinking away from her. The depth of the water turned her sister's flesh a pale peach. Amy exhaled, forcing the air from her lungs, making it easier to swim downwards. Even though the salt water hurt her eyes, she forced them to stay open, fixed on her sister's hands. Amy's fingers curled around her sister's limp wrist, and she thrashed her legs, dragging them both towards the surface. She allowed her eyes to scan the water, praying she wouldn't spot the shark.

But there was so much water, and it was turning murky with the dying light. Holding her sister's dead weight made it difficult to swim. Without the use of her arms, her legs were running out of steam. Her lungs ached tremendously, the lack of oxygen depleting her energy, and the coldness sank deep into her bones, adding weight to her limbs. As she broke the surface, she still heard Dave's terrified screams and the thrashing of water as the shark attacked him. She filled her lungs with fresh air and pulled Sandy's back onto her chest to get her head out of the water. Her sister's head lulled to the side, her hair billowing out in all directions.

"Breath, damnit," Amy cried, trying to reach out for the buoy. It rocked side to side as it bobbed up and down with the increasing swell, making it difficult to reach. "Don't give up on me." Amy's hand smacked Marker Twenty, sending a flare of pain up her arm all the way to her shoulder. She stifled a curse word and grunted, straining to lift her sister onto Marker Twenty.

Sandy's pale expression stared back at her, her lips purple and her eyes bloodshot. There was a deep crack on her forehead, exposing the bone beneath. A trickle of blood streaked down her ghastly face. The red stood out in stark contrast against the pale flesh.

A deadly silence caught Amy's attention. She glanced over her shoulder, finding nothing except a red slick dragged out across the blue surface. Dave was gone. Seagulls divebombed into the filthy water, the blood tarnishing their white coats. They drifted overhead, waiting for the next victim to meet their demise so they could pick at the remains. Amy scoured the horizon, searching for any sign of the shark. One gull emerged from the water with a hunk of severed flesh dangling from its beak. It soared high into the sky, then drifted down towards them, landing atop Marker Twenty. The scrap of flesh fell from its beak and slapped Amy in the face before it splashed into the water.

When she looked down, Dave's eye stared back up at her. A scream escaped her lips, drowning out the sound of splashing water behind her. Amy swatted the pulpy mess away and doubled her efforts to lift her sister out of the water. She pressed her back up against the buoy, and grabbed Sandy beneath her armpits, trying to hoist her up onto Marker Twenty. Despite her efforts, it was all in vain. There was no way that Amy could ever lift her sister up while still submerged in the water herself. She wrapped her fingers around her sister's wrist, her nails sinking into the clammy flesh.

"Don't let go," Amy shouted, praying for Sandy's purple lips to part and start speaking. The roar of the ocean was the only sound that greeted her. She took a moment to glance over her shoulder, expecting the fin to be right behind her. All she saw was the craggy shore, taunting her. If she made a break for it now, while the shark hunted a seal that had strayed from the pack, she had a chance to make it. Sandy's dead weight anchored Amy to Marker Twenty.

"Goddamnit," Amy cried. She placed her palm on the

buoy and pressed herself up, the rusty surface scrapping her chest, gouging her flesh. Tendrils of blood streaked down her stomach, dripping into the water. She leaned forward, placing her weight over the small ledge, and wrapped her left arm into the interlocking rails, bracing herself.

An elongated growl escaped her lungs as she strained against her sister's weight, dragging her up and over the side slowly. There was a moment when her sister appeared to be glued to the marker, her torn flesh caught along the rough surface. Overhead, the flashing lights repeated, seeming to speed up as time ran out. There was a thunderous boom, and the buoy rumbled. Amy hauled her sister up onto the flat with her. She locked her arms around her sister, not willing to let her go. Sandy's eyes fluttered open, catching the last rays of daylight as the sun dipped below the horizon. The stars overhead shined bright, piercing through the approaching darkness.

"You're going to be okay now," Amy lied. "Everything is going to be all right."

Her sister's mouth moved, her lungs only capable of producing a haggard croak. No words formed on her tongue, but her lips went through the motions.

"Don't say anything." Amy pulled Sandy's head into her bosom, caressing the back of her head. Her sister's hair was matted with blood and gore, the salt water drying it out. Amy felt something warm and sticky oozing over her thigh and feet. When she glanced down, blackened blood pumped from the gnarled wound. Where Sandy's thigh meets her knee, a mangled bite had stripped flesh from the bone, leaving the femur sticking out of the gore. In the dusk, it was difficult to see how deep the wound extended, but Amy knew her sister's wound was fatal.

Amy sobbed, drawing in a tethering breath. "I love

you, Sandy."

In the dusk, Amy watched several fins churning up the water, converging on the bloody slick that was David. Shadows cast over her from the cliffs along the shore, the black tips stretching out for her like fingers. Amy shuffled in towards the middle of the buoy, resting her shoulder blades against the rails, and tucked her head between her knees. She cried until her eyes burned, struggling to catch her breath, choking on the mucus running down the back of her throat.

She let go of her sister, her torso slumped over, before sliding off the flat and splashing into the ocean with a loud sploosh. Even as the night crept in, she admired the growing silver light of the moon against the pitch-black surface. The crest of the waves rolled over the buoy, washing away the blood left behind by Sandy's severed leg. Gulls cawed incessantly, and the shark thrashed its tail in the water, circling Marker Twenty. One shark surfaced, a sliver of moonlight caught in its eye. The creature appeared to be watching her, studying her. Amy shuddered at the sight of its jaw. Jagged rows of gnarled teeth protruded from the creature's bloodied gums. It watched her for what seemed like an eternity, then disappeared as suddenly as it had appeared.

Amy was cold, not from the dropping temperature but from the shock. She lost track of time. All she knew was the sun was long gone. A pale yellow orb hung high in the sky in its place. Clouds drifted past the moon. A stiff breeze blew in from the ocean, chilling her to the bone. Goosebumps riddled her flesh. She shivered uncontrollably. She tried to lie down, but the waves rolling over the buoy wouldn't allow her any peace. Her backside ached from sitting on the hardened surface for so long, and her joints throbbed, frozen stiff from the cold and inactivity.

Sleep escaped her, leaving her alone with her thoughts and the roar of the ocean. Memories of her sister flooded her mind, bringing fresh tears to her cheeks. They dripped from her chin and washed away with the waves.

Time no longer had meaning, and she suffered for hours. Her head pounded from dehydration, and her stomach clenched with cramps and hunger pains. A lack of sleep muddled her thoughts, compounding her troubles. The only thing holding her in place was fear. Below, the ocean was darker than the night sky. A rolling sheet of pitch black with unseen monsters waiting just below the surface. Depleted of energy, she didn't think she would make it to shore even if the sharks weren't stalking the waters. She only hoped that someone would rescue her. If she managed to hold out until morning, somebody would come to the beach. After all, it was a popular area with the locals. It had to be part of somebody's morning routine.

Overhead, the clouds blotted out the moon, enclosing Amy in a shroud of darkness, alone with the flashing beacon. The wind rocked Marker Twenty, the waves lapping against the side as the tide surged. Foamy saltwater sprayed her face as the waves crashed into the buoy. Drops of salt water ran down her face, stinging her cracked lips. Her tongue recoiled at the taste, but she couldn't stop it from exploring, drawing in the saltwater. It made her stomach urge, but she couldn't help herself. She didn't want to die of thirst, allowing herself a few drops before the saltiness became too much to bear. Her stomach ached, and her headache throbbed. Somehow, she kept it down.

A light drizzle started falling. It was warmer than the ocean and lulled her into a state of comfort. She fought a losing battle against sleep and drifted into a restless state of semi-consciousness. While she dozed, a set of headlights drove along the winding road leading towards the beach. If she had been awake, she could have tried to signal them. But she didn't hear her parents yelling out her name—or her sister's. She slept through it all, their panicked cries drowned out by the roar of the ocean. Her parents didn't recognize David's vehicle, so they went on searching for them. They called the cops, but they looked in all the wrong places. By the time they discovered where she was, it would be too late.

When she awakened, the sun was climbing above the horizon. A flaring orange semi-circle cast a brilliant glow over the ocean. The faint rays of light warmed her, rousing her from sleep. Her eyes were stuck together. She wrested them open with her fingers. A flock of seagulls gathered all around her, either perching on the buoy or drifting overhead. They cawed at her. The collective call was a high-pitched screech.

She strained to sit up, but her joints were locked in place. Everything hurt, especially her lower back and knees. The buoy wasn't rocking as much now, but she struggled to gain her balance. Her cracked lips throbbed, and her throat was dry. The glare off the ocean strained her eyes, distorting her vision; a million reflections of sunlight bounced off the surface. She scoured the surface for any sign of the sharks, but there wasn't any in sight. Cautiously, she edged herself across the Marker Twenty, peering over the side with weary eyes. The water was a deep blue, and she couldn't see very far into the depths. Anything could be lurking just out of view. If she didn't move soon, she would die of thirst or exposure. But she couldn't bear to stare into the darkened waters, terrified of what lurked beneath the rolling tide.

A loud grumble seized her attention. Hidden from view, an engine thundered and tires rumbled over the dirt road leading to the beach. She tried to pull herself up to get a better vantage of the beach. With her feet numb and the muscles taxed to their limits, the task proved arduous. She opened her mouth opened, and a silent scream escaped her throat. Unable to produce a sound, she licked her lips, trying to draw moisture into her mouth. Too afraid to look, she plunged her hand over the side of the buoy and stuck her fingers in her mouth, sucking off the salt water. She gagged and coughed, throwing up an acidic, clear yellow fluid.

"Help." Her voice came out just above a whisper. Slipping her hand back into the ocean, she forced more salt water into her mouth.

"Help," she screamed. This time, her voice was loud enough to be heard over the whistling wind.

But it didn't matter. The sound of the engine faded, leaving behind a trail of dust settling in the air as a dirt bike crested the road and headed back towards the main highway. Amy screeched, the shrill sound scaring off the seagull. It flapped its wings and soared high into the sky, catching the breeze, and headed off towards the shore.

She stared out across the dark blue water as the wind whipped across the open ocean, spraying salt water into her face and stinging her eyes. With no other options, she slid into the frigid ocean, kicking her legs and thrashing her arms, trying desperately to swim towards the shore. A shadow drifted beneath her.

ONLY A TRICK

Driven by the howling wind, a frigid mixture of rain and hail hammered the windows. The gutters groaned as torrential rainwater gushed through the leaf-clogged drain pipes. Even inside a dampness hung in the air, and Andrew couldn't get warm no matter what the thermostat registered. But soon that wouldn't be an issue. A sly smile crossed his face, pressing his lips thin against his yellowed teeth as he eyed the bottle of whiskey on the counter in the kitchen.

As the local news paused for break, the commercial blared through the speakers with an added tinge of static for good measure. "Goddamnit," Andrew snapped, rustling himself to a seated position to reach the remote laid on the dining room table in front of him. "Why do they have to make the commercials louder than the program?"

His wife didn't respond to his outburst. With a disdainful grimace, Andrew glanced at her slumped in the sofa's corner. Her hands worked deftly, the knitting needles click-clacking away as she watched the news. The springs in Andrew's worn recliner squeaked with every movement. Over the years, the faded fabric covering the armrests had become frayed. He muted the volume and tried to settle back into his groove, which grew more difficult to find with every passing day now.

"Are you going to be at that all night, Cynthia?" Andrew snarled.

Cynthia paused, letting out a deep sigh before she answered. "If I thought you'd give out the Halloween candy, I wouldn't be here." Her hands resumed the motion, the constant drone of needles growing louder now.

"Oh bleeding hearts for the poor children," Andrew groaned, placing his hand over his chest.

"Stop it," Cynthia lashed out. "It doesn't hurt to be kind."

Andrew patted his pocket. "Tell that to our bank account."

Cynthia shook her head in disgust. "Maybe the bank account would feel better if you contributed to it," she said, her tone curt.

Ignoring his wife's comment, Andrew continued as if she hadn't insulted him. "If you ask me," he paused, thrusting his finger into his chest for emphasis as if she didn't know him, "any parent foolish enough to send their child out into this weather deserves a slap on the wrist." He felt victorious when his wife didn't respond. "And another thing. How the hell did this holiday ever become about handing out candy to children? It's ridiculous if you ask me, and I don't feel one bit guilty about standing up to consumerism."

A sharp knock on the door brought a smile to Cynthia's face, and it made Andrew disgusted to watch as she skipped to the front door to hand out candy to those ungrateful snot rags. He had a mind to take an inventory of the candy and pass out bills to the families the next day. Shrill laughter and a frigid gust of wind greeted Cynthia as she threw open the door. She greeted each child with a jovial voice complimenting their costumes before dumping fistfuls of goodies into their outstretched hands. It made Andrew sick to the pit of his stomach. The best part of Halloween night was the leftover bars and candy, and

Cynthia appeared to be on a mission to ruin the one shred of joy he got from this horrendous holiday.

Waiting impatiently, Andrew eyed the digital clock on his cable box for the hundredth time in the last hour. Normally, he wouldn't have his first drink until puck drop; a tradition he picked up from his late father. He raised his empty glass to his old man in mock tribute, "May the bastard rest in peace."

"Leave the dead to rest in peace," Cynthia scolded him as she found her way back to the couch. "If you're going to be a miserable old miser, then drink your damn rum now and get it over with. It's not like the Leafs are going to win or lose if you break your father's stupid tradition." A sly smile crossed her face as she added, "It's not like they've won the Stanley Cup with it."

"What do you even know about it?" Andrew snarled, slamming the remote down on the armrest. "Keep running your mouth and I'll teach you a thing or two about it."

"Don't you talk to me like that," Cynthia said, her voice trembling. "I'm not your mother, even if you are your father."

Infuriated, Andrew sprang from his chair, sending the remote flying across the room. It slammed off the floor with a splintering crack and the batteries rolled beneath the couch. "Get out of my sight," Andrew yelled, glaring at his wife with bloodshot eyes. "Just get the fuck out of here before you come to regret those words."

"You're an asshole," Cynthia stated. She stood up, matching his gaze, her eyes wet with tears.

Andrew drew in deep breaths, his chest hitching as the anger coursed throughout his body. He balled his hands into fists until he caught Cynthia's eyes wandering down to them. "Don't let the door hit your fat ass on the way out of here," he barked, fueled by a brooding rage that had boiled over.

Cynthia stomped over to the porch, yanked her jacket from the hook on the wall, and grabbed her purse from the floor. "I'll be at my sister's until you've come to your senses." Without another word, she slammed the door as she left.

"Good riddance," Andrew called out.

Andrew stood in the living room, staring at the door, shaking furiously. Outside, he heard the engine rumble to life before settling into a growling idle. Drawn towards the bottle of whiskey, he wandered into the kitchen and poured himself a stiff shot in a dirty glass. He tilted his head back, drowning the amber liquid in one gulp. It burned all the way down then splashed into his empty stomach. Unable to contain his anger, he hurled the glass into the sink. It exploded in a barrage of sharp, jagged shards that rained over the kitchen floor. Not wanting to deal with the mess, he grabbed the bottle and made his way back into the living room, planting it on the table in front of his chair.

His stomach grumbled, brought to life by the flood of alcohol. Before he turned back to the kitchen, he spotted the bowl of Halloween candy beside the door. With a greedy smirk, he strolled onto the porch and snatched the bowl. As he turned to leave, a gregarious knock rattled the door.

"Forgot your keys, bitch," Andrew chuckled as he threw the front door open.

"Trick or treat," a teenage boy wearing a vampire costume announced, his voice deep. His cheap makeup ran down his face with the rain and his soaked cape clung to his body. The boy was almost as tall as Andrew, but his gaunt frame couldn't hide behind the clingy costume. He held out a pillowcase and shivered as a gust of wind pelted him with a slushy mixture of half-frozen rain.

"Aren't you a little old to be out trick-or-treating?" Andrew questioned, sizing up his guest with an accusing gaze.

"My brother is sick," he answered, which sounded rehearsed to Andrew. "And I promised him he'd get some candy tonight."

"Well, ain't you a sweet young man," Andrew said, unable to contain his sarcasm. Without saying a word, the boy stood in the door frame, leaning forward as the wind lashed out. Andrew stared at the pillowcase as it swayed in the wind, only half-filled with treats, which did little to add any weight against the blustery weather. "I guess you are having a rough night?"

The teen vampire nodded his head. The freezing rain wiped any trace of a smile from his face. He glanced up at Andrew then down at the bowl in his hands. "Most folk won't give out candy to a boy my age," he said, shaking his pillowcase and attempting to smile at Andrew.

"Here," Andrew said, reaching out for the top of the pillowcase. The boy jerked away from Andrew's outstretched grasp but not quickly enough. Andrew grasped the bag, holding it open. He dumped the contents of the bowl into the sack. "That's a treat."

A genuine smile crossed the vampire's face, revealing his plastic fangs. "Thanks, mister." The boy tried to pull the bag back but couldn't yank it from Andrew's grasp.

"And this is one of my favourite tricks," Andrew chuckled as he snatched the bag out of the kid's hands. The vampire stood in the rain with a shocked expression on his face. As his lips parted to protest, Andrew sent a swift kick to the boy's stomach, sending him toppling over the stairs. "Grow up, kid. Life will eat you alive if you walk around looking for a handout."

Andrew slammed the door shut, locking it before he walked away. The boy slammed his fists off the door, rattling the frame, cursing and swearing as he did. But the vampire gave up just as the hockey game started. Andrew drained a mouthful of whiskey and opened a bag of ketchup chips. "I don't know what Cynthia's problem is, but I love Halloween."

"You overpaid prick," Andrew cursed at the television set. "Haven't you ever learned that you can't score if you don't shoot the puck?" Drunk, Andrew staggered to his feet and mimicked taking a slapshot using the empty bottle of whiskey as the stick. The horn blew in the stadium, signalling the end of the first period. A highlight package played before cutting to commercials. Andrew admired the two goals by Auston Matthews as he drained the last of his whiskey straight from the bottle.

"There's got to be something else in this house to drink," Andrew said, slurring his words. He shuffled through the empty wrappers that littered the floor and made his way towards the kitchen. When he found himself in front of the sink, rooting through the cupboard above the stainless steel, his mind jumped back to earlier when he had broken the glass against the sink. He lunged forward, leaning his gut against the counter enough to lift his feet off the floor. Fearful of cutting his feet off a shard of glass, he inched his right foot down gingerly. When his foot touched the floor without incident, he sneaked a peek at the floor. A layer of crumbs and stains coated the floor, but there was no broken glass to be found.

Andrew scoured the area, searching for any signs of his broken glass. Unable to find even the slightest trace anywhere, even along the edge of the board that ran beneath the cupboards, he scratched his scalp. Flakes of dandruff drifted down to his shoulder, sprinkling his blue Maple Leafs sweater with pocks of white that matched the lettering. Confused, he leaned the small of his back against the counter and continued to do a thorough, albeit drunken, examination of the situation.

"Clever girl," Andrew said. "I knew you couldn't stay away for long." He rubbed the scruff on his chin. "Smartest decision you've made in a while." He stumbled over to the back door and twisted the knob, letting a blustery gust of glacial air into the kitchen. "Just as I thought." Certain of the sequence of events, he determined that if he checked the basement, he'd find Cynthia asleep on their pull-out sofa. She must have come in through the back door during the first period, cleaned up the mess, and headed downstairs. Her sister didn't want to deal with her constantly running away from home and sent her packing. That made two people in her life who had grown sick of her shit.

Andrew opened the fridge, pushed aside a jug of orange juice, and spotted three amber bottles lurking behind. "There you are," he said with a wide grin on his face, raising the bottle in mock salute. He twisted off the cap and tossed it into the sink. It clattered around, rattling off the dishes and steel walls. He stumbled back into the living room, making his way towards the curtain, pulling them aside to peek into the driveway. The car wasn't there, but he still knew Cynthia was home for the evening.

On the television, the referee dropped the puck for the second period, and the announcers started calling the action. Andrew slumped into his recliner, allowing his weight to carry him backward. The legs scrapped over the floor as the chair shifted with his momentum.

"Come on, boys," Andrew said, pumping his fist as his team gained possession of the puck. He peeled the wrapper off a Mars bar, screwing up his face at the size of it before popping it into his mouth. Glued to the television, he reached into the pillowcase, pulled out another treat, and tore the wrapper off without looking. His lips puckered at the sour taste. He took a giant swig of beer to wash the taste from his mouth then another for good measure.

"Can't win them all, I suppose," he complained to himself. "But beggars can't be choosers."

A hammering fist rattled the door, causing Andrew to jump forward in his chair. "Quit that before ye breaks me door," he yelled, his voice trembling with fright. He staggered towards the front door, trying to glimpse the stranger through the window. Just as he reached for the doorknob, a thunderous boom rattled the front door in its frame. The door jerked inwards, pushed to its limits, and the sound of splintering wood ripped through the air, piercing Andrew's eardrums.

A dreadful silence fell over the house, blanketing the sound of the rain and driving wind. Andrew's heart thrashed inside his chest. Cold sweat formed on his brow and ran into his eyes. He stood still, except for the uncontrollable trembling, and listened for a sound; any sound would be welcome.

"Who..." he tried to call out, but a lump stuck in his throat, choking him. He coughed, struggling to clear his throat, spewing a wad of phlegm onto the floor. Gradually, the sound of hammering rain came back, and the wind howled against the windows once more. After a minute, he recovered his fortitude and called out, "Who's there?"

This time, a mild knock answered his call. When Andrew placed his hand on the knob and turned, the wind forced the door open. He jumped back, not knowing what to expect. Standing all alone in the rain, a little boy who couldn't be much over ten held the hood of his yellow rain slicker down over his face. A pair of matching yellow rubber boots ran up to his knees with his weatherproof pants tucked into them. Rivers of rainwater gushed down the boy's jacket, cascading over his boots and splashing off the ground.

"And who are you supposed to be?" Andrew asked. Impatiently, he waited for the boy to answer, growing angry with every passing second. He tapped his beer bottle off his hip twice before raising it to his lips. "You don't even have a bag or anything to carry your treats in." Andrew tried to get a peek at the boy's face, but the child pulled the hood down over his nose and his hand obscured his mouth and chin. Andrew took another gulp of beer to occupy his idle hands.

"Last chance, kid," Andrew barked, "or I'll be slamming this door shut in your face."

The boy tilted his head up, still holding on to the brim of his hood. A soft sound escaped his lips, but not loud enough for Andrew to pick anything out. When he let go of the brim of his hood, Andrew watched his lips continue to move without offering a sound.

"Boy," Andrew snapped, "you're going to need to speak up. I can't hear you over the rain."

The boy's lips parted as he spoke, louder this time, but still inaudible against the howling winds. Andrew leaned forward, tilting his ear towards the boy. Frigid drops of rain splashed off the yellow rain slicker and sprayed into Andrew's ear, drowning out the sound and forcing Andrew to lean in closer.

"Did you leave any treats for me?" the boy asked, his

voice raspy. "Or did you eat them all?"

Andrew's cheeks flushed, and his eyes bulged in their sockets. "Are you trying to shame me because I'm fat?"

Despite the raindrops hammering the boy's face, he never blinked. "I want to know if you ate all the treats my brother worked so hard to get for me."

Shocked, Andrew remained silent; his tongue was tied in a confused knot. "Are you trying to tell me that little shit was your brother?"

Without saying a word, the boy answered the question by nodding his head.

Unable to contain his laughter, Andrew guffawed, holding the door frame and bending over at the hips. "That kid's a loser," Andrew started, then paused to allow another fit of laughter to pass before continuing his thought. "And you must be one too if you're out in this weather trying to get a sack full of cheap dollar-store treats." Andrew slapped his leg, punctuating his laughter. "What's wrong with your parents? Is your dad a deadbeat who can't afford to feed you or something?"

A cruel snarl bared the boy's teeth, but he said nothing.

"Don't you be growling at me, young fella," Andrew said, puffing out his chest. "I think your brother sent you to the wrong house or something. I haven't seen nobody all night."

"No," the boy snapped, "this is the right house and you're the man who stole my brother's candy."

"Maybe he gave you the wrong directions or something." Andrew hesitated, trying to come up with a good excuse. "It couldn't have been me. I just got back home from work, kid. So why don't you put an egg in your shoe and beat it?"

"Give it back to me. It's mine."

"I told ya, I don't have your brother's goddamn candy

kid. Now scram before I call the cops and have them come out here," Andrew said, raising the tone of his voice. He tried to close the door, but the boy jammed his rubber boot into the frame. "I'm about to lose my patience with you, kid. Get your fucking foot out of my door or you're going to regret it."

"What, are you going to hit me?" the boy answered.

"I don't know what your brother told ya," Andrew puffed, "but it's time for you to leave and never come back here. Whatever he told you, I don't have your candy, and I've never seen your brother." Andrew laughed before continuing. "I don't even know why I'm explaining this to a kid.

A bolt of lightning split the sky in half, casting a barrage of shadows dancing across the boy's face. The boy pushed his way inside, shoving Andrew aside with ease. With a vicious yank, he ripped the door out of Andrew's hand and slammed it shut, the blow rattling the entire foundation. His eyes glistened red, orange, and yellow.

"Now wait just a goddamn minute," Andrew stuttered, backstepping deeper into the house. "Whatever you think I did..."

"Shut up," the boy snarled, his voice raspy and deep. He held up a fist, his skin crawling with movement just beneath the surface. There was a sickening pop, followed by a wet splatter of blood across the door as gnarled claws emerged from the boy's hands. A pained scream escaped the boy's throat.

"It was only a trick,' Andrew cried out, shrinking into the corner as the monstrous figure stalked him.

"My brother only wanted to protect everyone from me," the boy snickered. He raised a clawed hand high in the air as a smile creased his face, pressing his lips thin against his teeth. "But now it's time for my treat."

With savage ferocity, the claws tore through the flesh with ease, sending a spray of crimson across the wall. Andrew clutched his stomach and collapsed to the floor, his weight driving into the wall. Holding up his hand, he pleaded for his life. Another swift blow scattered his fingers across the floor; blood spurt from the severed digits in clouts of bright red. With all the energy he had left, Andrew crawled away from the boy. He felt a sharp pain radiate from the back of his leg as the claws tore through his hamstrings. Razor-sharp claws slicked through the tendons with ease.

"It was only a trick," Andrew said, his words choking through the blood filling his throat.

He rolled over onto his side and gazed up, expecting to see the boy. But there was no one standing before him. His eyes dart across the room, searching every crevice and scouring every shadow. A haggard, hitching laugh rocked Andrew's body. His hands probed the wound on his stomach, his fingers stained scarlet from the superficial wound. Then he laughed even harder as he realized he had fingers.

"It must have been a drunken hallucination."

Andrew staggered back to the chair, his legs weak. Exhausted, he slumped into the chair and fell asleep.

Andrew awoke, suffering from a pounding in his head. He rubbed his throbbing temples. He glanced at the television and noticed that the hockey game was still going on.

"Must have been a nightmare," he said, rubbing his stomach. A handful of candy bar wrappers lay discarded at his feet.

Thump thump THUMP

"Trick or treat!" The boy's shrill cackle echoed outside as the door handle turned. A frigid breeze billowed through the house and heavy footsteps trod towards Andrew.

"But it was only a trick," Andrew sobbed as the boy staggered into view, his appearance having grown more grotesque.

MUMMERS: LET THE WRONG ONE IN

Outside, the wind howled against the side of the house, rattling the windows; every beam groaned in protest, having settled long ago. Hardened pellets of snow rattled against the window in rhythmic cadence, driven from the font lawn by the blustering gale in rapid bursts. A faint trail of wispy clouds rushed past the pale yellow moon in a never-ending stream, the shadows dragging across the front window as Meridith stared out the window. Fascinated by the surging storm, she sipped from a mug of hot chocolate, steam billowing from the cup, swirling around her face.

Nestled underneath a woven blanket, Meridith regretted not renting a cabin with a fireplace. Her husband Thomas didn't want to fool around with the mess and extra work involved, but the electric heat just didn't provide the same comforting warmth as a roaring fire. As a child, Meridith fell asleep effortlessly most winter nights, stretched out on the loveseat across from the hearth. The interior's pinewood walls were riddled with dark brown knots, offering a pleasant, comforting aroma that made her feel at ease. Beside her, her phone played the ambient noise of a crackling wood fire to set the mood.

"Do you think we will lose power?"

Thomas glanced up from his book. A slight grin poked out from beneath his bushy beard. "Something tells me you would enjoy that." Hidden amongst the tangle of gray hairs, the last few remnants of his natural chestnut colour poked out. With his head shaved, he appeared younger and more intimidating than his actual demeanour would suggest. An old soul, Thomas had settled into his golden years with a grace that Meridith envied.

Meridith nodded her head. "Actually I would. I remember being a little kid at my parents' cabin. We didn't even have electricity hooked up. It would be nice to disconnect for once." She twirled her fingers through her hair, admiring the jet black dye her friend Hannah had recommended and agreed it suited her tanned skin.

Thomas shook his head and knocked his book's spine off the coffee table. "But it's so hard to read in the dark." Without waiting for a response, his eyes wandered back down to the page, signalling he was finished with this conversation, intentionally making it known that this was not his ideal vacation destination. After years of living away from Crooked Creek, Meridith wanted to spend an old-fashioned Christmas back in Newfoundland. After finding out their daughter would be in Cancun with her new boyfriend this year, Thomas couldn't come up with an interesting excuse to avoid a trip home to be with his wife's family.

"I'll get some candles," Meridith said. She pushed herself up from the leather couch, groaning as her knees cracked. With a quick tug, she straightened out her dress, frowning as it hugged her midsection a little too tightly. The floor was frigid, the chill seeping through her wool socks, reminding her she should have splurged for the cabin with the fireplace.

The cupboards creaked as she pulled them open, searching through a random assortment of treasures left behind by the owners. On the first shelf, she pushed aside a mixture of shot glasses with various local phrases, amber plastic cups that reminded her of her grandmother's collection, and glasses that her father would have used for mixing his rum and cokes. Standing on her tippy toes, she rummaged through the items on the upper shelf. Her fingers ran over a box of matches, which she nudged down and let fall to the counter. The matches rattled around as the box clattered into the sink. Drawn towards the sound, she realized the owners had lined the candles up along the backsplash beside the sink.

Jammed into wine bottles, several layers of multi-coloured melted wax covered the candles from years of use. "Wow," she said as she twisted the bottle around in her hands, "this is neat. Maybe I should start doing this when we get back home."

Not bothering to lift his head out of his book, Thomas grunted his agreement. A brilliant beam of light swept across the front window, demanding Meridith's attention. She turned her head towards the clock hanging over the television, the bright light reflected towards her off the black screen.

"Are you expecting someone?" Thomas asked, a disappointed rasp infecting his tone.

"No," Meridith said, wandering towards the front window to get a better view.

"Your sister doesn't respect personal boundaries," he said, snapping his book closed. "It's getting late."

"I don't think that's my sister." Meridith reached out for her phone, awakening it to see if there were any notifications or messages she might have missed. There wasn't any, just a blank screen with the time displayed in large numbers. "She would have messaged me if she wanted to come over this late."

"Who else would it be?" Thomas barked. "No one else

lives close enough to walk here." Thomas stood up and tossed his book onto the coffee table. It slid across and tumbled to the floor in a fluttering crash of pages, drawing a slew of curse words under his breath in the process.

Meridith laced her fingers together, pressing her pinkie fingers against the glass, and stared out into the driveway. A young woman trudged through the freshly fallen snow, kicking up puffs of glistening white with every step as she made her way down the driveway. Tufts of straggly blond hair stuck out from beneath a purple and pink beanie, her head tilted down, her hand covering her face to shield herself against the wind. A flashlight dangled from the other hand, casting a dancing beam of light through the front porch window as she neared. Snow crunched beneath her boots with every step as she made her way up the porch stairs.

The young girl rapped her bare knuckles off the door, the sound all but drowned out by the blustering wind and creaking beams. Meridith rushed across the living room, towards the door.

"What the hell are you doing?" Thomas snapped, reaching out and grabbing Meridith by the wrist. "You don't know who that is?"

"Thomas," Meridith paused, staring into her husband's eyes. She didn't know if it was fear or anger lingering in his gaze. "It's a young woman who needs our help."

Thomas rolled his head towards the door then back to Meridith. "I'll get the door," he said, letting out a defeated sigh. "You get your phone and be ready to dial for help if needed."

"Thank you," Meridith said. When she grabbed her phone, she turned to find Thomas still standing there, hesitating. "Go ahead, Thomas, get the door now."

Thomas sighed, his shoulders slumping and rising as he reached out for the door. With his chest puffed out, he pulled it open. A frigid gust of wind swept into the cabin, ruffling the jackets hung from the hooks along the wall. "Can I help you?" he asked.

The girl shivered, her arms wrapped around her body. Meridith hadn't noticed until now, but the stranger wasn't dressed for the weather. She wore a dull gray sweater with the word Slipknot scrawled across the front in gory red letters.

"Invite the girl in and close the damn door, Thomas," Meridith said, scuffling back to her chair. She grabbed the blanket and hurried back to the porch.

Reluctantly, Thomas stepped aside and ushered the woman inside with the wave of a hand. Timid, the woman stepped inside, dragging snow onto the porch as she stepped over the door frame. Meridith held the blanket out in front of her, shaking her wrist to let the woman know to take the blanket. "What's your name, dear?"

The girl spoke, her lips moving, but Meridith couldn't hear a sound. She glanced up at Meridith for a moment, but her eyes darted away the moment they made contact, dropping to the floor.

"What did you say?" Thomas asked, leaning in towards the young woman.

"My name is Jessica. And my car ran out of gas down the road."

"You must be frozen, Jessica?"

Meridith stepped forward and draped the blanket over Jessica's shoulders. A thin smile pressed Jessica's cracked lips against her teeth, exposing painful cuts along her bottom lip. When she tilted her head back, the light cast shadows across her face that sank her eyes deep into the skull.

"Where is your car?" Meridith asked, leading Jessica towards the kitchen. "Can I get you a tea or anything?" She walked over to the stove, grabbed the kettle, gave it a shake, and placed it back down on the burner. The flames burst out as she turned the dial, licking the cast iron greedily.

Behind her, Thomas let out an exaggerated sigh. He rustled through the closet and got a broom, sweeping up the snow behind Jessica as it trailed her into the kitchen. When Jessica sat down, she pulled the blanket tight around her neck and rested her elbows against the edge of the table. The heat in the cabin quickly melted the snow from her boots and puddled around the chair.

"My car ran out of gas just before the turnoff to this road," Jessica said.

Meridith smiled. "You're lucky we're here."

"How did you know there'd be someone down this road?" Thomas asked, interjecting himself into the conversation. "Can't be any homes down this way."

"I'm not from around here," Jessica answered, her tone defensive. "Thought it would be safer than wandering down the highway in this storm."

"You don't have to be so rude, Thomas," Meridith scolded her husband as she pulled down three white ceramic mugs from the cupboard. The kettle whistled, spewing steam from the spout. "There's a can of gas in the back of the truck."

"Thank you," Jessica said, her voice gaining volume. "You don't have to do that. I'll call my friend to come get me if you can lend me your phone. Mine ran out of battery power." She held up her phone as evidence.

Without a second thought, Meridith handed her phone to Jessica before going about making three cups of tea. She poured a heaping teaspoon of sugar into her mug and a dash of milk into another for Thomas. As Jessica used the phone, Meridith placed the milk, sugar, and mug on the table in front of Jessica. Jessica added milk and sugar absentmindedly into her mug as she rummaged through her jeans' pockets. She pulled out a crumpled piece of paper, and did her best to fold out the wrinkles, revealing a phone number in smudged blue ink scrawled hastily perpendicular to the lines.

With shaking hands, she dialled the number.

"Hey." Jessica pauses, waiting for the person on the other end to finish. "Yeah, that's right. I made it here."

Thomas stared at Jessica, his brow furrowed as he listened to the one-sided conversation.

"You were right. They let me in."

"Wait," Thomas interrupted, his arms crossed over his chest. "Who are you talking to?"

"You can come pick me up now." Jessica ended the call and passed Meridith the phone. "Thank you."

Thomas snatched the phone from Meridith and held it in front of his face, his fingers fumbling across the screen. "Who did you call?"

"What has gotten into you?" Meridith asked, embarrassed.

"She said she didn't know where she was," he said, pointing his finger at Jessica. "But she expected to be let in here."

A nervous burst of laughter escaped Meredith's throat. "You're just being paranoid."

Frantic, Thomas screamed. "Where's the fucking redial button?" He turned his back to Meridith as she stretched out to snatch the phone from him.

Jessica slumped into the chair, her fingers clasped around the steaming mug of tea, staring down into the swirling vapour rising over her face. Before taking a sip, she pursed her lips together and blew onto the surface, sending a splash of tea dribbling over the side, staining the white porcelain a light brown.

Meridith turned back towards Jessica, leaning her hand on the kitchen table. "Jessica darling." She lowered herself until they were eye level. "Can you just tell Thomas who you called so we can straighten this whole thing out?"

"I'm sorry," Jessica whispered, a single streaking down her cheek.

The phone rang, startling Thomas. He dropped the phone, and it clattered across the tiled floor, sliding under the cupboard and slamming into the moulding. "Fucking Christ." Thomas dropped to his hands and knees, searching for the cell.

"What are you sorry for, my dear?" Meridith reached out, placing a comforting hand on Jessica's shoulder. "This isn't your fault."

"I'm afraid that it is," Jessica mumbled. "I chose your name from the phone book."

As the phone continued to ring, Thomas cursed and started pounding his fist off the cupboards in frustration. He found it and started pounding his index finger into the screen. "How do you answer this?" His voice was a panicked scream. He thrusts the cell phone into Meridith's hand. "Answer it."

With the phone held in her hand, she stared down at the screen, the words "unknown caller" scrawled across the screen. The cell phone didn't stop ringing, no matter how hard she stared at it or wished for it to stop. Vibrations numbed her forearm.

"Aren't you going to answer that?" Jessica asked with a sly grin, her facial features more animated now. She let the blanket drop to the floor. Her timid nature washed away in an instant, replaced by something more sinister and intimidating.

Even though Meridith didn't want to answer the phone, she felt compelled to. "Hello?"

"Any mummers 'loud in?"

THUMP THUMP THUMP

Meridith screamed, twisting to face the door as it rattled in its frame. Thomas snatched the phone from her, held it towards Jessica, and pointed towards the door. "Who the fuck is that?"

"My friends are here to pick me up," Jessica said. A cackle of laughter tainted her words.

"This isn't funny," Thomas barked. "You're scaring my wife to death."

THUMP   THUMP   THUMP

"Aren't you going to let them in?" Jessica's voice was a shrill scream.

Meridith struggled to hold the phone up to her ear. Gripped by fear, her entire body trembled. "Why are you doing this?"

"Any mummers 'loud in?"

THUMP THUMP THUMP THUMP THUMP THUMP

"Go on now," Thomas yelled, "get the fuck off my property!" He turned back towards Jessica, his chest huffing. The vein in his neck throbs with rage. "And you get the fuck out of here." He stomped towards her, but before he could reach her, a brilliant flood of light shone through the front window. Outside, two bright LED headlights blared from a hidden truck, the light so blinding that the world vanished beyond them. Two looming forms stepped into the light, their bodies silhouetted in a blurry contrast. Somehow, their bodies were disfigured by the shadows, but was clear they were holding weapons in their hands.

Distracted by the visitors outside, Meridith stopped

dead in her tracks. She seemed to watch the event unfold before her. Thomas raced past her, towards the front door in a frantic dash, throwing his shoulder into the door as he slid the deadbolt over with a dull thud. A guttural, growling howl outside echoed through the vast emptiness. Thomas braced his back against the door, squatting down below the tiny window so that no one could see him from outside, his hands gripping his knees as if he were holding it from falling. All Meridith could think about was that show she watched on wolves, and how they hunted in packs. Was this a signal to the rest of the intruders to come? Or was it because they had their prey cornered?

The door rattled in its frame, the wood splintering with every pounding blow, forcing Thomas to remain against it to provide support. Suddenly, Thomas's eyes grew wide and his jaw dropped in a harrowing, silent scream. He raised his hand, his arm trembling as he pointed at Meridith. *Look out*, he mouthed. A rattling of spoons, forks, and knives from behind her caught Meridith's attention.

Meridith turned around and screamed. Jessica was standing in the kitchen, swaying back and forth on the balls of her feet. She had draped a pillowcase over her head, two jagged eyes drawn in black and red marker to conceal the real ones underneath. Drawn at a demented angle, a sinister frown in crimson reached from her left shoulder to her right ear. The light from outside caught the edge of the kitchen knife gripped in her hand.

Jessica made a sudden lunge towards Meridith, driving her backwards. A fit of laughter burst from her stomach, low and booming. She juggled the knife between her hands with a steady, practiced ease that scared Meridith. "What's wrong? You don't want to play with me anymore?"

Tink tink tink tink screeeeee

A metal rake clawed at the window, the shadowed form outside more visible now. He wore a pillowcase with bloodshot eyes drawn on it. Freshly blown snow covered his blue-and-black checkered jacket. Brownish-red stains covered his blue jeans. He raised the rake, letting it clunk against the window, the glass splintering against the blow, sending a spiderweb of cracks racing in all directions.

Jessica held the knife to her chin. "Are we going to do this the easy way or the hard way?

"What are you talking about, you psycho bitch?" Thomas yelled across the room, his back pressed firmly against the rattling door. Beads of sweat dribbled down his brow from exhaustion. His legs wobbled as fatigue set in.

Jessica brandished the knife across her face and pointed it at her temple as if she were lost deep in thought. "The easy way is you unlock that door and let my friends inside. I promise, if you do that, you won't suffer..." Jessica paused, "too much."

Caught in the middle, Meridith was too afraid to respond, her feet glued to the floor. She stared back at the window. The mummer outside was looking in, waiting for a signal. Behind him, another veiled form sped past, running around the other side of the house. There was a single window around the back that led into the bedroom. Meridith believed the man was aware of it. Maybe this was some cruel prank being played by the owner. It was the off-season, and he couldn't get too many visitors this time of year. Either way, this was a cruel joke, and she just wanted this to end.

"No fucking way," Thomas responded, his voice full of venom.

Jessica clapped her hands together, bouncing on her heels. "I am so glad you said that. Now we get to do things the hard way... the fun way."

"What?"

Jessica took a step forward, the knife held by her side, gripped in a balled fist. "You know, where we make you torture you and make you both suffer." She pointed the tip of the knife at Meridith. "There's only one question I have for you. Do you want to watch your wife get mutilated or do you want to make her do it to you? I'll let you make that choice. I'm not a cruel bitch after all."

"Fuck you," Thomas growled, racing across the living room straight towards Jessica.

A resounding fear forced Meridith to watch the chaos take place right in front of her.

With his arms spread wide, Thomas lowered his head and drove his shoulder into Jessica's gut, knocking the wind from her. A pained gasp escaped her diaphragm. He pushed her backwards into the kitchen, crushing her spine against the countertop with a sickening snapping pop. Jessica folded in half, the pillow case nearly flying from her head. Strands of wispy blond hair fell over her shoulders. Winded, Thomas took too long to stand up straight, his back exposed to Jessica as she raised the knife and drove it into his ribcage. The stainless steel disappeared until only an inch remained visible. Crimson bubbles surrounded the blade, dripping over the floor in thick drops.

"Thomas!" Meridith cried, reaching out for her husband.

Thomas and Jessica fell to the floor in a jumbled heap with Thomas on top. Jessica's rib cage deflated from the impact, the bones cracking beneath his weight. She squirmed beneath him, grunting as she tried to roll him off. Thomas was still breathing, his ribcage expanding in shallow, haggard breaths. A whistling hiss escaped the wound as his punctured lung deflated.

A strange sensation washed over Meridith. She moved without thought of consequences. She braced her hand against the countertop as she straddled the tangled mess of bodies on the floor. Jessica was unable to move, still pinned to the floor under Thomas's heavy frame. Meridith stared down at Jessica, her knee rising to her chest as she raised her foot, hovering over the pillowcase. With all the force she could muster, she drove her heel between the sinister eyes drawn onto the pillowcase. Something hard gave way beneath the white fabric as the pillowcase turned a muddy maroon.

Behind Meridith, glass shattered, spraying across the floor in a wide arc as the mummer smashed the window beside the door. A hand reached in, fumbling for the deadbolt. Grunts and groans identified the mummer as another female.

But Meridith didn't turn around. She was determined to finish what she started. Jessica was no longer trying to push Thomas off. She drew her hands to her face, holding her nose as blood gushed from it. Meridith raised her foot again, driving it down in a piston motion. At first, she could feel Jessica's fingers snapping and breaking beneath the blows, then her arms fell to her sides. Meridith's heel found more flesh and bone. Driven mad, her vision blurred, and she didn't stop until she felt a hand on her shoulder, spinning her around.

"Into the bedroom," Thomas urged, dragging Meridith along.

BOOOOOM

A thunderous crash exploded from inside the bedroom, and a rush of air swept through the house.

"Any mummers 'loud in?" a booming voice called out from deep inside the bedroom.

"Jesus Christ," Thomas gasped, his breath growing

more laboured. He staggered towards the kitchen, droplets of blood splattering against the tile as he went, leaving a gory trail in his wake.

The front window exploded inwards. Shards of glass and pellets of ice scattered across the floor in a raging torrent, propelled by the howling wind. A golf club traced the window frame, breaking out the remaining jagged shards and clearing a path. Thomas realized this before Meridith. He yanked open the kitchen drawer. Forks, spoons, and knives rattled around inside, a clatter of metal that rang out above the madness. With a meat cleaver clutched in his fist, Thomas rushed to the window, swinging the blade blindly into the darkness.

"Get out of here, you bastards," Thomas growled into the night. The blustering wind flapped the surrounding curtains, creating a veil around him, making the scene before her surreal.

Meridith watched through the veil as a set of hands emerged from the darkness, grasping Thomas by the collar. Suddenly, he was jerked down, and his chin smashed off the windowsill. A pillowcased face with a snarling black grin appeared above Thomas. The figure leaned inside the cabin, wrapping a thick arm around Thomas's neck. Thomas swung the blade in violent arcs above his head. The stainless steel caught the figure's arm. Softened by the thick fabric of wool, the blade only made a superficial cut, drawing a trickle of blood that was instantly soaked up by the gray sleeve. But Thomas was relentless, the blade swaying back and forth as his face turned an alarming shade of scarlet.

Coming to her senses, Meridith grabbed a kitchen chair and raced across the living room towards her husband. Thomas' struggle was halted by a second set of hands that reached in, grabbing his flailing arm. In an instant, the two figures ripped Thomas from the cabin, vanishing into the night air. Thomas's pained cries were punctuated by sickening, wet blows. As she threw back the curtains, the ghastly scene unravelled before her. One man held Thomas upright by the arms as he used his heel to keep Thomas steady. The other mummer held a spiked bat, smashing the blunt instrument into Thomas, each arc casting a trail of blood over the freshly fallen snow. Each blow shredded Thomas's clothing, exposing the savage wounds left behind. Broken ribs and shredded flesh turned into a disgusting pulp as the mummer drove the spiked bat into Thomas' lifeless body. When they'd had their fun, the mummer holding Thomas let go. Thomas crumpled into the snow. A wave of red radiated around him. Meridith cried out for her husband, his unrecognizable face staring back at her with a blank expression.

"Get away from him, you bastards," Meridith screamed at the top of her lungs.

Determined to make the mummers pay, she turned to make her way towards the door, to confront them on her own terms. As she stepped towards the front door, a sudden force drove her into the wall, pinning her against it. A searing hot pain radiated from her kidney. Meridith gasped in shock. She twisted her body, coming face to face with a bloodied pillowcase. With wavering strength, she reached out and tugged at the mask. It slid over Jessica's face inch by inch. Ropes of blood and gore tried to hold the mask in place. Jessica stared back at Meridith with a crooked smile, her nose flattened against her face, a trail of dark red running over her split lips and down her neck.

"You let the wrong one in," Jessica cackled, driving the knife upwards.

Meridith's stomach ruptured. The contents splattered against the floor with a sickening plop. Jessica let go and

Meridith toppled to the floor, landing face-first in the gory mess. Out of the corner of her eye, she watched Jessica pick up the pillowcase and slip it on over her disfigured face. As the world around Meridith faded to black, she heard Jessica's footsteps fade. The door opened and closed behind her as the mummers left, still without reason as to why they ever came in the first place.

ABERRATIONS OF THE DEEP

Darkness shrouds us like a veil. Heavy smoke billows from the stack, silhouetting the steamer against the midnight horizon. Being led across the Cabot Straight by the Naval patrol vessel, these nighttime conveys wreak havoc on the nerves of all involved. A cold October night keeps most passengers and crew inside. The night is far colder than it has any right to be without a single light lit. But it's the safest way to make this crossing without drawing unwanted attention from the German U-boats lurking in these frigid waters. Over the last several days, the reported sightings have increased, putting everyone on edge.

"That wind is bitter," I complain. Unable to stand the eerie silence falling over the convey, I am compelled to break it. "And this coffee is even worse," I add.

Captain Benjamin Taverner glares at me, and a crescent of silver moonlight catches in his eyes. "Shouldn't you be down in the engine room?"

"I needed a breath of fresh air," I answer, wiping the soot from my face. "That coal-fired steam boiler is working just fine."

The Captain doesn't speak so much as grunts. "Find your way back to your station."

An uncomfortable silence settles between us. From beneath the engine's drone and the gentle lap of waves, an odd noise interrupts the methodical rhythm of the Atlantic. The Captain's breath is haggard and raspy from lack of sleep over the days leading up to the crossing. Between the painstaking planning and hundreds of intelligence reports, there is little room for sleep. "What do you think it is?" I ask, straining my eyes against the darkness.

As suddenly as it appeared, the noise vanishes; or blends back into the maddening melody that serves as the theme song of our crossing.

"It could be anything," Captain Taverner grumbles. He leans over the railing, his head bent low against his chest. A strong breeze gusts across the open water, carrying a spray of white sea foam, soaking into his beard. The Captain continues speaking, but the shrill racket cuts off his words, carrying them far away.

Every sound out of the ordinary draws our attention, as a strange sense of dread fills my bones. My mind is playing tricks on me. That odd noise lingers just beyond perception. Unable to push it out, the sound grows inside my skull like a blaring siren. Somehow, the sound interrupts the flow of the tide, splitting the waves in two. Hundreds of possibilities race through my head; none of them ease my racing heart.

"Something is out there," I say, "stalking us."

A long sigh escapes the Captain's throat. With a steady hand, he reaches out and grabs me by the collar, yanking me forward. "Unless you're absolutely positive about that," his breath is warm against my face, "it's best to keep thoughts like that to yourself." Before he lets me go, he continues, "I don't need anyone getting worked up. Ghosts will appear in the darkness when you're looking in all the wrong places."

I stumble backwards when he relinquishes his grasp on my jacket. I take a moment to recover my wits. "Aye, sir," is all I can muster.

Captain Taverner yanks at the hem of his jacket, straightening out the wrinkles and brushing off the salt water droplets forming on the exterior of the water-resistant fabric. "Make yourself scarce." He hesitates then adds, "Stoker Baker."

"It's Cook," I correct him, then add, "sir." I click my heels together and about-turn. Concealed in the darkness, I bump into the railing as I make my way towards the hatch. Once inside, the corridors are pitch black. Black curtains draped over the portholes block out the faintest trace of moonlight. Red light is the only allowed source of illumination on this deck. But with the looming threat, it's not worth it. Muscle memory and experience guide my feet to the ladder, and I slip over the ledge and make my way down towards the boiler,

The engine's grumble grows into a monstrous growl below deck. A passenger walks by, the red light from his lamp casting his face in sinister shadows. Without speaking, the man tips his hat at me as he passes. Holding his daughter's hand, he guides her down the narrow corridor towards the heads. One more deck down, I jump off the ladder and make my way abaft. The murmur of families filters down through the deckhead. Closer now, I appreciate the thunderous vibrations of the engines as I pass.

I continue past the engine room and continue towards my station. When I round the corner, the coal fire's blazing glare assaults my eyes. My pupils constrict, blurring the radiant orange and brilliant yellow flames as they burn savagely. Beads of sweat form on my brow; the intense heat is a sharp contrast to the frigid autumn air.

Charles' voice booms from somewhere inside the boiler room. "Ben," he grunts, "please tell me you are here to spell me."

"I'd wait a few minutes," I say as my vision focuses.

Charles is leaning his arms on the handle of his shovel, the metal head digging deep into the coal. Soot soils every inch of exposed flesh. Black suspenders hold his brown slacks, which blend into his previously white tank top. There's a sly smile on his face, the lines on his face outlined with grime. "The Captain must be making his rounds," he laughs.

"How'd you know?"

"It's plastered all over your face," he answers, cocking his head in the bridge's direction. "What did he say this time, Ben?"

"You know, after all this time," I pause, shaking my head, "he still doesn't know my name."

"Get over it," Charles snaps. "You have any idea how much pressure that man is facing? He's logged more time on these treacherous waters than you have sea time."

"Fair." I spit the word out, not enjoying the taste of it in my mouth.

"I'm going to wander around," Charles says. "Stretch out my back and see how everyone else is doing tonight." He leaves the boiler room, the dull echo of his footsteps fading down the hallway. Before the gregarious roar of the coal furnace cuts him off, I catch a bit of his trademark laughter. Only Charles would find humour in a situation like this.

Alone with the raging fire, I am shut off from the universe. With only my thoughts to keep me company, I push them aside and go about my work. The sound that the shovel makes as I drive it into coal is like nails scratching across a chalkboard. When I open the door to the furnace, a blast of heat floods over me. The fire roars and I can feel my skin searing as I feed the flames. Greedy, the red-hot coals burn with tremendous intensity, gobbling the blackened coal and spitting out smouldering embers that shoot outwards in a fanning spray. My weathered skin resists the attack, and the flankers fall to the grated floor beneath me. I stoke the boiler, close the glass door, and take a seat along the far wall. Unable to escape the rolling waves of heat, I embrace it. My mind carries me away to a tropical beach, far removed from the great war. The foreign shore fantasy envelops me.

KAAABOOOM

A thunderous growl rocks the entire ship, tossing me violently from my seat and across the deck. I can hear the metal girders bending and twisting. A gush of water floods the belly of the ship as the ocean races to occupy her newly claimed space. The grated decking does a number on my face. Rough metal edges dig into my cheek and scalp, ripping the flesh open. Dazed and confused, my head spins. Panicked voices meld together into a chaotic screech that surrounds me. Rivets bust, fires blaze, and water gushes all around me.

"Ben?" Charles calls out my name, his voice choked by the same billowing smoke smothering me. "Where are you, Ben?"

Behind me, I can hear him lurching towards me, but the smog is so heavy I can hardly see a hand in front of my face. And I'm disoriented; I can feel sticky blood streaking down my sullied face.

"Hey!" I cry out, stumbling across the deck on my hands and knees. I take a moment to realize the ship is listing heavily to port. Frigid water pours over me from the overhead hatch. "I'm in here, Charles!"

The only thing that keeps my focus is the boiler room. Even amongst the anarchy, the smouldering flames center me. The flickering yellow light waltzes amongst the smog, dancing a macabre jig around me. With the furnace window at my back, I trudge towards the door. My fingers whack the bulkhead. I get as low to the deck as possible and inhale deeply, drawing in gasps of fresh air, struggling to fuel my lungs.

"Ben!" Charles shouts at me, his voice as clear as day. "Keep the boiler going for as long as you can."

"What the hell happened?" I ask, already having a compelling idea of what just transpired.

"We've been hit," Charles cries. Water is pouring through the hatch, creating a savage waterfall on the ladder. "I'm going to buy you as much time as possible." His voice trembles. "Don't stop shovelling coal into that beast, no matter what."

"Get down here and help me!" I yell. The water level is rising fast and is already past my ankles.

"This hatch won't open if it shuts on top of us." His voice is stoic. "The longer we can stay afloat, the more lives we can save." He hesitates. "I'm sorry, but I can't help you."

The hatch slams shut, and the locking mechanism spins into place as I scream bloody murder. Choking on the thick smoke, my nostrils fill with the acidic stench of burning oil, tainted by the thick scent of salt water. My lungs ache and my throat burns. No one can hear me above the boisterous clamour and chaos gripping the entire ship's company. Behind me, a pipe bursts, unleashing a powerful jet spray of water that knocks me back, sending me stumbling towards the furnace. Another pipe explodes beneath the surface, sending a geyser spraying froth high into the smoky air.

My toes are numb from the Atlantic's glacial water sloshing up past my knees as the swirling waters splash against me. I trudge through the rising water, my pants glued to my legs. The coal furnace is on the starboard side and is rising above me as the ship continues to list to port.

When I reach the coal bin, I snatch the shovel and grab the door handle for the furnace, tossing it open. The heat from the fire battles against the frigid chill of the water for dominance over me. I ignore both and focus my mind on the task at hand, dumping coal into the greedy furnace as fast as my arms will allow. Blood and sweat trickle into my eyes. The stinging stabs of pain try to stop me from accomplishing my task, but I persevere.

A voice from above calls out. "Just keep shovelling!"

When I turn towards the hatch, a man I don't recognize is climbing through the hatch. Soot and sweat slather his shirt, the soiled fabric clinging to his wiry frame. His muscles ripple with every movement as he struggles to maintain his balance.

"Who are you?" I ask, dumbfounded.

"I'm here to help," the man answers, choking on every word. I hold out the shovel for him. He shakes his head and holds up his hand. His heavy cotton pants are stained deep crimson by thick clumps of gore. "I've shovelled enough coal in my time."

"What?" I snarl. "I thought you said you were here to help me."

"I am."

"Then what are you here for?" I ask.

"I'm here to encourage you."

"Encourage me?" I jam the shovel into the coal, the metal scraping against the hardened lumps. "You're kidding me, right? I don't need encouragement. I need some help." The fire roars as I throw coal into the furnace, a wave of heat applauding my efforts.

"There's nothing I can do for you," the stranger answers, scratching at his neck. Black filth forms under his nails, leaving streaks of white behind on his neck. He adjusts a plain silver wedding ring on his finger, staring at it as if he had never seen it before.

"Then get the fuck out of here," I growl in frustration.

The lights begin to flutter and flicker, casting the room in and out of shadows as they struggle to maintain power. A high-pitched electric warble whines, the sound building to a frantic crescendo before blurring into a single burst of sharp sound. Suddenly, the lights go out, and I know they aren't coming back on. Cast in the flickering yellow glow of the furnace, my shadow dances on the wall beside me.

The stranger lowers his head and shakes it, clumps of his matted hair sway with the motion. "I'm afraid we can't do that," he says, fanning his hand across the cramped room.

For the first time, I realize we aren't alone. There are sailors sitting all around me, cast in the dull glow, their expressions sorrowful. The ship lists dangerously to port, water gushing against the bulkhead in a torrential water-fall. Frigid, the ice-cold ocean water is taking control of the ship, threatening to immobilize me. Water has found its way into the coal. Every shovelful into the flame sends a hissing swirl of steaming vapour into the chaos. The rising smoke forces me to cover my face with my filthy shirt, and the taste of sweat and dirt soil my mouth. I gag on the putrid fabric and the stench of smoke fills my nostrils, choking me. Unable to continue, I toss the shovel aside, realizing if I don't leave now, I'll never have another chance to escape.

"Keep going."

"Don't stop shovelling."

"Never give up."

A chorus of voices rises from the mourning sailors, begging me to stay.

"There's nothing I can do to save everyone," I say, my

voice shaky with a mixture of fear and regret. A single tear tracks down my cheek, snaking its way through the build-up of soot on my face.

"You can still save more lives."

"What about my own?" I ask, the water numbing my entire body now. It's flowing over my knees and is only inches away from dousing the furnace for good. "If I don't leave now, I'll never make it."

"But you can save so many more."

The figures around fade in and out of reality, the colour drained from their appearance.

"Who are you?" I ask.

"They are the ones I've lost," the man who first appeared answers. With a trembling hand, he holds the shovel, the wooden handle pinned against his stomach. "After my fate was already sealed, I tried to save myself once. Selfishly, I left my post and tried to flee my sinking ship. You have a duty to fulfill." He thrusts the shovel towards me, pressing it against my chest.

"But..." I sob, staring down at the handle. My fingers trace the weathered wood, welcoming the familiar surface. I don't have to glance down to know where the cracks are, where every splinter awaits, threatening to pierce my skin. "What about the duty I have to my family?"

The man lets out a deep sigh. "What about their families?"

"I don't care about them," I shout, thrusting an accusing finger at the strangers crowded into the boiler room with us.

"Not them," he answers, pointing up towards the deckhead. "Listen." The roar of the flooding ocean water vanishes as if on command. Replaced by the panicked screams, frantic shouting, and the assertive voice of the captain ring out. "They all have families. Please redeem this old coward so I can rest."

I take the shovel from him and continue my duty until the water douses the flames. Cast in complete darkness, the ice-cold water rises over my waist, filling the compartment at an alarming rate. Before the water can consume me, I feel a clawed hand on my shoulder.

"Foolish man," a cackling voice snickers. "Another soul claimed by the devotion of duty."

The dying shouts above continue until the water consumes me.

SOMEBODY'S HOME

Pauline climbed down the steps, holding onto the rail until she got off the school bus. Her friend Janet jumped off the last step, landing beside her. It was a blistering June day. The sun beat down on them from a clear blue sky. There was no breeze in the humid air and it weighed over them like a wet blanket. After the crowd dispersed, Pauline and Janet stood by the stop sign. The lawn behind them desperately needed to be mowed. Yellow dandelions dominated the green backdrop. Weeds sprouted up all over the place.

"Come on," Janet said, tugging on Pauline's wrist. "I don't want to be out here longer than we need to."

Pauline held her bookbag against her chest. She unzipped it and rummaged through it with a sense of desperation. "What exam do we have tomorrow?

"History." Janet rolled her eyes. "Did you forget your books?"

Pauline nodded her head. Sighing, she said, "I'll go back and get it. You go on, I'll meet you at your house." She patted her pockets, making sure she had the keys.

"You don't have your keys either, do you?"

She pulled out the pockets of her jean shorts, the white fabric dangling over the faded blue denim. With a quick check of her schoolbag to confirm that she had forgotten the keys to her parents' house, she let out a defeated sigh.

"I guess not," Pauline admitted. "But they leave a spare key beside the back door. It's beneath a fake rock," she added.

"Okay." Janet buckled the chest strap of her backpack. "Let's go. It's not like I'm going to study without you."

"You two stick together," the bus driver called out. "That girl's still missing and they suspect someone kidnapped her."

"Yes, sir," Janet said, giving the bus driver a mock salute.

"Just be careful is all I'm saying," the driver said, ignoring Janet's gesture. He ground gears as he drove away, the muffler spewing a trail of black smoke as it gained speed.

"Everyone knows that Cindy ran away with her boyfriend," Janet said. "She's such a little slut."

"Didn't the cops question her boyfriend?"

"They did," Janet answered, "but he's just covering for her. They're having too much fun." A wicked smile creased the corner of her lips.

Both girls laughed, walking down Read Street towards Pauline's home. Her father was on vacation in Florida with his new wife. Not old enough to spend two weeks alone, Pauline begged to stay with Janet's parents. She didn't want to spend two weeks with her aunt Betty. Not because she didn't love her, she just wanted a little freedom. Sixteen was an awkward age. There were a lot of additional responsibilities being added to her daily routine. She had two younger brothers and a younger sister, but they expected Pauline to help cook supper and clean the dishes while her siblings played outside. Her new stepmother insisted that Pauline do the laundry. Last, but certainly not least, she swept and mopped the floors.

And what were her rewards? She never had time to get her license and she spent her free time catching up on her homework. Her stepmom refused to give her an allowance and expected her to get a job.

Twenty minutes later, they saw a two-story house resting on a hill, towering over the surrounding homes. The lawn rose from the sidewalk in three humps. Even though her father was gone, the lawn remained meticulously attended to. No doubt her father paid the neighbour's son to keep it that way. They walked up the long driveway and up the cement walkway that wound at an angle towards the front steps. A giant tree on the side of the house cast a looming shadow, the long black branches reaching out for the two girls as they made their way up the steps. Something made a dull thump from the upstairs window, but the giggling girls didn't notice the sound before pulling open the screen door. Fidgeting for her keys in her purse, Pauline sighed with frustration as she rummaged through old receipts and discarded wrappers. Distracted, she didn't notice Janet take a step behind her.

With a quick jerk, Janet grasped Pauline around the waist and screamed, "I got you."

Pauline let out a gasping scream, the contents of her purse spilling out over the steps. The keys clattered against the concrete. "Frig off," Pauline said, unable to contain her laughter.

"This place is so spooky." Janet tilted her head back, staring up at the upstairs window above the door. "I think there's someone in there."

Pauline knelt down to pick up the keys. "Knock it off," Pauline said, slipping her finger through the key ring. "My parents are on vacation and my brother is staying with our aunt."

Janet tugged at her skirt, pulling the hem down to

cover her knees. "I don't mean your family." Janet hesitated, searching for the right. "Something about this doesn't feel right."

Pauline put the key in the lock and turned the deadbolt. Before she could open the door, Janet reached out and grabbed her by the wrist with a sense of urgency in her movements.

"What's wrong with you?" Pauline asked.

Janet held up a finger to her lip, her brow furrowed in concentration. "Don't you hear that?" Janet asked, her tone serious. Her smile had departed, leaving no remnants of her joyous expression from only moments ago. "There's somebody inside the house."

Unable to ignore the serious expression on her friend's face, Pauline strained to pick up the sound. A gentle breeze whispered through the trees. The leaves reciprocated the low tone. From somewhere behind the house, a dog barked at something unseen, but there was nothing from inside the house.

"I don't believe you," Pauline said, her voice scarcely above a whisper.

She turned the doorknob, allowing the door to swing inwards on its own. She took a tentative step inside the porch. The familiar scent of her father's leather jacket greeted her. The shoes were all lined up with the heels against the wall from largest to smallest. Halfway through the door, she paused, tilting her ear at the ceiling towards a muffled noise; she swore there was a man's voice coming from her bedroom window.

"I got you," Janet growled as she wrapped her arms around Pauline's shoulder, dragging her back outside. Both girls busted out laughing, the screen door creaking as Janet bumped into it. Janet laughed so hard tears tracked down her cheek.

"You scared me to death," Pauline said, then added, "asshole."

"Come on," Janet said, pushing her way past Pauline and inside. "I'm starving. I hope your parents left some food behind to eat."

Pauline followed her friend inside, making their way to the kitchen, laughing the entire way. When they reached the kitchen, Pauline yanked on the fridge door, the contents on the door sliding around. A putrid stench wafted from the fridge; no doubt the half carton of milk had turned sour. She hauled the carton out and tossed it into the sink. A thick spray of white foam erupted from the cardboard and splattered over the stainless steel. The white goop defied gravity, refusing to roll down the sides.

Janet plugged her nose. "That's nasty."

"There's some juice in here," Pauline said, shaking a carton of Five Alive. Without waiting for an answer, Pauline carried it over to the cupboard, pulled down two glasses, and filled them, the cups sliding across the marble countertop until they were heavy enough to remain in place. She took a large gulp of the tangy juice; the flavourful flood awakened her thirst. Pauline topped up her cup, emptied the container, and discarded it in the trash, the cardboard bumping off the plastic walls all the way down.

"Wait, what was that?"

Pauline sighed. "Don't start that shit again."

Janet cocked her head toward the ceiling. "No," she whispered, "seriously."

"I'm not falling for that a second time," Pauline announced, mustering more courage into her voice than she had inside. "I'm going upstairs to grab my bag."

Without another word, Pauline turned towards the

stairs, which led to the second floor. A picture of her father and his second wife in Bermuda greeted them at the
landing where the stairs took an abrupt turn. The remaining run of steps vanished beyond the wall. With each step,
the staircase groaned in the house's silence.

Janet's footsteps scurried across the linoleum, the
heels of her shoes clacking against the hardwood as she
caught up to Pauline. She reached out, grasping Pauline
by the wrist and yanked, twisting Pauline around so that
they were face to face.

Unable to contain a pained yelp, Pauline snapped.
"What's wrong with you?" she demanded, rubbing her
shoulder and grimacing at the pain that radiated from her
entire arm.

Pauline glared at her friend, but the terrified expression on Janet's face caused a shiver to run down Pauline's
spine. Goosebumps riddled her forearms as her entire
body shivered. For the first time, Pauline realized the hand
wrapped around her wrist was cold and damp despite the
warm summer day. She shook her head, insulted that her
friend went to such lengths to continue a joke that had already run its course. But was there a noise upstairs? Janet
couldn't fake the clammy palms. Pauline turned back towards the stairs. The floral blue wallpaper of the upstairs
floor awaited her, inviting her to her childhood bedroom.
And when she turned to make her way up the stairs, Janet
gave her arm another firm jerk.

"Please," Janet pleaded, "let's get out of here before
something terrible happens..."

"Fuck off, Janet." Pauline wrenched her arm out of Janet's grasp and stomped up the stairs. "There's nobody
home."

"There is somebody home," a booming voice growled
from a bedroom upstairs. "And I'm coming to get you."

Heavy footsteps thudded across the hardwood floor, lumbering towards the top of the staircase. Both girls screeched as the surrounding walls rattled. Not waiting for the stranger to appear, the girls raced down the stairs and darted towards the front door. Behind them, the maddening crescendo of footsteps chased after them. A shadowed figure stalked them, howling obscenities as he pursued his prey.

Janet got to the door first. When she flung it open, the handle buried itself into the wall. The screen door rattled as she forced her way through, the black mesh tearing at the seam from the panicked lunge. Pauline forced her way through the edge of the screen door, clipping her elbow. The voice boomed, looming closer, urging Pauline to run faster. Somehow, both girls made it down the staircase, neither feeling the cement beneath them. Before Pauline realized it, she felt the ground beneath her feet, and she clipped the back of Janet's heels, sending both girls tumbling down over the bank of the front lawn.

But somehow, they kept their legs churning despite the searing pain that racked their entire bodies.

Pauline glanced over her shoulder and saw the man standing on the threshold of the front door, his piercing blue eyes boring a hole into her brain, engraving his image into her memory. The man's mustache glistened in the sunlight, the black mop of hair atop his head a matted mess. A cruel smile stretched his lips thin against his teeth, baring a strip of tobacco-stained teeth.

Janet's arm brushed against Pauline's, drawing her attention away from the man for a moment. When she looked back, the door remained open, but the man had vanished back into her home. Instead of the familiar warmth of her home, the doorway led into a haunting nightmare. They kept running straight down the middle of the street, hollering for help.

Pauline sat at the kitchen table, a cup of tea clutched in her grasp and pressed against her chest, the warmth doing little to soothe her. Janet's mother, Elizabeth, draped a blanket over Pauline's shoulder, rubbing her hand in concentric circles over her shoulder blade.

"Everything is going to be just fine," she said, her tone soothing and calm.

Pauline couldn't stop shaking. The tea dribbled over the edge of the cup, the piping hot liquid burning her flesh. But she ignored the pain, desperate to force the image of the man's piercing blue eyes from her mind. Upstairs, the water gargled through the pipes as Janet sat in the shower, trying to warm herself up.

"I hear Arnold's car," Elizabeth said.

To Pauline, her voice sounded miles away. Afraid that she would see the stranger from her home had stolen Arnold's car and had driven straight here to find Pauline, she stared down into her mug. Steam swirled around her face, the vapours wetting her nose and forehead with condensation. She sucked in quick gasps of air as someone outside walked down the stone path, the pebbles shifting beneath the steps.

"Well," Elizabeth said as the door swung open, "what did the police say?"

"They didn't find anyone there," Arnold answered.

Not trusting her ears, Pauline faced her fears and glanced up, finding Arnold's hazel eyes there to greet her. She let out a breath she hadn't realized she'd been holding. "Did they find anything?" Pauline asked, not recognizing her own voice.

Arnold reached out and gave her shoulder a gentle

squeeze. "Did Cindy loan you any of her clothes?"

Surprised, Pauline furrowed her brow and shook her head. "What?"

"The cops found a torn black skirt and a Rolling Stones' tee-shirt covered in blood in your parents' bedroom." Arnold knelt down on one knee. "Cindy's mother described the same outfit to the cops when she first went missing."

Pauline stared at Arnold and disbelief.

"Maybe they're yours?" he asked. When Pauline didn't answer, he placed his hand on her knee and gave it a good shake. "Pauline, are they yours?"

"Could be," Pauline sputtered. "I guess. I don't know."

"This is important," Arnold said, his voice stern.

"Arnold," Elizabeth snapped. "Not now. Can't you see she's upset?"

Janet and Arnold argued, their voices blurring into a droning background noise as Pauline tried to remember. Yes, she had a Rolling Stones shirt and a black skirt; what teenage girl didn't?

"Did you say covered in blood?" Pauline asked, her voice distant in her ears. She didn't need to hear Arnold's answer; she already knew the clothes belonged to Cindy.

"And there's something else I need to tell you," Arnold said, establishing eye contact with Pauline. "I don't know how to say this, so..."

"Spit it out, Arnold," Elizabeth demanded.

"They found Cindy's body in the bushes behind your house."

Hitching sobs rocked Pauline's body as she realized how close she came to walking in on Cindy's killer. And how close she came to death's door today.

MAL'CHIK

The sunlight's deteriorating rays lingered on the horizon. As the sun faded below the mountains, they cast looming shadows across the valley. A cruel wind rattled the branches at the edge of the clearing, tugging at the leaves and tearing away the dead ones. Snow carried across the sky in heavy sheets, swirling around and disorienting the landscape. The woods offered shelter from the bitter temperatures, inviting the stranger into its embrace. The young boy rushed in, eager for relief from the frigid elements. Darkness enveloped the boy, casting him into the shadows far beyond the reach of the fading daylight. At first, the boy's laboured breath drowned out the melodies of the forest. When he got his breathing under control, the noises distinguished themselves.

Crack

A tree branch snapped somewhere in the ruthless blackness, drawing the boy's attention and luring him deeper into the woods. A bright orange blaze swayed in the distance, casting a dreary light over a slender frame as the carrier wandered away.

"Help," the boy cried out.

Shivering, he pushed deeper into the forest's depths. The cold settled into his bones. Prickles of pain raced up and down his limbs, emanating from his extremities; his fingers and toes were already numb. Trudging through the deep snow, his feet felt like two cement cinder blocks. Every step was a struggle now, his muscles getting ready to give out.

At the edge of the boy's eyesight, the burning light illuminated the vague form. The figure took long strides, tufts of snow exploding in his wake with every step. The boy tried to run faster, but no matter how fast he ran he couldn't seem to gain any ground. The cold air burned his lungs as he sucked in large gulps.

"Please help me." His pitiful scream died in the seclusion of the woodlands as the wind howled, drowning him out.

Snap

The sound stalked him from the shadows. His teeth clattered together. He tried to speak, but he couldn't control his jaw.

CRACK

Much closer now, the commotion made the boy jump and swing around. Hidden within the blackness, hideous forms and threatening shadows slithered towards him. A scream caught in his throat. He stumbled over a buried stump, falling hard on his backside. The sounds of boots crunching in the snow drew closer. A horrified howl escaped from his lungs.

"Derzhis' podal'she, mal'chik," a deep, gruff voice spat out.

"Stay away," the boy begged as he tried to back away, pulling himself backwards. His numb fingers dug through the snow, the ice scraping away at the flesh. "Why won't you leave me alone?"

"Uyti ot neye," the stranger yelled, "ona opasna."

The flickering flame stopped fading away, the wind pushing the lamp back and forth in the stranger's hand.

A woman's voice called out. "Is somebody out there?"

With a surge of energy, he scrambled to his feet. "Please help me," his voice cracked, "they're going to get me!"

"Who is going to get you?" Her voice was soothing. The light swelled as she walked towards him.

Snap crack crack

The boy's heart skipped a beat as the ominous noises surrounded him. A faint trickle of light reached out for him, drawing him towards the woman. "The monster," the boy warned as a high-pitched shriek filled the forest. A thunderous thump rocked the ground, sending the boy hurtling face-first into the snow. Footsteps marched towards him. When he craned his neck up, the light from the flame was close enough that the boy could feel its warmth.

"You're okay," the woman cooed as she ran her fingers through his hair, "there's no one here but us." A fur coat draped over her slender frame ruffled with the wind. Fragments of light caught in the slick fur as the flames melted, the snow catching on the hairs of her jacket. Long, black hair framed her face, running down and blending into the wild animal furs. For a moment, she looked more animal than human, but the soft features of her face calmed the boy.

The boy turned his head around, finding the light stretched deep into the trees. At any moment, he expected a shadow to jump out from behind a trunk or from the shadows. "They were right there." His finger pointed towards the vast darkness.

The woman pulled him closer. "Relax, my child." She patted his back. "Everything is going to be okay." She pulled him closer into her warm embrace and rocked him back and forth. "Let's get you out of the cold and warmed up. My cabin is just ahead."

He glanced over his shoulder one last time, still expecting some cruel monster to be waiting for him. After a moment passed and he discovered the darkness was no longer moving, he allowed himself to relax. He nodded his head, his voice too weak to say anything. With a deep sigh, the woman cradled the boy in her arms and stood up. A stiff breeze brushed the hair away from her face, revealing emerald-green eyes. Her skin was a shade of pasty white, unblemished, and rosy. Tears welled up in his eyes.

A guttural growl roared in the blackness. The boy's heart leapt into his throat, but the woman remained calm, not breaking her pace. "We are almost there now." Her voice didn't show any strain, remaining tranquil and soothing.

The boy turned his head towards a pair of glowing lights in the distance. It took him a minute to realize it was actually just light spilling out through two windows. As they neared the house, he realized the hut was suspended above the ground on bone-white tree stumps that looked like scrawny chicken legs. Dilapidated boards formed the misshapen walls. Scarce straw did its best to cover the hut's roof. Bare patches stood out like sore spots.

Crack

The footprints echoed once more, approaching, accompanied by heavy breathing. They were getting closer to the hut now, but the boy feared that the haggard door would offer little resistance to the monster stalking them. Smoke billowed from a chimney, the wind carrying it towards them, burning the boy's eyes. He coughed uncontrollably, tears filling his eyes and stinging his cheeks.

"Ne khodi tuda," the gruff voice called out with a maddening sense of urgency.

"Mal'chik moy," the woman screamed back, her accent thick and raspy.

It astonished the boy that the woman spoke the same language. "What is he saying?"

The woman didn't respond but quickened her pace as the footsteps neared. He thought he recognized the word mal'chik. Didn't his grandmother call him that?

"Pozhaluysta, poshchadi yego." A burly man wandered into the light. He gripped an axe firmly in his hands across his stomach. Sweat matted his thick black hair and lumberjack beard. Sinewy muscles bulged beneath the man's red and blue plaid shirt. He limped towards them, bent over at the hip, but still casting an intimidating presence.

"Ya goloden," she hissed at the man as they reached the porch steps, which groaned beneath her as she carried them towards the rickety door. The boy wondered if the steps could withstand the man's weight.

"Mal'chik," the man stared at the boy with sad eyes, "ona ved'ma."

The woman opened the door. A fetid stench billowed over them, gagging the boy. Thrown into the hut, the boy landed hard on his shoulder. A sticky red paste coated the floor where the boy landed.

"Mal'chik, ona baba yaga," the stranger warned as she slammed the door shut.

"Baba Yaga," he shuddered as the lock thudded shut. Those words he recognized. His grandmother had warned him about the child-eating witch who lived in the woods. When she turned around, she tossed the lantern into the fireplace. A bright spark ignited the wood, and the flames engulfed them with a thunderous whoomph. Without the glow of the lantern embracing her face, the woman's exquisite beauty melted away before the boy's eyes. Festering wounds riddled her face, oozing a sickly greenish-white puss. Her nose was long and crooked, and her once emerald eyes were now a piercing yellow and sunken deep in the sockets. She let out a hideous cackle. Her lustrous, jet-black hair turned a deathly shade of bone-white.

"Stay away, witch." The boy's voice was a mere whimper. He backed away from her, his backside thumping against the kitchen cupboards. He let out an agonized grunt, pushing himself to his feet. When he stood up, his knees locked then went weak and buckled. His hand shot out for balance, bumping against something on the counter and knocking it to the floor. A ceramic bowl shattered over the floor, spilling a thick concoction of reddish-brown liquid over the boy's feet. Amongst the shards of glass and red paste were teeth and fingernails.

"I'm hungry, little one," the witch hissed, "and you just spilled my dinner." Baba Yaga lurched for the boy. He darted to the side, nearly tripping over his feet but avoiding her grasp. The witch let out a pained howl as her knuckles wrapped off the cupboards where the boy had huddled.

Bang bang bang

A thunderous pounding rattled the door. The man's laboured voice outside was muffled, sounding far away. With a desperate lunge, the boy tried to make his way towards the door to open it, but Baba Yaga cut him off. Her feet scuffled over the boards, thumping off the floorboards like pistons. Hideous laughter filled the hut.

The boy scanned the room, hoping to find a place to run, but the whole hut was one room. Where does she sleep? Windows alongside the house were the only other way out. He dashed towards the window, throwing himself into the glass pane. An intense pain radiated in his shoulders as he slammed off the window, falling backwards onto the floor. Baba Yaga let out a terrible cackle.

"Where do you think you're going, mal'chik?"

"I just want to go home." A tear ran down the boy's cheek. Baba Yaga reached out; her bony finger scraped his flesh to wipe the tear away. She stuck her finger in her mouth, and a sinister smile crinkled her weathered skin. He refused to look at the witch, deciding instead to stare out the window. Her warm breath fell over his neck, as the putrid smell of rotting flesh flooded from her mouth. Outside the hut, the boy watched the man slam the Axe into the window over and over, but the glass remained intact.

Baba Yaga's jagged nails dug into the boy's shoulder, pulling him into an insidious embrace. The boy's heart thumped loudly in his chest. The witch placed her ear against her chest, the phlegm grumbled in her chest as she breathed.

"Are you afraid, mal'chik?"

The boy stared out the window at the man refusing to give up. A crack formed in the glass, the lines reaching out in random directions forming a spider's web.

"Not anymore," the boy cried, closing his eyes as the window shattered inward. Baba Yaga released the boy, turning her attention towards the man as he climbed through the window.

"Run away," the man bellowed in broken English as he swung the Axe in a wide arc towards the witch. The blade sliced through the flesh of Baba Yaga's cheek, opening up a nasty gash just below her eye.

The boy sprinted towards the door as Baba Yaga cackled. A thunderous thud shook the hut as the boy reached the door. His hand fumbled with the lock. The heavy iron was rusted in place. The man let out an agonized grunt. Looking over his shoulder, the boy watched as the witch stood over the man. With her hands wrapped around the man's neck. Every muscle and vein stood out as his skin turned reddish-purple. Spittle formed at the corners of his pursed lips. His jaw opened into a silent scream.

After what seemed like an eternity, the lock slid over. The door flew open, and the boy's momentum caused him to stumble down the stairs as he fell face-first into the snow. He scampered to his feet quickly, praying that Baba Yaga wasn't finished with the man.

"Where are you going, mal'chik?" Baba Yaga cackled. "I want something sweet for dessert."

The boy dashed into the darkness of the forest. Behind him, the door slammed off the wall of the hut as the witch threw it open. The stairs groaned and creaked as she raced down them, her laughter a piercing sound that echoed in the woods. He sprinted blindly through the blackness, unable to see anything, fear propelling him forward.

A fierce wind pushed at the boy's back through the edge of the forest and into the clearing. Without looking back, he raced back towards the village where he first encountered the man he had believed to be a monster. He could only hope there would be someone in the village who could save him from the hungry witch.

THE WITCH'S CABIN

A rock shattered the placid calm of the lake, sending a spout of frothy water into the air reflected off the glossy black water. An inverse image of the sky wavered with every ripple, distorting the crystal-clear image. Another rock plunged into the lake, surpassing the first and reaching the edge of the expanding waves. I clasped a rock tight in my chubby fist, reared back, and slung it with all of my might. A pained snort escaped my pursed lips, brought up by the exertion created to keep pace with the others. For an instant, the rock defied gravity, sailing high against the clear sky before plummeting down into the lake. Accompanied by a chorus of sneers, it landed laughably short.

"Good throw, Tommy," my brother said as he held his hand over his face to conceal the spreading smirk that contorted his upper lip into a curl.

"Thanks, big guy," I responded in a condescending tone.

Born just fourteen months apart, Aaron appeared years older than me thanks to the aid of puberty. A scruff of whiskers covered his face in patches, but he refused to shave, so they had begun to fill in his beard. Even the locks of chestnut hair on his head had grown thick, aiding his mature appearance. His faded denim shorts hung low, revealing his scrawny torso framed by two sharp hip bones jutting out of the waistband of his underwear. Another reminder of his rapid growth spurt that left me behind and sitting at the kids' table during family gatherings.

With my gaze held low, I scoured the beach in search of a better rock. My eyes wandered across Aaron's black work boots. I could tell that he'd already turned his attention back towards the lake by the angle, allowing me to tilt my head up. Our cousin Jim was standing at the edge of the brackish water, poking a stick into the muddy bottom. A layer of silty water covered his legs, the dirt clinging to the thick tufts of hair. Oblivious to our sibling rivalry, Jim gazed out over the pond with a blank expression, unaware that the Samson brothers were both staring at him with a sense of awe.

Aaron hitched up his jeans with a quick tug and turned back towards me. "Don't be a sore loser, little buddy."

I felt a flush of jealous anger redden my complexion and my eyes grew wide, allowing the sunlight to flood my vision. In a gust of rage, I scuffed my feet as I turned and sped away, sending a barrage of rocks skittering over the craggy shoreline. No matter how much the rocks hurt my toes, I refused to allow the pain to take away from my scorned expression.

"Wait up," Aaron called out to me as he dashed across the beach to catch up. His hand snatched my wrist, twirling me around so that we were face to face. "Mom will have a fit if she finds out I let you wander off by yourself out here."

With a sudden jerk, I wrenched my arm out of his grasp. "You're not the boss of me."

Behind us, the methodical clatter of Jim's lumbering footsteps meandered towards us. "Knock it off," Jim demanded. His deep voice boomed amongst the trees that ran along the edge of the beach.

Aaron twisted towards Jim with a betrayed expression, his mouth hanging open in a wide gap. He mouthed words that tumbled silently out of his mouth, but I could see his hot breath lingering in the cool morning air. Dumbstruck, Aaron backed away from me as Jim inserted himself between us.

"We're all stuck here for the long weekend," Jim started, then paused. He shoved his hands into his pockets and pulled out a pack of cigarettes, placing one in the corner of his mouth. "Remember what happened the last time our families came up here? You two fought all weekend, and we had a miserable time."

Wide-eyed, Aaron pointed towards the open pack. "Where did you get those?"

A thin grin crossed Jim's face, pressing his lips flat against his teeth. "Grabbed them out of the dashboard of your old man's truck. He doesn't need them with everything that's going on. I'm doing that prick a favour." He shifted his attention towards me. "You ain't going to snitch on me, are you?"

Speechless, I nodded my head back and forth deliberately.

"Give me one," Aaron said, holding a hand out with the palm facing up.

When Jimmy dropped a cigarette into Aaron's grasp, it didn't take me long to realize that it was his first time holding one. The incoming pressure to join in pressed in on me. I didn't want to smoke; I'd seen what it can do to a person's lungs; two blue oxygen tanks lived next to my mother's chair, waiting for her at the end of the workday, which had recently become shortened. But I didn't want to disappoint Jimmy. Neither of us does.

Jim reached into the back pocket of his jeans, retrieving a silver Zippo with a blazing skull emblazoned against the shimmering background. With the flick of his wrist, a blaring yellow flame erupted as the top snapped open.

Puffing, he lit his cigarette, creating giant puffs of gray smoke that encompassed his face. Jim thrust the Zippo in Aaron's face, the dancing flame kissing the tip of the unlit cigarette still clutched awkwardly between Aaron's fingers. Aaron drew the cancer stick to his lips, cupped his fingers around the flame, and inhaled. As the first tendrils of smoke reached Aaron's lips, he broke into a coughing fit.

"Dude," Jim laughed, "you're supposed to savour it, not inhale it."

I couldn't contain the smile forming on my lips at the sight of Jim's exultant grin. The sight of Aaron trying to catch his breath made it even harder to suppress my smirk. It felt wrong to laugh, but I just couldn't help myself.

"Here, Tommy," Jim said, holding out his cigarette for me. Wisps of smoke braided into the air, hanging between us.

As I reached out for the cigarette, Aaron's hand lashed out and slapped my wrist.

"What is wrong with you?" I yelled.

"You're not smoking," Aaron grunted, clearing his throat. "Not on my watch, little brother."

Jim flailed his hand in a lazy circle. "Don't be such a tyrant. If he wants to try it, then you should let him." With the stern thrust of his wrist, Jim jabbed me in the chest, knocking me back. "Maybe it will put a little hair on his chest?" he said, turning towards me before continuing. "Isn't that what you want?"

Before I could answer, Aaron said, "If you want to put some real hair on your chest, there's something you could do that will do the trick."

"Are you thinking what I'm thinking?" Jim's voice rose with excitement.

The two boys chattered amongst themselves, some hidden code that I couldn't decipher, their voices rambling and filled with giddy laughter. And the more they talked, the more uncomfortable I felt. I enjoyed a sense of relief that the pressure to take my first drag had passed and Jim had moved on, but the dread of the unknown outweighed every other sense in my body. My stomach cramped, twisting into a tight knot as I could only imagine what dreadful stunt they had in store for me.

Growing anxious, I interrupted them before this could go on any longer. "Earth to Aaron and Jim," I said, waving at them. "You want to fill me in on what you guys got planned, or are you going to let those cigarettes burn to ashes?"

Jim stared down at his hand as if he had forgotten what he had been holding and took a long drag before speaking. "I don't want to ruin the surprise." As he spoke, smoke billowed over his face. He gave Aaron a sly smirk. "Probably best to just show you."

Aaron nodded his head in agreement, lending his support. "Want to go for a little walk down the beach with us?"

I tried to think of what was up on the beach that they could get me to do. There was the cliff around the cove that I refused to leap from last summer. Or the underwater cave in the quarry that I was terrified of. "Sure," I said, mustering as much confidence as I could. "Lead the way, boys."

Without a word, Jim made his way down the beach. Aaron followed, matching him stride for stride. I struggled to keep pace, stuck between a shuffle and an awkward jog. The beach curved inward after we rounded the cove. The cliff loomed high in the sky on the other side, blotting out the sun and casting a dark shadow over the still, black water. A chill raced up my spine at the sight. But I was determined to make the leap of faith this year.

"Too easy," I said to break the silence.

They didn't respond to me. Instead, they kept their frantic pace as the beach narrowed. Tree branched jut out, threatening to push me into the water as they reached out for the lake. Jim and Aaron brushed the branches aside with graceful ease, but I struggled with every twig. Sharp thorns and jagged slivers of broken wood scratched my forearms, drawing a scribble of red lines across my flesh.

Ahead, the boys stepped into the woods and vanished from sight. My heart fluttered in my chest. To avoid the branches, I stepped out into the frigid lake and my legs plunged into the ice-cold water up to my knees even though I was only a few feet from shore. As I rounded the corner, the trees gave ground. Jim and Aaron were already walking side by side as the beach pushed the trees aside. Suddenly, they stopped in unison and turned towards the forest. I'd been down the path before, and I realized what they'd stopped to stare at.

Nestled amongst a tangle of overgrown brush and trees, the two black windows of a forgotten cabin stared out at us. The strange glass absorbed every ray of light the sun could offer. Weathered siding concealed the once vibrant red paint; only a few chips of paint remained scattered about the face of the cabin. Below the two windows, a large sliding door offered a veiled glimpse inside the dilapidated abode. A couch with the cushions shredded by vermin faced them, having long ago offered a brilliant view of the lake. No one could remember who owned the cabin. It was only referred to as the Witch's Cabin.

"Hey, Tommy," Jimmy began, inhaling deeply on his cigarette. "I bet you don't have the guts to step inside that cabin."

"Neither do you, loser," Aaron answered on my behalf.

"Shut up, dickweed."

I didn't believe in witches, but the inside of that cabin gave me the creeps. Just thinking about all the mould and rotten wood was enough to keep me out of there. And don't forget the rats and other ghastly creatures that dwelled within.

"Let's just get out of here," Aaron said, tugging at Jimmy's elbow. "I'm not in the mood to play this game today. Let's just get to the cliff, and at least we can have a little fun." He motioned towards Jimmy, pointing his finger back and forth between them, leaving me out.

I didn't want to go inside the Witch's Cabin. But I really didn't want to leap off that cliff. I knew if I volunteered to go inside, the other boys would chicken out and at least they wouldn't be able to tease me about the cliff.

I pointed at Jimmy. "I'll go in first as long as you come with me."

Jimmy chuckled and took another drag of his cigarette before tossing it to the ground and snuffing it out with his foot. "Let's go."

Without another word, he pushed past me and headed straight towards the rickety steps leading to the sliding door. As I followed him, I had to keep my arms up to block the branches as they flicked back at me. The thin branches lashed my forearms and left red marks on my skin. Aaron kept close behind me, his footsteps keeping me company as we stepped out of the sunlight and into the shadows.

Aaron reached out and grabbed me by the shoulder, jerking me around, and whispered into my ear. "You don't have to do this."

"I don't care," I said back, meaning it. All I had to do was step inside a filthy room for a few minutes, poke around at a few things, and it was all over. "It's not a big deal."

"We can go back to the cabin." Aaron's voice warbled, filled with a sense of apprehension. Maybe he believed the stories that our uncle had been telling us around the campfire.

Jimmy yanked on the sliding door, pulling it out of the track. A loud metallic screech sent a cluster of birds fluttering from a tree and into the sky. He covered his face with his shirt, pinching his nose closed, and waved his hand in front of his face. "This place needs to be fumigated." The cotton fabric muffled his voice.

"Tommy!" Aaron raises his voice, trying to sound stern and in control. "Let's get out of here."

"No way," I said, shaking my head.

I turned and climbed the steps, the boards swaying beneath me as I made my way up. The boards creaked and groaned with every deliberate, hesitating step. The air that spilled from inside the cabin was nauseating, so I pulled my shirt up over my nose to block the stench.

Jimmy was holding the door open for me, waving me inside with his free hand. "After you."

"Thanks," I grumbled as I step past him.

My feet stuck to a greenish-brown substance coating the floor. It was mould or something that hadn't finished rotting away yet. Neglect covered everything in a thick layer of dust, giving the inside an ethereal appearance beneath. Discarded dishes and broken cups lined the counter along the far right wall. The former owners had filled the sink with a rusted-out pot that had a layer of black mould coating the inside. Tufts of torn couch cushion littered the floor, dragged all over the room by the vermin that occupied this house.

Behind me, Jimmy made his way inside. "See if there is anything worth stealing, then let's get out of here before one of us catches the clap."

"What's the clap?"

Jimmy laughed but didn't answer me. I decided that whatever the clap was, I didn't want it. I kicked at a kitchen table chair, the legs glued to the floor by rot and mould. There was no way I was going to find anything inside this place that I was willing to pick up with my hands. The stairs leading up to the second story creaked and groaned, drawing my attention. I glimpsed Jimmy's legs just as they vanished upstairs.

"Hey, Tommy," Jimmy's voice called out from upstairs, distorted and hoarse. "You've got to come check this out, dude."

"Fuck," I whispered to myself. I considered turning around and heading back outside with my brother. But I couldn't face Jimmy's ridicule, and I had even less interest in diving off the cliff after stepping foot inside this cabin. Filled with unease, I made my way across the living room, discovering that the rug had fused with the rotten wood and a cluster of maggots had taken up residence there. Before I headed up the stairs, I took a deep breath and tried to calm my nerves.

"Come on, Tommy, get up here."

"What is it?" I called out, trying to play it cool but my voice cracked.

"You've got to see it to believe it." Unwavering excitement filled his voice. I couldn't remember hearing that from him before.

I made my way up the stairs. Someone had covered the walls in blackened hand prints, small enough to belong to a child. There was a part of me that wondered if there had been other kids who had broken into this cabin and gone upstairs to view whatever had had Jimmy so excited. The other part of me didn't want to think about those hand prints. And where they were leading me.

"Tommy." Jimmy's voice was low and raspy now, urging me up the stairs.

As I crested the stairs, there was a large open space with a closed door straight across from me. This room was far cleaner; there wasn't even any dust, and someone had painted the walls a vibrant shade of blue that reminded me of my room back home. The floor was bare, and the wooden boards barely had any scratches on them. There were pictures of the lake on the wall and one of this very cabin from its early days. The ruby paint shimmered in the sunlight that was trickling through a glass slit in the ceiling, offering a splendid view of the sky above.

"Get in here, Tommy." Jimmy's voice faded in from behind the door.

No longer afraid, I rushed across the room and threw open the door. Someone was sitting in an old rocking chair by the window, but as I stepped into the room, the door slammed shut behind me. I spun around and tried to open it. The knob turned but nothing happened. When I turned around again, the chair was empty.

"*Welcome*," a harsh voice rasped from the walls.

"Jimmy!" I screamed at the top of my lungs.

"Aaron, help me."

"*They can't hear you, boy.*"

"Who are you?" I asked

There was no answer. I could hear my brother and cousin outside talking to someone. They were hooting and hollering. Drawn towards the window, I pressed my face against the filthy glass to get a better view outside. My brother was talking to a boy the same size as me with the same shaggy haircut. I noticed him point up at the window and laugh. Jimmy was beside him, staring up at the window too, tears rolling down his cheek as he slapped the boy's shoulder. Rubbing his shoulder, the boy seemed to shrink away from Jimmy.

"They pranked me," I groaned to myself, "and now they're making fun of me." My face blushed red with embarrassment and anger. I slammed my fist against the wall to display my displeasure with them, but they ignored me and started walking back towards the beach.

"Hey," I called out, slamming my fist against the wall, "wait up for me."

Aaron and Jimmy didn't even glance over their shoulder at me. They walked out of view without waiting for me. But the kid stopped and turned around. When he turned to face me, I saw my reflection staring back up at me with a wicked grin.

"*Goodbye*," the witch said to me from outside the cabin, her voice coming from inside my head.

I slammed my fist against the window and screamed at the top of my lungs to warn my brother. But the glass didn't break and something trapped my panicked cries inside this cabin with me. Outside, the witch waved goodbye to me and turned, heading down the trail to join my brother and cousin, leaving me to rot inside this hell hole.

THE MAN WHO LIVED IN THE BLACK POND

A young girl strolled down a forest path, singing a tender melody. The stone path shifted beneath her feet as she made her way down the winding trail. Above, the sun drifted behind sombre clouds that threatened rain. The path levelled out at the bottom and stretched far into the forest. A flock of birds trilled pleasantly all around her. She skipped along, humming in tune with the birds. Rays of sunlight struggled to break through the canopy of branches hanging overhead, leaving thin rays falling to the ground.

Below the sheltered area, the ground turned soft and mucky. A pungent, earthy aroma rose from the ground. Water trickled over the path just ahead from a hidden pond just to the right. The girl felt a cold chill race down her spine. A flock of birds darted above her head, rustling the tree branches as it fluttered out of sight. For a moment, she wondered if something had spooked them. Another scent lingered in the air. Something she couldn't quite put her finger on. It was like burnt metal, singing the hairs inside her nose as it wafted deep into her airways. Hidden on the swampy edge of the trail, a chorus of frogs croaked. Flies buzzed around her; she swatted them away from the front of her face.

As the girl reached the tiny stream flooding across the pathway, she dithered. Pacing back and forth, she stopped and judged the distance across. She stepped back and made a running leap, landing in a thick pile of sludge on the other side. Her feet slipped wildly beneath her, threatening to spill her onto her backside. Something inside warned her not to touch the water, making her heart race. Forcing herself to fall forward, the girl's hands slid across the mud and the potent aroma of soiled earth filled her nostrils. She spat a wad of phlegm onto the ground as she pushed herself up to her knees. She brushed her muddy hands off her filthy blue jeans, her shirt soaked through with moist soil. Tears formed at the corner of her eyes. A sobbing cry choked her as she thought about what her mother would say when she saw the state she had gotten herself in.

A hoarse voice sprang from the darkness. "Don't cry, little girl."

The girl glanced down the path, expecting to see a man standing in there but found it deserted. Beside her, the pond was exquisitely still. The surface was pitch black, like a glass tabletop. Bare white trees emerged from the pond like gnarled fingers.

"Hello." The girl's call was nothing more than a soft whimper.

"What are you doing all the way out here?" the man asked, his tone demanding.

The girl's heart leapt into her chest, sticking in her throat. An eerie silence fell over the pond as the wildlife vanished. She strained her eyes to see where the voice was coming from, but there wasn't anybody by the side of the road that she could see. A stiff wind blew across the path, rustling the tree branches and tearing off leaves. She found herself battered by the dead leaves and assaulted by a sickly, nauseating aroma. Somehow, the water remained still against the sudden chaos.

"I was out for a walk." The girl found herself compelled to answer. "With my brother," she lied, scouring the area for the source of the voice.

"It's a long way from home." The man accentuated home with a sharp H.

A sudden ripple cut the black pond in half as if shattering a layer of ice. The bone-white trees shivered against the waves as if repulsed by the sudden shift in the pond's dynamic. It settled quickly, the last remaining movement folding into the calm surface. Then, materializing out of thin air, a reflection formed on the surface.

"What's your name?" His high-pitched voice was a wicked snarl.

"Annabelle." The words slipped out of her mouth before she could think about why she was responding as if someone else was controlling her thoughts. The white branches parted with an unseen wind, revealing the stranger hunched amongst a nest of gnarled roots. Large clumps of earth clung to the wood, dried out from the sun. Dressed in a filthy white shirt and tattered black jeans, Annabelle immediately thought of him as homeless. His hair was a dishevelled mess, clumped together and matted to his deathly pale skin.

"What's your name?" she asked.

"You can call me anything you like, it won't matter." A smile waned on his face. He glared at her with yellow, cat-like eyes. Behind his gaze, there seemed to be a dull, burning glow that reminded her of a dying ember. A sickly green tinge tainted the white of his eye. Beads of sweat dripped down his placid skin, rolling down his neck and soaking into the collar of his raggedy shirt. "Some people say I'm the man who lives in the black pond."

The reflection in the pond seemed to swell and grow, stretching out towards her. Annabell took a step back; an irrational fear of the sinister shadow settled in. "Where do you live?"

A cruel fit of laughter gargled through the phlegm in his throat. "I live here."

"You live here?" Annabelle asked, suffering a deep sense of pity for the man. "All by yourself?"

Black crevices creased the man's face, and his dark ruby-red lips added an evil layer to his sinister smile. "I get..." He paused, the silence deafening. "...visitors from time to time."

A shiver ran down Annabelle's spine. Far in the distance, she thought she heard a bird chirping, but it sounded muffled and distressed. The man reached out, his elongated fingers stretching across the length of the pond, and appeared to rustle the grass along the edge. She watched with morbid curiosity, her heart beating sporadically. There was no rhythm as her pulse climbed and wavered. Fixated by the shadowed, clawed reflection of his hands, she couldn't turn away. Vivid details of dirt beneath his fingers appeared in the pond as if beneath a microscope. Festering blisters covered the skin on his hands, a clear puss oozing from them.

Annabelle broke her trance. "I'm going to leave now."

"Don't you want to say and have a little chat with me?" His smile stretched wide across his face; wrinkles ran from the corner of his mouth all the way to his temples. The trees in the pond shuddered back and forth. They cracked and splintered, producing a sickening sound like breaking bones. There was no breeze, but that didn't matter. Something else was moving them. The water didn't ripple despite the movement, the surface remaining perfectly still, a mirrored image of the clouds scrolling across the sky reflected on the lake.

Annabelle backpedalled, too afraid to take her eyes off

the man. Patches of rough dirt and gnarled roots threatened to trip her up. Half buried in the hard-packed soil of the path, a stone with a flat face tripped her up. She fell on her backside, bracing herself with her hands. Her wrists bent backwards at a painful angle, and she let out a pained whimper. Overhead, the sky disappeared, replaced by a snarling tangle of dead branches that formed a ceiling, blotting out the sun. Enveloped in blackness, she held her breath for what seemed like an eternity. Only the sporadic beat of her heart interrupted the deafening silence.

Thump.... thump.. thump. thump.......... thump... thump... thump.. thump.....

The fetid stench of sulphur wafted over her, weighing down the atmosphere and crawling over her skin. A rapid series of bright flashes sparked close by, creating a shuttering effect. The light shimmered off the surface of the lake. In the intervals of darkness, the bone-white tree branches changed places. The black pond remained still.

"Did you hurt yourself?"

A brilliant spark fizzled just feet from Annabelle. At the edge of the pond, the man was resting between two trees. He pressed his back into a tall stump, while his legs rested atop a shorter stump. With his feet crossed and a cigarette nestled into the corner of his mouth, he almost looked relaxed. Suspended over the pitch-black liquid, his gnarled fingers scratched at the branches, creating the bright flashes. A flickering red flame remained on his fingertip. He used it to light his cancer stick. The tip flared a deep orange as he inhaled. Annabelle felt helpless to move, her eyes fixed on the orange flare.

"It's okay to talk to me, little one." Smoke drifted around the man's face. "Would you like a smoke?" He pulled it from the corner of his mouth and held it out for her. All she could do was shake her head. "Suit yourself."

He placed it back in his mouth.

"My mom says that they are bad," Annabelle said. "That they can kill you."

"There are a lot of ways to die," he stated with a thin smile. "Trust me." He inhaled deeply, filling his lungs and letting out a thick cloud of smoke through his nostrils. "This isn't the worst," he sneered.

"What do you want?" Annabelle asked, not expecting an answer.

"Answer me one simple question," he paused for dramatic effect, "and I'll let you go on."

"What if I don't know the answer?" Annabelle contested. "What if it's a trick?"

"It's not a hard question." He tapped his temple with a jagged nail. It dug into his flesh, drawing blood. But he didn't seem to notice. "You will know the answer."

Annabelle pondered his offer. Maybe I'll just run away, she thought to herself. He seems to be trapped in this pond.

The man answered her unasked question. "You could try, little one, but I wouldn't do that." His voice turned into a growl, snapping off the last word.

"Please." Tears welled in the corner of her eyes. Giant globs trekked down to her cheeks. They fell from the edge of her jaw, landing on the soil with an audible plop. "I just want to go home." Her voice trailed off into a whisper.

Cackling laughter erupted from the man. "I just want to go home," he said in a falsetto full of phlegm.

"Stop it," she screamed. Her fists curled into tight balls. She punched the ground beside her. Shock waves of pain raced up her arms and up to her shoulders.

"So, the girl has some fight." He accented the last word, making it sharp. "Answer my question and I'll leave you alone. What do you say, Annabelle?"

"Fine," she screeched. Courage allowed her to lock eyes with the stranger. They were darker than the darkest of night, void of any light.

The man jumped down from his place between the trees, landing at the edge of the shore. Behind him, the tree sank into the black liquid and vanished from sight. He was unbelievably gaunt, his legs nothing more than skin stretched over bone and sinew. Somehow, he moved with an eerie grace. A palpable heat emanated from his mouth, carrying with it a putrid stench. It was a horrendous concoction of rotten fish, damp soil, and sulphur. The foul odour was nauseating.

Annabelle struggled to fight back the tears. "Don't come any closer."

The ground trembled with every footstep the man took. He stopped inches away and knelt down to eye level with her. The man's head tilted back and forth, his dead eyes scanning left to right, studying her. He remained silent. There was a deep grumble in his throat that surged with every breath. His chest thrummed like a furnace powering up.

"What's your question?" Annabelle asked. She just wanted this man to go away.

When the stranger smiled, his blood-red lips stretched from ear to ear. An extraordinary burst of orange and yellow exploded behind the oily black of his eyes. "Mom," he laughed, "or Dad?"

"What?" She felt like she must have blacked out and missed the bulk of the man's question. Maybe it was hiding behind the laughter that boomed from his throat.

"I told you it was a simple question," the smile widened on his face, baring his teeth. "Mom or Dad?"

"I don't understand," her voice trembled.

"You got a fifty-fifty choice." He slapped his scrawny

leg with the palm of his hand. It snapped like a clap of thunder. "There isn't a right or wrong answer either, you just have to say one."

Annabelle tried to think of all the reasons the man would ask her that question. There weren't any options that put her mind at ease. "Neither." The word caught in her throat, choking her. She couldn't draw breath, the bubble of air lodged tight against her larynx.

"That's cheating little one." A scowl twisted the man's features. Dark circles formed beneath his eyes. His skin grew white and pale as his eyes sank deep into two black voids that filled his orbital socket.

He snapped his finger. The curt noise broke the bubble in her throat. She sucked in a sour mouthful of air. It made her sick, but she forced herself to draw in as much air as she could. "I'm not cheating." She gagged on the last word, expecting the word to lodge in her throat once more. When the word left her mouth without sticking, she took another quick breath of relief.

"There are only two answers," he snarled. "Mom, or Dad."

"I don't want to play this game anymore," Annabelle cried.

Above, the sky lit up in a brilliant display of purple lightning, spreading across the horizon like spiderwebs. Thunder rumbled in tune with the man's growling breath. "You can't stop playing now. If you quit, you get penalized. We don't want that, do we?"

Deep hitching sobs sent shudders through Annabelle's body. "Please, mister, I just want to go home." She stared down at her feet, unable to face the stranger's maddening glare.

"Do you want to have one of your parents home when you get there?" the man growled. "Choose one," he demanded, "or I'll kill them both."

She knew he was telling the truth. "I can't," Annabell sobbed. "Can't you take something else? You can have anything but them."

A rumbling bout of thunder rattled the ground. But the pond remained still, reflecting the purple jolts like glass back at the sky. "My choice?" the man questioned.

"Yes, you can have anything except my mom and dad," Annabelle begged.

"Look at me girl." The man who lived in the black pond reached out. His finger tilted her chin up. His blood-shot eyes studied her. A sulphurous vapour poured from his mouth, his putrid breath riddled with burnt fish and decayed flesh. "I will spare your mom and dad." A cruel snarl contorted his face, dark black cracks scared his ashen flesh. "But I need you to make sure this is what you want. I need you to think about it."

Annabelle clamped her eyes shut and nodded her head. "You can have whatever you want," she repeated herself. In her young mind, there wasn't anything else that mattered as much as her parents.

"Run home, little one." the 'an's voice sounded distant.

When she opened her eyes, the stranger was no longer standing next to her. She found him sitting on the far side of the pond, his hands and feet buried in the muddy bank. An icy chill coursed through Annabelle's body, riddling her flesh with goosebumps. Sunlight fell on her back, the warmth of the day drawing her away from the pond. Overhead, the clouds parted, the shadows unravelling from the pond. From across the pond, Annabelle could see the man's sinister smile. As the sun crept over the reflective surface of the pond, a flash of bright white filled Annabelle's sight. She covered her eyes with her hand, blocking out the light.

When she opened them, the man was gone. Annabelle

turned and raced back down the path, the rocks scattering behind her as her feet kicked them out. Her heart raced so fast that the beats blended into a solitary hum. Her lungs ached, but she refused to stop, afraid that the man who lived in the black pond would beat her back to her home and renege on their deal. Trees swept by her in a blur as her troubled mind lost track of time. She was out of breath when the mouth of the path opened into her backyard, the blue siding of her family's two-story home welcoming her home.

"Dad!" Annabelle cried out when she reached the yard.

The back door swung open, and her father raced over the patio and down the stairs. He swept her into his arms. "Annabell, where have you been?" His voice was harsh with anger.

Overcome with emotions, Annabell broke down, her shoulders hitched with a deep sob. "Where's mom?"

Her father shook her back and forth, her hair flailing in front of her face. "Answer the question," he demanded. "Where did you go?"

"I went to play in the forest and got lost..." her voice trailed off.

"What have you done?" He pushed her back to arm's length, his eyes examining her.

Annabell shook her head, not understanding her father's tone. "Nothing."

"Go on up to your room and wait there. Your mother and I will be in to speak to you shortly." Her father spat out the words as if they soiled his mouth. With a disgusted expression plastered on his face, he turned away from Annabelle and pulled his cell phone out of his pocket, pressing it against his cheek. "Yeah, she's back home." He paused, waiting for the voice on the other end of the conversation to finish. "No, I don't think she remembers doing it."

Without another word, Annabelle headed inside the house and made her way upstairs. As she passed her brother's room, she smelled the sickening stench of sulphur and rotten earth from the pond.

Annabelle screamed her brother's name, her nails digging into her scalp as her fingers entwined into her hair. Black soil and ashen soot stained the once pristine powder blue walls. Clumps of mud led to her brother's bed. A gruesome crimson blotch of viscous fluids that soaked through the thin cotton and dripped to the floor ruined the white sheets of his bed.

Outside, she heard the faint blare of sirens approaching. She stared at her hands, noticing for the first time the deep scarlet stains beneath the muck that coated her hands. Unable to hold back her tears, she sobbed into her hands, remembering the words of the man who lived in the black pond: *my choice.*

IRELAND'S EYE

Settled amongst the trees of Random Island, the community of Hickman's Harbour staggered into another fall season. The ocean thundered against the craggy shore, pounding the shoreline with ferocious aggression, turning the harbour into a treacherous trap. A wayward wind rustled the eaves of The Mess Deck, the lone drinking establishment on the island. Most of the summer residents had already left for their winter homes in Clarenville, not wanting to get trapped on Random Island during the lengthy winter months that lay ahead. Angus sat at the bar, a double whiskey from Ireland, reminding him of home, clutched in his grasp. With the glass tilted towards him, the ice clattered against the side as he rocked back and forth on his elbows. Like most fall nights, The Mess Deck was vacant. Angus contemplated how this place stayed open after tourist season other than Friday nights.

"You waiting on me again, Harold?" Angus asked, already knowing the answer.

As Harold rubbed a white dishcloth around the rim of a beer stein, he tapped his heel fervently against the tiled floor. "Seems that way," Harold growled as he shined the glass to a glistening sheen.

After all the tumultuous years that had passed since they forced Angus from his home of Ireland's Eye, he still felt everyone owed him. He could still feel the damp sensation against his skin from the deep sea air that blew across the shore, and he missed how the air filled his lungs. Even with the putrid stench of the fish processing plant implanted in his memory, his childhood home tugged at his heartstrings with nostalgia.

"I'll be moving along then," Angus slapped a $20 bill on the bar. "Will this be enough to cover me tonight?" He lost count of how many drinks he'd put away. Twenty seemed fair. His vision was still straight.

Without hesitating, Harold's weathered hand slid the green bill across the bar and stuffed it in his apron pocket. "It'll do." He propped his elbow against the bar, leaning in close to Angus. The sweet aroma of his cologne was overpowering, making Angus's eyes water. "I wanted to talk to you about the rent," Harold whispered.

Angus looked around, wondering if somebody had wandered in while he got lost in his drink. Not surprised, he found them alone in the bar. "What is it this time?" he grumbled, too loud for Harold, who grimaced as if someone had slapped him across the face.

"Some outsiders arrived this morning," Harold kept his tone low, forcing Angus to lean in. "They're looking to take a brief trip to Ireland's Eye."

Angus banged the bottom of his glass on the bar, the ice cubes making a boisterous racket. "At this time of year? They're either foolish or young and foolish. The waters are colder than a witch's tit," he guffawed. "And treacherous for an inexperienced sailor. No outsider could ever navigate the random currents and rough waves."

When he wasn't drunk, the locals regarded Angus as an accomplished and reliable sailor. Since Ireland's Eye had once been his home, they considered him the local tour guide; it was also how he made a living around these parts. When the government forced the residents of

Ireland's Eye to move, it created a lot of animosity and speculation amongst Newfoundlanders. Locals avoided the island, as rumours of the real reason behind the resettlement sparked fear. Those same rumours drew curious outsiders to the area. Years of poverty didn't push away the fear, it only allowed room for desperation to take root and flourish. There were enough treasures waiting for him around his childhood home to keep his belly and glass full. The yearning for relics from the past provided value to discarded household items in Ireland's Eye. Not one to crave modern comforts, Angus was simply content to scrape by as long as he could continue to keep a roof over his head. He lived in the apartment below Harold, and as long as he did his chores for Harold, Angus didn't need to worry about the rent.

"Two hotshot kids from Maine." Harold continued to maintain his hushed tone. "And they've been asking questions about the island and they even asked for you by name."

"So what?" Angus sighed, his shoulders slumping forward.

"They know too much," Harold snapped. "If they keep digging, they're going to find out our little secret."

"Now it's our little secret," Angus said, rolling his eyes in revulsion.

Oblivious to the cynicism, Harold continued his rant. "We can't have the world discover the truth behind all of this. They know enough to be dangerous on that island."

Dumping the remaining ice into his mouth, Angus ground the ice into shards with his teeth. "Can't I just talk them out of it? Or take them somewhere else? There are several small islands around. They won't even know I took them to the wrong one."

"They'd know," Harold countered, cutting Angus off

abruptly.

"Well," Harold said, rolling his tongue around his mouth. "Maybe I'll refuse to take them."

"They were very insistent," Harold stated. He slid the bottle of black spiced rum out from beneath the counter. "And so am I." He poured two shots into a stubby glass filled with ice. The ice splintered and popped, then Harold topped the glass off with soda. A barrage of bubbles fizzed in the glass. "We have a duty to keep our town's secret, don't we, Angus?"

Angus cradled the fresh drink in his hands as bubbles fizzed over the side and tickled the flesh on the back of his hands. He stared down into the dark liquid, wishing for nothing more than to get lost in the dark void. "It's bound to get out." Angus lifted the glass from the table and took a greedy gulp. "One way or another I suppose." The glass clinked as he slammed it down, half empty.

"Not on my watch." Harold's eyes flickered with a flaring orange hue. When the strange hue subsided, contempt and hatred remained. "If you're no longer up for the task," he slid the bottle of rum out of view, "I'll find someone else."

"Quit your belly aching," Angus snapped. A flash of regret took hold of his mind. "Sorry, sometimes I forget my place."

"Don't you ever forget where you live." Harold reached out and placed his hand over the top of Angus's drink. He slid it across the table towards himself. "If you want to stay here, you need to protect the Eye. It is your home, after all. And you're the last surviving member of the community. You're the gatekeeper of this extraordinary secret."

Angus suppressed his anger. "I wish I could forget it."

Harold laughed. "If only it were that easy Angus."

His lips pressed against his teeth in a slanted grin. Filed, cannibalistic teeth pressed into his lips, drawing a trickle of blood from the soft flesh. "Now, why don't you go on home and get some rest? You have a long day ahead of you tomorrow."

As a blustering wind swept down the mountainside, it carried the chilly promise of snow with it. In the background, the subdued roar of the ocean collapsed against the craggy shore at the mouth of the bay. Angus stumbled down the street, a vague mist suspended in the pale yellow street lights. He zig-zagged between the spotlights, afraid of the blackness outside of their feeble grasp. The town was asleep and he found himself alone after midnight once more. When he crossed the convenience store, his eyes wandered towards the dark interior, wishing that it was still open. His stomach growled in protest. He could see the porch light over his door just ahead. Maybe there was something that could tide him over until morning inside.

Angus fumbled with the keyring, the frigid night air numbing his fingers. "Come on, you bastard," he grunted, struggling to find the key to his apartment. When he found the right one, he slid it into the grove and turned it. The worn metal would soon snap. The door to his apartment bounced up and down as it swung inwards. He flicked the light on. Overhead, the bulb buzzed and tinkered as it struggled to guide the electricity through its coils.

The sporadic assortment of discarded furniture cluttered the open space. An old cork-board counter was the only thing that separated the kitchen area from the messy room. Bare shelves lined the kitchen pantry. Without a second thought to the grimy floor, Angus kicked off his boots and threw his jacket over the back of his recliner. At the back of the open room, there were two doors. His bedroom door was slightly ajar. A stiff breeze from the open window inside chilled the room. Behind the other door, the toilet continued to make random, gurgling noises as the sewage system below threatened to wreak havoc on the plumbing.

He stumbled towards the fridge, a grumble in his stomach demanding food. A pale light cast over his face as he yanked the refrigerator door open. As his eyes adjusted to the light, the stained glass shelves appeared all but empty, mocking him. There was a block of butter on a white dish, the lid long shattered and tossed into the garbage. In the vegetable crisper, a block of mouldy cheese was melding into the plastic. The horrid stench made his stomach clench. He slammed the door shut with disgust. A random assortment of magnets fell to the filthy floor.

Angus knew once he completed his task tomorrow, Harold would make sure that he got enough money to live for another few months. If he was smart about it and laid off the booze, he could stretch his food allowance for six months. Once more, he promised himself he'd stay away from the rum and get himself as far from Ireland's Eye as he could, knowing he would be making that promise again when his money ran out. He stumbled into his bedroom and threw himself into the unkempt bed, not bothering with the light. Falling into a restless sleep, terrible nightmares flooded his thoughts. Another horrendous night, the alcohol solving none of his problems once again. He would try again tomorrow; of that he was sure.

The dreadful secret of Ireland's Eye watched over him, haunting his restless sleep.

A sharp rap on the door woke Angus up. He bolted upright. A thin sheen of sweat covered his body and a dull, throbbing pain radiated from his temples. He tented his fingers, resting his forehead into the palm of his hand. Slowly, he opened his eyes. A trickle of daylight seeped in through the blinds, softened by the sullen clouds that filled the sky.

"Wakey wakey," Harold's voice called out, "eggs and bakey."

Angus scratched his head, unable to comprehend if Harold's voice was coming from outside or the kitchen. A mouthwatering scent of maple accompanied by the familiar aroma of drip coffee tingled the hairs in his nose. Still dressed in the same clothes as yesterday, Angus pushed himself out of bed. His knees cracked and his back ached, but the sweet smell of sizzling bacon was enough to lure him into the living room. His door fluttered open with a creak, the sound of bacon frying in the pan growing louder with every step.

Harold stood at the stove, a giant bow tied into his apron, flames kissing the frying pans from the crackling wood beneath. Angus wanted to ask him why he was standing in his kitchen, uninvited, but his stomach dreaded the thought of losing another meal. Wisps of hazy steam rose from two mugs on the counter. Harold poked empty plastic bags into the corner, an open egg carton laid on top, holding them in place.

When Harold heard a board creak in the living room, he twisted around. "How are you this morning?" he asked, a sly grin plastered across his face.

That smile made Angus uncomfortable as if it were painted on there to help conceal the truth behind those hideous eyes. He ran his fingers down the front of his old dress shirt, fiddling with the buttons along the way. Next, he checked his fly. "What time is it?" There was no working clock in his apartment. He told the time by how thirsty he was.

Harold checked the watch on his wrist, "A quarter past six." He turned back to the stove, flipping the eggs with a silver spatula. Angus couldn't remember owning a spatula.

Then it all came back in a jumbled memory. It wasn't clear yet, but he knew that he'd be going to Ireland's Eye today. Back home. Harold was here to ensure that Angus remained sober. "What time do I have to be ready?" he whined, knowing what lay ahead.

"Not until ten," Harold started, turning the bacon over in the pan. The fat crackled and eased into a steady, simmering sizzle.

Angus scratched his head, his nails jagged from biting them. Flakes of dry skin fell over his shoulders. "What in God's name are you doing here so early, Harold? Can't you just let a man get some rest?"

"Sit down." Harold motioned towards the coffee cup sitting on the counter. "I think we need to go over some things before you head out today." He shuffled over to the fridge, yanking the door open and grabbed a purple container of creamer.

With Harold's body in the way, it was hard to see, but it appeared that the shelves were full. Angus walked past the coffee, stepping on his jacket. It must have fallen off the back of the chair during the night. He reached down to pick it up. A square lump filled the pocket. He reached in and hauled out a pack of Export A Dark Blue, the plastic wrapping still on the box. He eagerly tore the red ribbon, ripping away the plastic and letting it fall to the floor along with his soiled clothes. The sweet aroma of tobacco was strong and comforting. "I don't have a light?" He

tucked a cancer stick into the corner of his mouth, deciding to take a seat by his coffee.

Harold laughed. "Your filthy habits are going to send
you to an early grave." He rummaged through his jeans'
pockets. They didn't fit him very well, too tight around
the thighs and much too short. A long patch of his white
socks peeked between the hem of his pants and his shoes.
After considerable effort, he tossed a blue Bic at Angus,
who fumbled with it, catching it against his gut.

Harold didn't wait for Angus to say thanks. "These
two men are very insistent," he explained. "They're here
because they've been digging into the government's reason to relocate the residents of Ireland's Eye. We both
know that anyone who does any research into it will see
the cracks."

Angus nodded his agreement, inhaling deeply on the
cigarette and blowing a ring of smoke towards the ceiling.

"Most people give up before they realize they don't
want to know the truth," Harold said, rambling. "But not
these two. No sir, they're hell-bent on discovering the
truth behind Ireland's Eye and exposing it to the world.
Apparently, they've done this kind of thing before."

Sucking back on the cigarette, the tip flared a bright
orange. Angus could feel the heat on the tip of his fingers.
"What do you expect me to do about that?"

"We have to stop them from discovering our little secret," Harold said, thumping his fist against the counter.
"You need to stop them if you want to keep out of trouble."

"No matter where I go," Angus spat on the floor, the
wad of phlegm landing with an audible splat, "trouble
follows."

"You can't even begin to imagine how terrible it will
be for you if you let them discover our secret," Harold

hissed.

Everyone in town knew the rumours, but no one ever spoke a word about it out loud. Angus simply nodded his head, lighting another cigarette with practiced ease. A trail of stale smoke rose over his face, clouding his vision. Through the smoke, Harold appeared as a phantom. As Harold spoke, Angus tuned him out, taking pleasure in the smoke while pouring cream into his coffee. Once the black liquid turned into a muddy brown, he placed the carton back on the counter. He sipped his coffee with the cigarette dangling from the corner of his mouth; smoke billowed through his nose even as he drank.

"They arrived with the correct GPS coordinates." Angus tuned in near the end of Harold's speech. "So, there's no fooling them. You'll just have to think of something else. We can't let this secret get out."

Harold started taking the bacon out of the frying pan and placed them on a pile of napkins to soak away the grease. Before he cleaned the pan, he cracked two eggs into the bacon grease. The yolks bubbled as the scraps of bacon absorbed into the whites. Angus couldn't remember telling Harold that was the way he liked his eggs. He also didn't remember having smoked in Harold's bar or how he could have known his favourite brand of smokes. Harold always read his mind.

"What's there to figure out?" Angus growled. "We are just going to do the same thing we do to everyone who comes around, poking their nose into our business. The only question is, do I have to do this myself or are you going to help."

"No need to get angry with me. This should be a happy day for you," Harold said, a grin stretching the skin across his cheeks. "You are going home."

Angus hacked up something awful, borne in the depths

of his throat. He wandered into the bathroom, spitting a yellowish-brown wad of phlegm into the porcelain bowl. It swirled around counterclockwise, something that was supposed to be reserved for the southern hemisphere, but every town has its secret.

Water sloshed between the ten-foot fishing boat and the dock on the port side, the rough seas slapping against the starboard side. The droning sound was maddening, growing louder with the rising sun. Angus squinted and groaned; the last of the lingering side effects of his headache refused to leave him. He heard the rustling noise from the foreign yacht as the occupants prepared to depart for the day. They were checking the lines, making sure they'd tied them off before they left with Angus for Ireland's Eye. As the town's visitors approached as the boards creaked and groaned beneath, their weathered surface wilted a pale gray. Conflicted, Angus wanted to warn them to turn around and forget this place ever existed and to take him with them. Angus felt Harold's eyes burning into the back of his head from atop the hill, glaring down at him. He tilted his head up towards the cliff, knowing he wouldn't see him standing there.

Thump

A youthful voice drew Angus's concentration. "Hey, you're our guide?" a tall, blond-haired man asked, his expression full of doubt. His jawline was carved from stone and his bronzed skin was weathered by the sun. At his feet was a knapsack filled with camping gear and survival gear. Another thump rattled the dock as a man behind him dropped his gear alongside.

Angus kept his calm. If Harold saw any hint of emotion on his face, he'd see fit to interfere with himself. "Listen, feller, water's frigid and the current's strong this time of year." He pronounced it ear. "There are some icebergs just offshore. I can get ye close to those."

"That's not what we came here for," the other man interrupted. They must have been brothers, sharing the same skin tone and vivid blond locks. His hair was considerably shorter, but the trace amount of sunlight sparkled in it just the same.

"Yeah, man," the other brother joined in. "We came here to visit the Eye."

"Ireland's Eye isn't much to see," Angus said then added: "just a few abandoned homes. Strangers have already claimed all the valuable trinkets."

"Listen," the long-haired brother stepped forward and placed one foot on the gangway. "Me and my brother Henrick will pay for whatever it takes to get to the island. We don't even need you to step foot on the island. Just get us there and wait for us to come back."

"What's your name?" Angus asked, pointing at the man standing on his gangway.

"Weston," he replied as he stepped down into the fishing vessel. He was broad, laden with muscles but still lean. "So, what do you say, old man?" Weston waved Henrick aboard the fishing vessel.

Angus heard a splash in the water beside the boat. It didn't catch the brothers' attention, but it caught his. "You two ain't from Maine." Angus eyed them. They didn't dress like it. Weston wore a bright orange rain slicker over his dive suit. Henrick's was a shade of red that reminded Angus of a boiled lobster shell. "Where are you boys from?"

"Los Angeles," Henrick said with a stubborn sense of pride.

"We sailed here from Maine," Weston added, as if it

was supposed to impress Angus.

"Now what's a couple of hippie dippies doing all the way out here?" He swept his hand over Hickman's Cove. Waves capped by white tips rolled in through the mouth of the harbour. Overhead, a gull cried its high-pitched call as it drifted in the breeze. Below, something awful slithered through the waters with eerie grace and speed. Angus heard it, but he noticed they were oblivious. He also knew if he got them to look over the side of the ship, all they would see was the waves crashing against the edge of the fishing vessel and a few empty lines floating atop the ocean. "There are a lot of abandoned towns around Newfoundland. And all of them are easier to get to than this one. What's your goddamn fascination?"

"We know who you are." Henrick glanced at his brother. "Angus O'Leary, last remaining survivor of the incident at Ireland's Eye."

"Incident?" Angus felt his heart skip a beat. A bead of sweat rolled down his backside despite the frigid winds coming off the water. He heard that hideous breathing of the creature as it breached the surface, then slapped its tail off a cresting wave as it dove below once more.

"In 1958, locals spotted a UFO in the skies above Clarenville," Henrick recited from memory.

"So, what does that have to do with anything?" Angus turned his head, praying that he would see Harold standing on the cliffside, eavesdropping on them. A strong breeze ruffled the bushes at the edge of the cliff, leaving no doubt the hilltop was barren.

"There were hundreds of eyewitnesses," Henrick responded.

"All of them corroborating the same story," Weston added. "They all witnessed it hovering over Random Island before dipping below the horizon. No one ever saw it rise above the island again."

"I don't see what this has to do with anything?" Angus understood he could not distract them. They were determined to go snooping around. All they were going to find was their demise.

"Just a few months later, the residents of Ireland's Eye were forced to resettle across the island." Weston's lips twisted into a sly smile, revealing his pearly whites. "But there are no traceable records of where they ended up settling."

"Almost as if they're covering something up," Henrick added.

Angus forced laughter, trying to convince the brothers they were being ridiculous. When he glimpsed their stone haughty stare, he realized they weren't buying it. "What do you think? That an alien spacecraft landed on Ireland's Eye and whisked away the townsfolk?"

"That's exactly what I think," Weston said in his West Coast surfer tone. "I think the aliens killed everyone except you and that government tried to cover it up.

If only they appreciated the consequences behind the real truth, Angus thought, they'd give up this foolish quest.

A momentary wave of relief washed over Angus, false hopes that they had enough of him and were going to head back to their yacht. It didn't matter to Angus if they went searching for whatever it was they thought they were looking for. He recognized it was only a matter of time before it found them. He was just glad that he would not be a part of the conspiracy. Henrick grasped his knapsack, his muscles flexing beneath his jacket as the wind pulled it tight against his slender frame. Then all hope fled from Angus's lungs in an exaggerated gasp. Henrick walked across the gangway onto the fishing vessel as he ordered

Weston to hurry.

"Now, old timer." Henrick approached Angus, getting in his face. "You're going to take us back to your home." He paused and waited for Weston. When his brother was standing beside him, he continued. "Back to the Eye." He thrust his finger into Angus's ribs, pushing him backwards.

Angus's eyes wandered beyond the brothers, up towards the drab clouds. A clap of thunder tore them open. Rain splattered on the dock, falling in huge, frigid droplets. A tear streaked down his cheek, hidden by the rivulets of water running down his weathered face. He watched the townsfolk walking down the road, their presence going unnoticed by the brothers.

"Won't be any problems, fellers," Angus steadied himself, doing his best to remain calm as his heart fluttered in his chest. "I'll get you there soon enough." Angus needed them to understand what was coming for them, even if they couldn't see it yet. "Haul in the heaving lines and get that gangway aboard. I'll get the engine going."

Henrick sneered at Angus with a crooked smile, his face disfigured by the leering gesture, the smooth features replaced by sharp, jagged lines. Angus expected him to say something, but he went about working the lines with his brother. Neither one noticed the citizens of Hickman's Cove approaching them, or the strange fog rising from the ocean to greet them. Angus readied the controls, preparing to turn the keys. Thick, black smoke billowed below deck as the diesel engine sputtered to life.

He dreaded what awaited them on Ireland's Eye.

Angus's heart sank as the decrepit remnants of the Eye sprung from the opaque mist. The weathered, decomposing remains of his childhood blended into the dismal horizon. Vestiges of the rotten past staggered through the monstrous shadows as the fishing vessel bobbed in the turbulent ocean.

"I can't get us ashore, boys," Angus stated, keeping his voice indifferent. "The waves will pin us against the shore and tear us apart."

Weston sighed, raising his hand to his eyebrows to shield his eyes from the driven rain. The waves crashed against the shore, the dark blue waters beaten to a frothy white against the rocks. "Just get us close enough. It's not that deep here."

"Yeah," Henrick added, "we are so close to the truth."

Angus caught movement amongst the shadows from the corner of his eye. "You don't understand how close you are," he muttered to himself.

The entire ship rattled as the savage waves threatened to tear the fishing vessel apart. Henrick and Weston grabbed the anchor, hoisted it to the gunwale, and tossed it over the side. The wind ripped away the sound as it splashed into the shallow water and dug into the sea. Weston jumped over the side first, plunging into the water up to his hips. The receding current tugged at him, yanking him out towards the depths and pinning him against the boat. When the tide flowed towards shore, he stumbled forwards, the depths diminishing to shallow puddles after only a few staggering footsteps.

"Come on," Weston called out over the roaring ocean, waving his hand.

"You first, old man," Henrick demanded.

Angus sat on the edge and swung his legs over the side, waiting for the tide to be in his favour. Even after all these years at sea, he still feared drowning beneath those unrelenting, merciless waves. There was only one thing he feared more than drowning.

Angus dropped over the side, the current guiding him to shallow waters as he stumbled forward. He heard a loud splash as Henrick jumped into the tide behind him, his legs churning through the deepening waters.

"There," Weston called out from the shore with a finger pointed towards Angus's childhood home.

Two fierce, glaring orange orbs glared at them through the upstairs bedroom window for an instant before vanishing into the shadows. Excited, the brothers encouraged each other and embraced; the blistering winds and pelting rain couldn't dampen their spirits.

"That's enough, boys," Angus called out over the wind. "Time to go back before it's too late."

Weston pulled back his sleeve, revealing a slim black watch. "It's only early, old man," he yelled back. "We have lots of time before the tide comes back." The brothers turned their back to Angus and hurried towards the house.

Angus rushed to catch up with them. He reached out and grabbed Henrick by the shoulder, spinning him around so that they were face to face. "Trust me," Angus pleaded. "You don't want to go in there."

Henrick batted Angus's hand away with ease. "Tell us the truth, old man. What happened all those years ago when you were just a boy? What happened to the people who lived here?"

"Abducted by aliens and taken back to their home world," Weston said with a knowing smile.

Angus shook his head. If only Harold weren't so paranoid. He would have never brought them here. They had strayed so far from the truth they would have never found it, even with his help. "You're right boys, it's a huge government cover-up. Now, let's head back. There's nothing left to discover here."

"Nothing left to discover?" Weston mocked Angus. "People just didn't know what to search for."

"Are ye' listening to yourself?" Angus roared. "Don't you understand? The government already gathered all the evidence and got it hidden away someplace no one will ever find it?"

"The Eye is still here," Weston announced. "We just witnessed it with our own eyes."

"Come along, brother," Henrick said, tugging at his brother's wrist. "We are going to be famous."

"Don't," Angus demanded. "The secret of Ireland's Eye is too much to bear. If only people realized how far its vision stretched, you would leave it alone."

The brothers paused for a moment then broke into a fit of uncontrollable laughter. Without another word, they turned and headed towards the front door. It creaked a final warning as they yanked it open, vanishing inside the house. Angus turned his back to the home and stood silently in the rain, the wind carrying the brother's screams to him. When the screams died down, he wandered aimlessly towards his boat, refusing to turn around. As much as he longed for home, they took it away from him years ago. Left bitter and alone, his heart yearned for the family that remained here, even if they weren't really his family anymore. They would welcome him back with open arms. And that's what scared him the most, how much they wanted him to come back home... and how much he wanted to join them. He would feel Ireland's Eye upon him no matter where he went for the rest of his life.

Angus trudged through the swirling water towards his fishing boat, staring down at the blackness engulfing his boots. He stood there for hours as the tide rose around him, pouring over his boots and passing his hips. The voices of his family whispered in the wind behind him, begging him to come back home. Despite his desire to return to Ireland's Eye, he realized he needed to move on. Angus took a step forward. The ice-cold water only stung for a minute. It felt good. With one last glance over his shoulder, he said goodbye to home and kept walking.

MUMMERS: SPREADING CHRISTMAS JOY

Blustery wind howled in the darkness, and the two-story Cape Cod style house answered with groans and creaks. Sixteen-year-old June stood at the kitchen sink, steam ascending from the hot water as she washed the baking trays. The fragrant smell of molasses and cinnamon filled her grandparents' home. June could hear the incessant click-clack of her grandmother's knitting needles over the evening news. Her grandfather was, as usual, voicing his opinion toward every story. He didn't limit his commentary to the facts: he also provided his take on each of the reporters' attire.

Trees lingered along the edge of the backyard, the exposed branches hanging in the wind casting shadows across the snow in the dying daylight. It was another typical winter's night in Crooked Creek, Newfoundland; the kind with a chill that kept you inside once the sun went down early in the evening. Heat poured out of the traditional wood stove nestled in the corner of the living room, just out of sight. June could have sworn that, in late November, once winter finally set in, her grandpa had lit a fire in the hearth and refused to let it die out. Obsessed with keeping the fire burning, her grandfather spent most his days stocking wood in the woodshed indoors or splitting logs in his shed.

Tibb's Eve, or as her father often called it, Tipp's Eve, was a day she had always spent with her grandparents. This year was no exception. Against her many protests, her parents had gone out with their friends. It wasn't that June didn't love her grandparents; she was just growing older and didn't want to be treated like a child anymore. Deep inside, an increasing compulsion to hang out with her friends overshadowed her desire to spend time with her family.

Red, green, and white lights strung underneath the kitchen cabinets, the colourful shades catching in the fake snow resting on the windowsill ledge. Cookies placed on raised steel racks to cool obscured the festive red and green floral pattern of the tablecloth. With the noise of the running water and television to conceal her actions, June snuck a cookie while they were still warm. She stuffed it in her mouth and chewed quietly as she fetched her phone from the pocket of her jeans. "You got to be kidding me," June whispered to herself, disappointed. Despite the increasing prevalence of modern amenities around town, there was still no cell service at all on the outskirts of Crooked Creek, nor scarcely any in downtown on the best of days for that matter. Even if she could gain permission to head out, she wouldn't know where to go, anyway.

She stared at the last text message on her phone from Jacob. He had been hounding her for a date ever since *that* party, but she wanted nothing to do with him. She had avoided him at every avenue. It was easy to ignore his texts, but she dreaded going back to the school where it was much more difficult to avoid his advances. They had been working on an English project together. He had used it to his advantage more than once to get a little too close. She begged him to let her work on the project alone, finish it, and let them both take credit. He insisted on finishing it with her. They had been doing a book report together on *Donovan's Brain*, a novel of his choosing by Curt Siodmak. She had grown to love it, the book sitting next to the kitchen sink even now; she could barely put it down. She had memorized her favourite line, recognizing it as quoted in a movie she had recently seen, though she couldn't remember which one.

"Amidst the mists and fiercest frosts, with barest wrists, and stoutest boasts, he thrusts his fist against the posts, and still insists he see the ghosts."

She could picture Jacob now at that party, standing head and shoulders above her, peering down at her with that awkward glaze in his eyes. Alcohol made you do stupid things you regretted; he was her first harsh lesson in that particular subject. Whatever she had seen in him that night at the party, it was her fault she let things progress so quickly. Abruptly ending things probably wasn't the best idea either, but she had left him there with his hardened desires in his hand. Thankfully, classes had ended for the Christmas break. She was left praying that the whole sordid ordeal would blow over by the time classes resumed.

A fierce squall pelted snow against the window, making her look up abruptly. Just beyond the light spilling out the kitchen window, prowling in the shadows, June swore she saw a pair of eyes following her. She leaned towards the glass, a slight chill seeping in from the drafty glass pane window. Something was standing in the woods; a slight reflection of moonlight caught in the black pupils of some critter, she told herself. She stayed tethered to the spot for a moment, her legs unwilling to move until her brain convinced the muscles that there was nothing to be concerned with. After all, it was probably just another moose wandering aimlessly towards the scent of society.

After brief deliberation between her gut and her mind, June's senses came to an agreement. She stepped to the side of the sink, obscuring herself from any potential woodland voyeur. A bowl of chicken bone candy tempted her from the other edge of the double sink. Red flowers decorated the stained glass dish her grandmother brought out "special for company," but she allowed herself a taste. The sharp cinnamon made a welcome effort to bring her back to the present.

"Do you guys want a cookie brought out?" June called to

her grandparents.

The rhythmic clicking of her grandmother's knitting needles paused briefly. "Yes, my love." Her voice carried down the short corridor and into the kitchen. June reached up into the cupboards and dragged down a plate without awaiting her grandfather's response. June knew full well he was asleep and would have one or two when he woke up.

The molasses cookies steamed, not entirely cooled off yet, but that didn't stop June from gingerly retrieving some from the cooling rack. She liked them fresh out of the oven, not quite hot enough to burn her fingers but just on the cusp of it. She placed four of them on the ceramic plate and walked over to the fridge. With a vigorous yank, the refrigerator door opened and a bag of gingersnaps slid from the top shelf, giving her a slight fright. Instinct took over, her reflexes jumping into action to brace the plate against her stomach.

A hard bang echoed sharply in the kitchen as the frozen cookies collided with the plate. June laid the plate on the kitchen counter, fought with the Ziplock bag to grab four gingersnaps, then resealed the bag and shoved it back into what seemed like a more secure spot. Momentarily forgetting herself, she found herself face-to-face with the dish of chicken bone candy. She reached out and placed one in her mouth, staring out the window at the storm brewing outside.

A sense of dismay washed over June. Her eyes were immediately drawn to the brink of blackness. Something was out there, or someone. Snow was beginning to fall faster and heavier outside, and she swore she could see the frilled edge of a maroon scarf dancing in the squall. She squinted to make out what it was attached to, but between the encroaching darkness and the growing storm her efforts were fruitless. She stared out the kitchen window transfixed, drawn to identify the unknown.

BANG, BANG, BANG.

"Any Mummers lowed'in?"

If June had been holding onto the plate of cookies, she would have thrown them across the room. Her heart vaulted into her throat, choking out her startled shriek. Her fingers gripped the edge of the steel sink, the cold surface a sharp contrast to the flush of warmth that coursed through her body now. Quickly turning away from the window, she looked down the hallway that led to the mud room. Shapes formed behind the fogged-up window of the front door, their shadow looming across the threshold.

"Harold, would you get that," her grandmother urged. June heard her putting away her knitting. "June, be a doll and throw the kettle on."

June's grandfather grumbled, the springs in his chair crying out emphatically as he pushed himself up. His tired feet scurried across the floor.

*BANG, BANG, **BANG**.*

"ANY MUMMERS 'LOWED'IN?" a deep, growl boomed on the other side of the door with an excessive application of fury.

"Lord thundering Jesus," Harold snapped back. "I'm coming. Hold your horses."

June was still overwhelmed by the sense that something lay waiting just beyond the treeline, a piercing glare burning a hole in her back. She glanced back once more, half expecting to see whatever had been watching her to have made its move while she'd had her back turned. Snow obscured her vision more than ever though, the treeline now invisible from the kitchen window. June's grandmother's rocking chair rattled noisily. The telltale sound of the woman struggling to rise from her chair diverted June's attention back to the present. June snapped to attention as the front door creaked eerily on its ancient hinges. Three mummers stood in the porch light, silhouetted by the whirling snow behind them.

"Any mummers 'lowed'in?" a disguised voice inquired, placing a lot of significance on the last syllable.

"Shake the snow of yer damn boots," Harold grumbled. "I don't need ye tracking snow through the damn house." Her grandfather stepped aside, letting the mummers pass the threshold.

June felt a shudder course through her body. One of the figures nearly had to crouch as he trod into the house, his broad shoulders making the pillowcase insignificant on top of his head. He had cut two tiny slits in it for his eyes, outlined in red with black splotches that resembled triangles. Drawn in black, a wide grin stretched from ear to ear. The largest mummer wore a blue lumberjack shirt and a pink brassier over his red tee. The other two mummers wore black rubber boots, but he wore an obnoxious bright yellow pair with his blue jeans tucked into them.

The smallest mummer wore a sweatshirt that was two sizes too big for them; the drab grey fabric came to a halt somewhere below their knees. They kept to the back; June figured they were begrudgingly participating in the tradition for the sake of the other two. Their grey pillow case with a black frown and black eyes looked dull compared to the others.

In the front, seemingly taking charge was the third mummer. They wore a yellow rain slicker pulled over a black knit sweater that had orange pompoms running up the front of it. They wore a pillow case tucked into the collar of the sweater, the eyes dyed pitch black. What stood out most about the threesome sent shivers down June's spine: the leader's pillowcase bore a sinister looking crimson smirk.

"Is the kettle on yet, June?" her grandmother called out as she walked into the hallway, her tone full of Christmas joy. "Come on in, you must be cold from the weather outside."

"What are ye fools doing out on a night like this?" Harold snorted. "Catch your cold ye will." He shut the door closed behind them.

"Now, Harold." Her grandmother tried her best to sound

soothing. "You welcome them with warm arms," she scolded him. "Never you mind my husband. He's just old and contrary."

"Christ, Mabel, I opened the door and let them in," Harold grumbled.

June grabbed the kettle from the stovetop. She brought it back to the sink, letting the hot water run for a minute so it would boil faster, and then filled it up. She kept a vigilant eye trained outside, waiting to glimpse the red shawl. The house groaned against the breeze. The snow that pelted off the windows and twirled around in the backyard kept her from seeing clearly. Bristles scraped against the linoleum floor of the porch as her grandfather meticulously swept up the snow behind the mummers. Their heavy rubber boots thumped against the hardwood as they made their way down the hall. One of them had jingle bells hidden on their person, the bell rattling as they walked. Something still didn't feel right. She tried to push it off as just an overactive imagination, but June couldn't shake the building sense of anxiety in her abdomen. Each jangle echoed in her skull, plunging deeper into her subconscious, warning her to run. Her eyes wandered over a knife she had just washed. Fear compelled her to pick it up, turning it in her hands, allowing the light to glisten off the blade.

"June, my love, would you take down some mugs and lay some cookies out on the table?" Mabel's voice was giddy with delight, catching June by surprise. June hastily placed the knife back on the counter next to the sink as her grandmother bustled into the kitchen. Hardly able to contain her excitement, Mabel moved through the room with practised grace, disregarding her aching joints. "Harold, don't be an old grump. Grab the extra chairs from the cellar."

Harold stomped down the stairs, his voice trailing off as he complained to himself. June wanted to call out to him; she felt uneasy without him. The three mummers loomed in the kitchen, standing silently together. "Tea?" June offered, tilting a mug in their direction. No response. The trio didn't move, didn't make a sound, their outlandish outfits concealing any signs they were even breathing. Regardless, June could have sworn they were all peering at her.

Much to June's relief, the high-pitched whistle that indicated the kettle had come to a boil broke the tension in the room. She shifted the kettle across the stovetop and off the burner. Mabel rifled through the cupboards, opening and closing doors as she took out tins of candy, jars of jams, and biscuits to lay out on the table. Instinctively, June poured her grandmother a cup of tea, adding milk and extra sugar and leaving the Tetley tea bag in. She looked out the window as a powerful gust of wind rattled the house. The storm picked up once more, burying any evidence of life in the yard. There was no red scarf, just trees and darkness.

Thump

Startled, June leapt around just in time to see her grandfather bending over to pick up a chair he had dragged from the cellar. "Hey, uh, would you mind helping my grandpa?" June stuttered, motioning toward the largest mummer with the sugar spoon still in her hand. For a moment he stood there, resembling a menacing statue. He swayed on his foot for a moment before finally lumbering down the hallway. Harold held out a chair, and the mummer took it into his meaty hands, making it look like doll furniture in comparison. He walked back to the kitchen with it, never once saying a word.

"Thanks," Harold mumbled as he turned the chair away from the table, taking a seat. He rubbed his hand over the stubble on his chin, generating a distinct scratching noise. The day's growth stood out as white whiskers, concealing some of the deep wrinkles that had formed on his weathered skin. Mabel settled in a chair next to him, a giant smile plastered on her face. Harold looked at her, a sly smile on his face as he tried to hide his anticipation and maintain his grumpy disposition. "Ye fella's forgot yer instruments?"

The mummer with the snarling red smile parted his yellow rain slicker slowly, revealing a harmonica nestled into the inside pocket. The behemoth withdrew a tambourine from underneath his sweater, the other mummer reached behind his back, pulling out a small ukulele. They tuned up their instruments before breaking out into a solemn rendition of "Any Mummers 'Lowed'In." Harold and Mabel stomped their feet, disregarding the slower beat and hummed the song to keep pace with the traditional version. The mummers began to shuffle, the movements a far stretch from a jig, closer resembling a rigid, macabre dance.

"Who do you think it is, sweetheart?" Mabel leaned in towards Harold, her long silvery hair resting on his shoulder.

Harold sat in the chair, his legs crossed and his elbows resting on the table. "That big fella there ain't from 'round these parts," he surmised. "I'd recognize a man that magnitude."

"He must be from the next town over." Mabel took a sip of her tea. "The relative of someone in town, perhaps?"

June thought she heard someone trudging through the snow, approaching the front door. Moments before the door opened, the red smiling mummer locked his elbow with hers and twisted her around, escorting her away from the corridor and further into the kitchen. He wasn't being rough, but he wasn't being gentle either. Her grandparents continued their vain effort to determine who the mummers were, not paying any attention to the front door opening. It had to be her parents, June rationalized, a tide of relief washing over her.

"Dad?" June called out, but the only response she received was the clunking noise of his boots as he stumbled up the stairs. *Great* she thought. Drunk as a skunk and headed straight to bed for the night, dragging Mom in tow by the sound of it. One last spin and the mummer released his clutch, depositing June back next to the kitchen sink. Her hand glided across the counter as she caught herself, and a sickening dread welled up in her gut again.

"I betcha it's the butcher," Mabel announced triumphantly

Harold furrowed his brow. "Now what would make you think something like that?" he said with disdain.

"Look." Mabel pointed at the mummer with the grey pillow case. "He's carrying a butcher's knife. That's you, isn't it Sam?" She giggled like a school girl, proud of deduction.

June wasn't laughing, and neither were the mummers. They all stopped dancing. June stared, disbelieving eyes going between the empty counter where she had laid the knife and where it now was held firmly in the small mummer's hand. Her jaw dropped open as if to scream, but only a choked whimper escaped her parted lips.

"You know the rules, Sam," Harold snorted. "Take off that stupid pillow case and join us for tea."

The mummer held the knife up to their throat, pressing it into the pillowcase fabric, causing the sheet to go tight against their face. June could see the delicate features of a woman beneath, licking her lips. "Dad!" June raised her voice and cried desperately for help.

"What's the matter, Sweetie?" Mabel didn't seem to recognize what was happening, but June's grandfather had finally caught on.

Harold gripped his cane tightly, his knuckles turning white as he pushed himself up. "Now, whoever is under that mask, take it off now. Yer scarin' me granddaughter, and I won't have it." His frail frame shook, not with fright, but with old age. Frail bones long past their prime struggled on the best of days to keep him steady on his feet. The mummers stood together, blocking off the exit to the hallway.

Mabel still didn't understand what was happening. "Harold, that's no way to treat our guests," she chastised, sounding ashamed and resentful at the same time. She tried to stand up, but Harold held her down with his free arm. The mummer raised his hand, pointing the knife towards June, the tip of it lined up with the bridge of her nose. June backed into the counter, the sharp edge digging into the small of her back. The giant mummer reached out with his massive gloved hand and smashed his fist into the telephone. The plastic pieces exploded into oblivion against his mighty blow. "Harold, where's your gun?" Mabel's voice quivered.

"We'd never get to it." Harold stepped in between the knife and June. "It's upstairs in the spare room."

For what seemed to June like an eternity, the mummers stood quietly in the hallway, swaying back and forth on their heels, slanting their heads at a disturbing angle to stare at them. "What do you want?" June screeched at the top of her lungs, the ligaments in her neck tensed. Her face burned with rage, despair and desperation; tears welled in her eyes. Harold made a move, not certain of what he was trying to do. Maybe he had been trying to console her, or perhaps defend her, but it didn't matter. Before June knew what was happening, a flash of yellow darted towards her grandfather's face. Harold's head jerked backward and to the right. A resounding pop burst forth from his jaw sending fragments of teeth, blood, and spit flying across the kitchen floor. Survival instincts took over. Harold swung his cane upwards, narrowly missing his attacker's face but sending an unmistakable message.

June made a quick decision, opening the top drawer, reaching blindly, her fingers probing for the handle of a knife. Her fingers quickly discovered a thick, wooden steak knife, and she thrust it out in front of her. "You better get out of here right now."

Rather than instilling fear in the trespassers, as she had hoped, snickering started from beneath the pillowcases. A low, gurgling chuckle from the biggest mummer boomed the loudest in the room. The red-grinned mummer chuckled. "We aren't going anywhere just yet."

"You're sick," Mabel sobbed. "What do you want?"

"I just want to watch the slaughter," he said slowly, without emotion.

"Get out of here," Harold bellowed, swinging his cane at the mummer's still outstretched knife. A loud clang echoed in the kitchen, shattering the tension and sending the bladed utensil skittering across the floor. "Now, goddamn it."

"We'll miss all the fun if we go," the smallest mummer bemoaned.

"Don't worry, dear. We'll be back to play once they've had a chance to meet our friend," the red-grinned mummer replied.

"That'll be when the real fun starts anyway," the third mummer said. The mummers talked to themselves as if they were alone in the kitchen, ignoring Harold's threat. June's breath lodged in her chest, the pressure building up, making it harder to breathe. Stars filled her vision; agonizing panic filled her mouth with a bitter, copper taste. Her stomach urged, demanding to release the pressure as the acid gurgled and started to rise. Silence smothered the house like a blanket thrown over a fire.

Without a word or another action, the mummers turned and sauntered down the hallway, their rubber boots thumping against the hardwood floor. They opened the door and closed it cautiously behind them, as if nothing sinister had just happened. June looked to her phone, the sudden impulse to toss it against the wall came and dissolved in an instant. "No signal." The words sounded distant, the delicate sound resembling a child's sigh. Jacob's text was still open. She cursed herself, recognizing that it was probably him behind one of those veils. He hadn't taken the rejection well, and now he was taking it too far. June felt guilty. Her grandfather had been severely hurt because of her.

Mabel rushed over to Harold, caressing his face with her hand. "Oh Harold, are you okay?"

"Don't you mind me. You get upstairs and get my gun before they come back." Harold brushed her off. "Wake up Micheal and Bethany. I don't care how drunk they are. We are all getting out of here."

"Who were they talking about?" *Have you seen our friend? He said he was coming here to slaughter you.* June couldn't get the phrase out of her head. It kept repeating like a fragmented record.

Mabel left the kitchen, and Harold followed closely behind. June crept down the hallway behind them. Her grandmother went upstairs and her grandfather stood at the window, holding the curtains open with his cane. "A car's coming up the road." His voice trembled as he spoke, unnerved by the encounter.

June's whole body seized as her eyes saw the red scarf draped on the coat hook in the porch. It was possible her imagination was running wild, but she was positive that was the same scarf she had seen in the back yard.

"Oh thank Jesus, it's your mother and father," Harold announced.

"What?" June was confused. "It can't be, grandpa." They both glanced towards the staircase, fear choked their warning cries.

THUMP

June sprung backwards at the sickening sound. Her heart leapt with it but didn't come back down, sticking in her larynx. Her chest rose and deflated rapidly, a whistling sound emanating from her lips as short breaths passed over them. Tires crunching snow outside came to a halt as it pulled in the driveway. Her mother stepped out of the driver's seat, while her father nearly toppled out of the passenger side, the unbuckled seat belt the only thing keeping him upright. June rushed to the door as her grandfather made his way towards the staircase. Conflicted with thoughts for the security of her parents and grandfather, she made a snap decision to reach out for her grandfather. With a handful of his sleeve, June spun her grandfather around, tears welling in her eyes. "Don't go up there," she pleaded.

Heavy stomps echoed overhead. The vibrations of the floorboards creaking against the weight frightened June. A car door slammed shut outside, followed by a low murmur. Her grandfather resisted her grasp, freeing his arm with a swift jerk. He swung once more to head towards the staircase and halted. A vulgar, dragging sound drifted down from upstairs. "She's dead," he uttered, confident of the statement.

"I know," June cried as they listened to the lifeless weight of her grandmother being dragged across the floor. "We need to get out of here now."

Harold took one last look towards the stairs and reluctantly agreed. He turned the doorknob, and a swift gust blew snow and cold air inside before being snapped shut. Startled, Harold struggled to open the door once more. The tendons in his neck stood out as he tried again with both hands. "What the hell?" Confused, a distraught expression drained the colour from his face.

A tapping on the glass caught June's attention. A grey pillowcase and black eye popped into view at the window, the mummer holding the door closed. "They're still here." A terrified groan escaped her throat.

Tap tap tap

The mummer was taping the glass window with an icicle. June darted to the window, flung open the drapes. Her mother was putting away her car keys as she strolled down the front walk. The giant mummer was supporting her father, helping him stumble his way towards the front door. June slammed her hand against the cold glass, catching her mother's attention. With an angry look on her face, her mother scolded her with her emerald green eyes. Her shiny red lips the same colour as the scarf hanging from the peg hook in the porch. *The same colour as blood.* The strawberry blonde hair sticking out from underneath her wool knit cap waved in the breeze around her face. June thumped the glass again and pointed at the door. A slight grin crossed her mother's face, holding back laughter, the terrified expression on her daughter's face not registering. A gust of wind spread a squall across the front yard.

When the wind slacked, the first thing June saw was a blur of yellow running across the lawn towards the walkway. An explosion of wintry air poured through the house as her grandfather ripped the door open. "Bethany!" He tried to warn her.

Realization finally came into view, turning on like a light switch. Beth looked at her father, too late to do anything, only enough time to say goodbye with her sorrowful eyes. The yellow blur collided full force into Beth's shoulder, sending her spiralling face first into the snow, a wisp of powder erupting from the impact.

"Fuck." Harold groaned as he lurched backwards, slamming the door closed in the same motion causing him to fall flat on his ass. He launched his feet into the door just in time to prevent it from swinging open. He held his hand over the shard of ice sticking out of his shoulder. "Close the deadbolt."

June wouldn't take her eyes off her mother. The mummer knelt on her chest, plunging the knife into her over and over again. A pool of blood spilled into the white snow, spreading into a large mess underneath her. In her last desperate attempt to shield herself, she held up her hands to block the murderous blows. The blade sliced through bones of her fingers with ease, severing the digits on her hand. Her mother never gave up, holding up her bloodied arm until the bitter end. The mummer slashed her neck wide open, and a spurt of arterial blood showered over his rain slicker. With one final blow, the handle of the knife was all that showed, the steel blade buried deep in her mother's heart. He peered up, the red sinister snarl taunting her.

"June!" her grandfather cried out over the scrapping of the door over the floor as he battled to keep it closed, the hinges moaning in protest.

With one last chance of hope, June looked at her father, and any chance of survival escaped her mind. She seemed to drift outside with them. Everything was so vivid. She heard her father's choked gasps. He was being held off the ground. The large mummer had him captured in a bear hug. Her father's eyes bulged out of their sockets, his face turning red and his lips purple as the pressure continued to intensify. He kicked his legs vainly against the meaty flesh of his attacker. Every visible vein on her father's exposed flesh stood out. They looked ready to rupture if you touched them. Spit and long ropes of saliva frothed from his mouth. His flailing limbs went limp, and his struggle was over without much of a challenge, tossed into the snow bank like a rag doll, left to lie under a blanket of snow.

"June!" Harold bellowed.

June snapped back into her body and looked over at the struggle taking place at the threshold to their home. One arm violated the entrance, the hand searching for something to grasp. Her primitive instincts guided her like a puppet to the assailant's arm. Her jaw sprung open and she bit down as hard as her jaw would allow. At first the filthy taste of unwashed fabric filled her mouth. Not to be deterred, she persisted. With a sickening movement, her teeth dug into his flesh, and the coppery bile of blood coated the inside of her mouth. The arm jerked back; the door crashed shut; and she closed the deadbolt. Her grandfather struggled to get to his feet. Sweat ran down his face from his hairline in rivers. His chest heaved up and down. He held out his hand for June to help him to his feet as a fist pounded against the front door.

"Any mummers lowed'in!"

BANG BANG BANG

"ANY MUMMERS 'LOWED'IN!"

THUMP THUMP THUMP THUMP

"ANY MUMMERS LOWED'IN!"

"Get the fuck out of here!" June screeched in defiance. The door rattled, the wooden frame splintering against the assault. Gusts of wind howled outside, drowning out the sounds of the other mummers as they crept along the edge of the house. A tap on the front window made June jump. She looked over as the vicious red smile pressed against the window, booming loudly as it struck the glass. Suddenly, it seemed that tapping sound, joining with disturbed laughter to form an awful symphony, was coming from all around the house.

"They are tormenting us," June cried. "They can break that glass and get in anytime they choose."

"I realize that," her grandfather agreed knowingly. "We only have one opportunity."

If June was able to snag her mother's purse and make a break for the car, maybe they could still get away. She looked at her grandfather's feeble legs and cane. *It would be easy for her to escape.* "No." She knew what he was going to do.

"It's the only way," he replied matter-of-factly. His old, tired eyes looked at her without another thought. Their paths now determined, he looked out the window and placed his hand on the doorknob. "On the count of three."

"One." A loud thunk rattled the upstairs floor.

"Two." Ice crunched underneath the rubber boots as the mummers circled the house.

"Thr…"

"Stop." June reached out and snatched another fistful of fabric.

"Damn it, June." Smacking her hand, his callused hands still had strength left in them "What is it?"

"We can try for the shotgun," she whispered, not taking

a chance on one of the mummers overhearing them. "Both of us."

"Don't be a foolish girl." He had already committed, ready to make the ultimate sacrifice so that his granddaughter could get away. "This is how it has to be. It's yer best chance."

"No." June spat out the defiant response through pursed lips. "Look." She pointed at the large mummer, lurking near her parents' Honda Accord. "He's waiting for us." Her voice was more calm. "That's what they are expecting." She was beginning to figure out the game. Even though she was an unwilling participant, there was no reason she couldn't win.

Harold furrowed his brow, still seeking to comprehend the new facts as they had been presented. He just shook his head, not in defiance or understanding, but because he didn't have any alternative way to communicate what to do. "We can't both die."

"I know." June tried to sound brave, her insides twisting into knots, her knees trembling. "Is there anything in the cellar?"

Taking a moment to remember, Harold's eye's lit up. "The garden tools are down there. A metal rake and spade."

"Good, you stay here. I'm going to run down to get them." June didn't wait for a reply.

She got to her feet and bolted for the cellar door. It opened to expose darkness. She held her hand out for the metal chain that dangled from the light leading down. Her fingers fumbled across it awkwardly then yanked it down, the pale yellow light casting shadows down the stairs. There were only six stairs, but they were steep, and the aged boards were coarse and full of splinters. June nearly toppled down the stairs as she flew down, a sliver of wood digging underneath the skin from the railing as she caught herself. At the bottom there was another switch. She flicked it on, expecting another mummer to be laying in wait for her. The cellar was a cluttered mess, but at least it was vacant.

Metal handles had been screwed into the wooden poles, and the gardening tools leaned against her grandfather's old workbench. She wasted little time rushing over. An old, rusted utility knife rested on the desk. She snatched that up and crammed it in her pocket before grasping the shovel and rake. She ran back up stairs, skipping two at a time.

Her grandfather was in the same place she left him, except now he was standing up, preparing himself for the battle to come. "Hand me the spade." He held out a jittery hand.

Tap tap tap tap tap tap tap tap

It started slow and soft then began to rise in a maddening crescendo. The mummers were tapping against the windows, each note louder and more threatening than the previous. Windows began to rattle in the frames. June spun around and saw a gloved hand balled into a fist, hammering at the glass relentlessly. Her grandfather reached out and grabbed her by the shoulders. "Pay no attention to that." He tried to shake her back to the task at hand. "We need ta'get upstairs right now."

June felt the weight of the rake. Unbalanced, the bulk of the tool laid in the metal rake at the bottom, each metal tip to be used as a deadly weapon.

Smash

The kitchen window shattered, fragments of glass sprinkled into the sink and across the floor.

Smash

A blast of frosty air tugged at June's hair as the living room window exploded.

Smash

Another window somewhere gave in to the relentless pounding, breaking inwards and creating a draft that slammed the cellar door shut with a loud bang. A vortex of snow blew into the house. Pictures blew off the wall, smashing into the ground. Christmas cards that had been taped to the wooden door frame of the kitchen flapped in the wind.

Smash

A hunk of ice collided with the TV, toppling it over, crashing into the floor.

"We can't wait for them to get us." Her grandfather ushered her towards the stairs, not waiting another second. Snowballs hurled against the house sent shudders through the pane glass windows before finally breaking, splintering into frigid pieces of deadly glass. Wind carried snow throughout the house from all angles, making it challenging to see. Windows upstairs could be heard breaking apart, adding to the pandemonium surrounding them.

Amidst the mists and fiercest frosts

Harold took the first step, the stairs groaning with old age underneath the strain. June followed him up the stairs. Both of them made no attempt to disguise their approach. Hopefully they would catch the upstairs assailant off guard. Creaks and groans accompanied the melody of high pitched, howling winds. It was deafening, piercing deep into her cerebellum, working hopelessly to warn her against the menace lurking upstairs. She let the head of the rake thump against the stair boards, the ominous sound meant to be a threat.

The top of the stairs opened into a long hallway that stretched the length of the house. A long blue carpet that stretched the entire length accented the pin-striped wallpaper. Old paintings placed on the walls years ago, outdated and in desperate need of cleaning, hung crooked, even after years of adjusting. Five doors lined the hallway, two each on the left and right and the bathroom door at the end of the corridor. All the doors had been closed. June imagined playing Russian roulette, visualizing the barrel of an old-fashioned revolver pressed against her temple. She was ready to pull the trigger.

Harold stomped down the hallway. June kept her hand on his shoulder so they wouldn't get too far apart. She could feel the cold air seeping out from beneath. He threw open the first door on the left. June's eyes grew wide at the gruesome sight. Acid rose in her throat, burning the whole way up, filling the back of her throat before she retched.

"Lord Jesus." A faint sob escaped Harold. To June, he sounded miles away. The reality of what they were dealing with was unfathomable.

Mabel lay on top of the covers, her white hair soiled by the blood, the whole left side of her skull caved in. Her left eye was popped out of the socket, dangling down by the optical nerve, resting in a thick, red mucus on her cheek. A coin was placed over her right eye, and a swatch of fabric was shoved into her mouth, contorting her lips into a hideous smirk. Underneath her, a puddle of blood soaked into the white linens extending to her knees. Laid to rest with her, they'd fastened the shotgun to her chest by crossed arms, her wrists bound by a braided twine. The moonlight gleamed softly in the dark against the grey gun metal, the barrel facing towards her feet.

"I'm going to make them pay for what they did to you," Harold promised his dead wife, placing his hand over hers. He laid the shovel down and gently removed the gun from her death grip. He cracked it open, the red facing of a shell seated in the chamber. He closed it with a loud clang.

A heavy thumping noise approached, the upstairs floor boards groaning loudly in protest. June turned just in time to see a man sporting a red pillowcase over his head barge into the room. Before she could make a move, he swung a baseball bat towards her. Reflexes took over. She raised the handle of the rake to defend herself at the same time as she took a step back. The bat knocked the rake out of her hand and sent her toppling over backwards into the dresser.

Harold raised the gun towards the man and screamed inaudibly. "You fucken bastard." He'd discovered his voice. "I will send ye straight back to hell." Harold pulled the trigger. A grimace passed over his face, drawing back his lips to reveal his yellow-stained teeth.

The mummer held out a piece of hardware and snickered. "You seem to be missing the firing pin." Each word was saturated with dread and venom. The mummer began walking towards Harold, chuckling loudly. His red pillow case accented by black eyes and a black, demonic grin. He was dressed in a black striped suit, a double-breasted jacket and a long red tie that hung around his neck like a noose. His pants were tucked into a pair of red rubber boots. Under normal circumstances this would have been comical, but June thought he looked like the devil.

With barest wrists, and stoutest boasts

Harold pulled the trigger repeatedly. A weak metal sound permeated the gaps in the delirious laughter. Each time he pulled the trigger it was like an exclamation mark to the deep chuckling. June scrambled to her feet and made a move for the gun. The mummer paid her no consideration. The bed stood in the middle of the room. June had found herself on the left side. Harold was on the right, and the mummer was now at the head of the bed. His deathly glare was fixed on her grandfather, bouncing the head of the bat off the floor as he cut across the foot of the bed and made his way to the right side. In an attempt to defend himself, Harold swung the butt of the shotgun wildly at the mummer. The hard wooden stock found its mark, and a sickening pop echoed noisily in the bedroom. The savage blow didn't even stagger the attacker; he stayed the course and wrapped his fingers around Harold's neck.

He thrusts his fists against the post

June gripped the handle of the rake tightly and lunged onto the bed, swinging the metal head down. Metal tips dug into the flesh of the mummer's shoulder, burying itself inches into the muscles, but he refused to let go. Blood began to seep out from beneath the mummer's bare fingers, his nails tearing through the skin and into Harold's throat. Harold spat crimson spit into the pillowcase, his eyes bulging out of the sockets, his cries gargled by the fluids choking his throat. June tried to pull the rake out to no avail. She needed leverage to dislodge it from the taller man's shoulder. The fingers around her grandfather's throat tightened, getting closer together with every passing second. The trickle of blood turned into a flow. A loud crunch as the fingers completely crushed Harold's throat made June scream with madness, the disgusting sound triggering a primal reaction.

"Fuck YOU!" June screeched, the last syllable drawn out and punctuated. She drove her foot into the mummer's manhood. There was no satisfying cry of agony, and she didn't get to see the grimace on his face, but he dropped to his knees. Now, with leverage, she hauled the handle of the rake, the metal teeth tearing through the flesh and sending a torrent of blood spilling onto the floor. She stretched her arms behind her head, building up enough momentum to kill the man with one deadly blow. In a wild arc, she drove the metal tips down into the top of his skull, the pillow case bunching up as the teeth of the rake lodged into his skull with tremendous force. His body twitched and gyrated for seconds, resisting the urge to collapse. He turned his head towards her and chuckled heartily in her face. Thrusting her foot in his chest, she yanked the rake back. "FUCK YOU!"

The red pillowcase turned a darker shade, the blood soaking through it. He slumped onto the floor, never once attempting to brace his fall, and a resounding clunk rattled the floorboards. Curiosity reared its head, compelling her to determine who was underneath that mask. On bended knee, she reached over and tugged at his shoulder, trying to roll the man over. The dead mummer was the same build as Jacob. It couldn't possibly be him though, *could it?*

And still insists he sees the Ghosts

"Who the fuck *are you*?" Bewildered, June was sick to her

stomach. She reached out for the crimson hood with a trembling hand, ready to yank it off, revealing the identity of the mummer.

She never heard the approaching footsteps.

Her only warning was the shadow cast over her. Before she reacted, a hand snatched a fistful of hair and began to drag her out of the bedroom. Her hands grasped the door frame, the resistance yanking out most of the hair from her head. Her assailant lost his grip on her. A low cry escaped her throat as she stumbled to her feet. As she tried to turn around a powerful blow over the head knocked her back down again. She collapsed at the feet of the mummer wearing black boots. "Get the fuck away from me," she cried then realized that this was the smaller mummer. Energized with hope, June rolled into the mummer and collided full force into the terrorizing figure. They both tumbled into a heap in the door frame. June had caught them off guard and landed on top. In full control, June began to smash her fists against the flesh underneath the pillow case, the blood staining through in random blotches.

June leapt to her feet. Fueled by a ray of hope, she stomped her foot down into the woman's stomach. A gush of air, escorted by ropes of blood, spilled from beneath the hood in long chords from the blow. A young girl lay dying between the threshold of the bedroom, her chest swelling and deflating in shallow breaths.

"Who are you?"

Lips moved underneath the stained hood but no words came out, just a choking, gargling wet grunt that caught in her dying throat.

June left her there to die slowly, walking out of the room and back into the hallway. June was resolved to finish this night now. "Where are you?" she taunted, her voice carrying loudly in the confined corridor. In her rage, she had left the rake behind, stomping down the stairs like something possessed, hunting for the others. "You can't hide from me." Snow had begun to cover the floor, leaving behind a trail of footsteps that led back to the kitchen. She followed them around the corner and was struck viciously in the face. Blood sprouted from her nose like a blossoming flower. Her feet skidded out from underneath her, slamming her head against the tiled kitchen floor. Stars danced in her vision. Once the stars cleared, the two remaining mummers towered over her. The giant mummer grabbed her by the leg and started to drag her out of the kitchen. Her fingernails dug into the hardwood floor, bending back painfully at the quick before tearing off.

A loud creak groaned from the hinges at the mummer opened the front door and dragged June outside. Trails of crimson flowed from her bloodied finger tips in the white snow, leaving a trail behind. Shock had seized jurisdiction over her body. She wasn't shivering against the cold anymore. The mummer wearing the yellow jacket followed closely behind, twirling a kitchen knife in his hand. June wasn't going to give up. She slammed her numb hands into the mummer's legs, and a painful shock wave rang forth from her forearms. The mummer continued to drag her with ease, her attempts against this behemoth failing to register. June screamed into the empty night, her voice carrying far in the cold air but falling silent before it reached help. Snow began to fill June's pants as the mummer dragged her into the deeper snow. June reached out, praying that her hands would come across a piece of ice, a stray rock, anything she could use to break free. Her fingers frantically searched despite the throbbing pain that had replaced the numbness. Every time she thought she found something, her fist would come up empty.

"Why are you doing this?" June didn't expect an answer, it was her curiosity forcing her to ask. "You can still let me go." Heavy breathing rushed her words. "I have no idea who you are." June's fingers stumbled across something hard. "I haven't even seen your face."

The mummer let go of her leg, towering over her like a statue. Snow swirled around him, each flake standing out against the pitch black winter's night. She heard the other mummer approaching, the crisp snow crunching underneath their rubber boots. Her fingers traced the solid mould. Her skin was too numb to understand what it had discovered, but she just recognized it was her last chance. It felt heavy as she picked it up, leaving her hand planted in the snow, a desperate attempt to camouflage her intentions. "If you will not let me go," June was trying to distract the large man, "reveal your identity to me. I want to learn who my killer is."

"Now, why would you want us to spoil our fun?" A thin voice crept up from behind, slightly high pitched. A low grumble acknowledged the statement with booming laughter. The mischievous smile hovered over her face, a flap of the loose pillow case dangled down towards June. She reached up, clutching her fist over the hideous smile, tugging at it. The fabric pulled tight against the outline of his face, and his long nose twisted sideways against the force. A tuft of blond hair rolled out, resting atop his shoulder. "Tsk tsk, little one." His hands batted her grip away with ease. She let her hands collapse beside her. Her frozen fingers clawed through the layers of snow, searching for a rock on the path buried beneath.

June's heart skipped a beat. A sense of trepidation and self-pity washed over her in waves, giving her the illusion she was suffocating in a foreign fluid. "Who are you guys?" she asked, trying to buy herself more time. Her fingers tracing the form of rock.

"Just a couple of hooligans out for a stroll," he spoke, his tone stern, yet tender. "We were out hiking the pathway and my friend saw you in the kitchen. Some would say it was love at first sight. He literally wanted to be the one to kill you." He snickered, kneeling down to her eye-level. Moonlight caught in the blade, giving it a celestial radiance.

She thrusts her fists against the posts

June swung her arm. The weight of the rock felt right. Her fist smashed into his temple at full force. He collapsed into the snow, a gush of blood spilling through his mask and into the white blanket of snow. That was the last time June ever got to see the night sky. A harsh growl behind her roared at the moon, before a thunderous blow to the back of her head caused the world to go black.

And still insists she sees the ghosts.

Her vision ebbed and flowed, her memory holding onto key moments, flashing vividly inside her head like a spark of lightening. The images and sensations erupting like a jolt of electricity bringing her back to life every couple of seconds. A hard thump as her head dragged over metal doorstep brought with it a thousand painful memories. She blacked out for a moment then felt carpet against her head. A pair of knitting needles sat on the floor next to her head. Thundering footsteps lumbered behind her. A wave of heat from the fireplace forced her to sleep.

Weightless, she rose from the carpet, a hot burning sensation scorching the back of her legs forcing her to wake. She opened her eyes. Her grandparent's living room spread out in front of her behind the mummers head. "Now little miss," the hideous smiling mummer spoke from beyond her line of sight, "this will only hurt for a minute."

Bang bang BANG

A sharp, throbbing pain erupted in her palm. She felt the mummer release his grip on her, but she didn't fall to the ground. Painfully, she tilted her head to the side and saw a trickle of blood falling from her hand, running down over the side of the fireplace. The back of her legs screamed at the heat, scalding her skin. "You got a little blood on your face." June mocked the mummer she had struck. Dried blood streaked the right side of his hood.

He ran his fingers on the dried blood. She must have been unconscious for some time now. "I'll be okay. It's you I'm worried about. Our friend here wants to decorate for Christmas."

"Is that so?" June answered bitterly.

"Yeah, he couldn't find no boughs of holly to deck the halls with." A sly fit of laughter erupted beneath the hood. "Sorry about this, I really am. Even I think this is taking it a bit far."

The other mummer ripped June's shirt open, tearing the fabric with ease, exposing her stomach. Jagged nails tore into the soft flesh, and she felt a warm trickle spill over her lower abdomen. A sickening tearing sound erupted as he ripped open her stomach, followed quickly by a loud splatter at her feet. She watched as a pair of hands pulled her intestines out. Her vision faded into blackness. Wet, slimy squishing noises were the last thing June remembered as the mummers spread her insides over the fireplace mantle.

BEFORE I FORGET

A tender song, as pleasant as an angel's kiss, carried on the sea breeze, speaking through the blowing grass. The balmy air was laden with the fragrance of the deep ocean, crisp and clean with just an exquisite hint of brine. Golden hues accented the primrose sand, sweeping out to embrace the undulating tide. Gentle rolling waves washed over the shore, the ebb and flow adding a delightful harmony to the notes of nature all around. Overhead, the whine of gulls blended into the low rumble of the crashing waves, creating a relaxing symphony. Without a cloud in the sky, the luminous canvas of blue rose from the vivid green ocean waters. The sunlight was mirrored in the tips of the waves, spawning thousands of brilliant sparkles across the surface.

Ryan lounged in his stained red oak Adirondack chair, his shirt flayed open and flapping in the breeze. His bronzed skin glistened with perspiration against the strong sunrays. Chilled beads of condensation ran down the neck of the transparent beer bottle, rolling over his calloused hand. With his feet buried in the soft, golden sand, his widening grin built towards a broad smile. He took a deep swig of his beer; the lemon wedged in the bottle's neck added a welcome Mexican-style flavour. All of his friends warned him to add the lemon to protect against the contaminated waters. But truthfully, he enjoyed the sour flavour. He scratched his five o'clock shadow; the fresh growth was itchy. His fingers ran along an old scar that stretched from his left ear to his chin. Unable to remember how he got it, he traced it back and forth, enjoying the rugged edges beneath the stubble.

His new bride strolled along the lacy waves. Foam crashed over her sandals before the withdrawing tide washed them clean. Her white shawl hugged her shoulder and danced gracefully around her. The hem of her satin green dress hugged her curves while displaying ample tanned thighs. She grasped a glass of red wine elegantly in her hand, the vibrant maroon liquid a sharp contrast to the crystal clear waters. She spun towards him, her pink lips stained crimson by her drink and her beautiful sapphire green eyes aglow in the daylight. The wind whipped her hair over her face in a veil. Tangled locks of intense red hair glowed as golden rays shined through. Their eyes met and her cheeks blushed. She winked at him with a come-hither look, raising her hand and gesturing for Ryan to accompany her. Without waiting, she turned and started wading into the swelling tide. She gave him one last glance over her shoulder before spinning to face the horizon.

Caroline sang out for Ryan to follow. The temperate breeze lifted her charming voice. Her tone was a soothing octave, sweet and elegant. The words she sang blended together, forming a harmonic symphony that rivalled birds chirping after a summer's rainfall. Her seductive words filled Ryan's heart with lust, driving him mad. Unable to control himself, he planted his feet, pushed himself up from his chair, and sprinted towards Caroline, the beach shifting beneath his bare feet. Before he reached the tide line, the water was over Caroline's hip. Her white shawl trailed behind her like a train. There was a slight chill to the water, but nothing that would stop him from going in after his wife on their honeymoon. Silt and sand rushed over his feet as the surging tide crashed over the beach, breaking against the shore in a deafening roar. Ryan raced into the flooding waters, losing his balance and staggering sideways as the current opposed him.

After regaining his balance, it took him a moment to find Caroline; she was much further out than he expected. The water level rose over her shoulders. All that remained was her long, flowing hair drifting behind her in a coral fan.

"Wait up!" Ryan yelled.

A surging wave crashed over Caroline, vanquishing her from view. His only thought was that she had stepped into a riptide, and the powerful current was dragging her out to sea. A shrill shriek pierced Ryan's head. His skull throbbed as the racket tore through his cranium. He could still hear her voice, faint and withering away.

"Caroline!" he howled, panic riddling his voice. He plunged into the ocean, struggling against the current as he swam towards her. As he kicked his legs and thrashed his arms, his heart froze in his chest, depriving him of the drive he needed to defy the current. The saltwater stung his eyes, but he forced himself to keep them open. He remained below the surface until his lungs ached, detecting no trace of her.

When he broke the surface, the sun was bleeding into the horizon, casting a crimson glare over the rolling waves. The sky was on fire; ash drifted lazily across the horizon. Floating along the surface was Caroline's shawl, turned scarlet red by the dying sunlight. It took him an eternity to reach it. Twilight filled the sky. Behind him, the shade tinted the beach sepia. The golden sands turned to rustic orange by the fading light. Everything disappeared from the beach, his chair nowhere to be found. The world was turning to hell around him.

Gales swept the sweet sound of Caroline's voice away. A scream drowned out all other sounds. The hideous noise pierced his eardrums; his head was ready to burst as the sound filled his skull. He focused on Caroline's shawl, pushing through the intense agony. Determined not to give up, he swam until his shoulders ached and his legs felt like dead weight, threatening to pull him down.

He held Caroline's shawl in his hands, inhaling her perfume deeply, the pleasant scent sullied by the putrid tinge of deep saltwater brine. Tears tracked down his cheek. The bitter taste of salt blended with the brine. Dread crashed over him like the relentless pounding of the waves. Then something tugged at his leg. The water was too dark to see much of anything beneath his waist. But a faint tinge of red compelled him to dive below the surface. Entombed by darkness, he found himself disoriented. Out of the blackness, a hideous snarl, rimmed by jagged teeth, opened up to swallow him whole. He opened his mouth to scream, and the coldness consumed him.

"For Christ's sake, Ryan," a gravelly voice snapped.

With his heart still fluttering in his chest, Ryan bolted upright. Sweat-soaked sheets clung to his flesh. He awakened in a groggy haze, confused and not recognizing where he was. Still trapped in his hellish nightmare, his pulse raced. He rubbed his eyes with the back of his hand, squinting to see through the sleep caked in his eyes. "What's happening?" he grumbled.

"You're having another night terror," John answered. His hand rested on Ryan's shoulder, still shaking him. "If you don't get it under control, none of us are going to get any damn sleep." He closed Ryan's curtain, then sauntered away, his footfalls heavy on the wooden decking.

Ryan's courtesy curtain hung from the hooks. It had broken free from the last three rungs, allowing the soiled grey sheet to collapse over itself at the corner. His bedsheets were balled up in a heap at his feet. Slowed by the cold settled into his joints, he pulled on his socks. Still damp from the day before, he checked the duffle bag at the foot of his bed for a dry pair. The bag reeked of filthy underwear awaiting a wash that was too far away.

"It was about Caroline again," Ryan replied. It was invariably the same nightmare. His own personal living hell to experience every night. There were always slight alterations to his vivid visions but repeatedly the same result. He couldn't remember the last time he didn't have a night terror. Heavy black bags formed under his eyes, sculpturing his eye sockets into dark shadows. The crew avoided eye contact with him. He understood the murmurs as they ate their meals. Always the outcast, he sat alone, John his sole surviving friend aboard.

"Now, son," John stood in the door frame, "you've never been married nor met this Caroline. Maybe you should just do us all a favour and get over her. Whatever got you so worked up, it's all in your imagination."

Steam rose from a mug clasped in John's hands. A strong, fragrant bouquet of spice tickled Ryan's nostrils. John placed it in an alcove in the bulkhead fashioned into shelves by the carpenter along their bunks for extra storage.

"But I can still hear her voice plain as day, as pleasant as strawberry wine." The memory of the blood-curdling shriek rested heavily on his mind. "She sings to me sometimes, calling me to her. I've met her, she's not made up.

And every time I think I've left moved on, she haunts my dreams before I forget."

"In another lifetime, perhaps," John mumbled, not sounding convinced. "But you're too young to know a woman's touch. I don't understand how you've gotten so much experience sailing. That's a bigger mystery to me than this Caroline." John vanished from view, fumbling through the dishes in the galley just out of sight.

Ryan sat on the edge of the bed and stretched his hands over his head, shaking off the cramps set in by the cold. It didn't take him long to recognize something else was wrong. Others were already up; half of the bunks were empty, and the coat rack was all but bare.

"The ship's hardly moving," he said. "We're stuck in the ice again," he added, knowing it was a fact. John nodded his head in agreement as he went about his business of making his bunk.

After sailing on many ships over the years, spending his entire life at sea, Ryan had grown accustomed to the routine sounds a ship made. He could tell the sea's state by the sounds the ship made, never having to leave below deck to confirm. Now, he observed the buildup of ice around the hull, applying pressure, testing the integrity of the ship. The hull groaned in protest, the keel twisting and yielding to the force generated by the slabs of arctic ice pressing in on both sides.

Despite being just above the coal furnace, he never warmed. Everything outside the furnace room held a perpetual chill, and Ryan couldn't wait until they found their way out of this frigid hell. This was his third time through the Northwest Passage. He was accustomed to the chill that settled into his bones and refused to leave for weeks after he left the Arctic Circle. But it never got easier.

"I made you tea," John said, holding out a mug, the

steam still billowing from it.

"No thanks," Ryan said, brandishing his hand dismissively.

"You're going to want it," John insisted, pushing the mug into Ryan's face, the white vapours dampening his coarse beard.

Ryan sighed, accepting the tea. "I don't want to go into the suit. It's not my turn," he complained, knowing it was a fruitless endeavour from John's stone-cold eyes.

"Captain Welsh said it has to be you," John explained. "You have the most diving experience of anyone aboard."

"Except you," Ryan interrupted.

John passed his fingers through his wispy, white hair. His weathered skin was scarred from a lifetime at sea. Brown blotches peppered his complexion. The flickering lamp cast deep shadows over his face, sinking his tired eyes further into his skull. "I'm too old to be going down into the frigid drink."

Before John turned to leave, Ryan got out of his bunk, the boards ice cold against his bare skin. "Are they going to heat the suit this time?" he asked.

"I'll get the boys working on heating the joints," John answered.

Ryan took a sip of tea, the spicy chai creating a warmth beyond just temperature. Bitter, the black tea ate away at his stomach lining and the hot water burned his lips. Not realizing how much his body craved the warmth, he downed the rest of the tea in three big gulps.

The ladder creaked as John walked above deck. When he opened the hatch, the wind howled, seeking to force its way inside the ship. It slammed closed with a sharp bang that made Ryan jump. Angry, he cursed out loud, attributing his agitated state to his nightmare. Not wasting any more time, he pulled on his dry suit, preparing himself to climb into the atmospheric diving suit. Above, he heard them dragging the suit across the deck. The iron suit was arduous to maneuver out of the water, and still a challenge once submerged. He pulled his hood on, zipped his suit up, and pulled his winter slops and boots over to stay warm until he clambered into the ADS.

It didn't take him long to climb the stairs. The dry suit was better suited for movement than his normal winter gear but provided scarce protection against the frigid temperatures. And once he got outside, the Arctic winds cut right through him, chilling him to the bone. His breath hung in front of his face in plumes of mist that turned to ice in mid-air. As the cold settled into his bones, he began shivering. He made his way towards the gathering crowd.

Everyone looked the same dressed in their outdoor gear, bundled up, covering all exposed skin to ward off frostbite. They were all gathered around the suit like an entourage waiting for him to strut on stage. The rigid brass joints kept the form of the suit as if there was already somebody inside. Beside the ADS, the helmet was a bulbous monstrosity ripped out of a science fiction comic; a rusty golden shine rimmed four glass viewing windows. Connected to the backside of the helmet, they coiled the length of the air hose into a chaotic, rigid heap.

Covered in ice, his boots fought for grip as he navigated along the treacherous decking, his hand slipping on the railings. His body wanted him to move fast, but he forced himself to move cautiously. Every movement was deliberate.

"Mister Salvani," the captain called out, his jovial voice laden with false enthusiasm despite the horrid predicament his ship was in. "Right this way, sailor," he motioned for Ryan to hurry, "time is of the essence, young man." Bundled in his winter slops, the captain still stood out amongst his crew, his mustache twirled into two thin twists.

Ryan rushed forward, his rubber boots scraping across the frozen boards. The air hurt to breathe. Three men waited to help him into the ADS, all of them glad they weren't going overboard; Ryan saw the relief in their eyes. They already had the zipper down, and Ryan climbed in as fast as he could. The heated brass joints provided warmth in the suit. It was soothing, even though he realized it wouldn't last.

"Edwards," the captain called out to the engineer, "come over and explain what needs to be done."

"Sir," Edwards chirped, clicking his heels together.

"No offence, sir," Ryan injected, "but I think I know what needs to be done." He waved his hand towards a break in the ice. "The screw is stuck. Am I correct, Edwards?"

Edwards bowed his head in agreement.

"Because if it wasn't, we'd be sailing towards the open water. Not waiting to be trapped and crushed in the winter ice," Ryan spoke, a knowing harshness tainting every syllable. "Let's just get this over with."

The captain glared at him, the venom in his blood contorting his pleasant expression into a snarl. Ryan bit his tongue, holding back some choice words. They raised the helmet over him and lowered it down over his head. He squinted through the smudged, scratched glass. Not enough to obscure his vision but just enough to make him work harder to see things. As they sealed the helmet, the air from the hose filtered inside; the stagnant air caused him to gag.

Muffled by the helmet, the captain barked an order.

Ryan felt the tension build on the ADS as the men struggled to hoist him over the railing. The line holding him pulled taut as he lifted into the air. He thumped the back of his foot off the frozen railing before descending towards the water. Slabs of cut ice piled up away from the hull of the ship. Members of the ship's crew waited alongside. They built a fire to warm themselves while they waited near the hole. Inky black water awaited him below. Jagged shards of ice resembling teeth lined the hole, bringing back a flash of his nightmare.

He peered into the blackness, his heart beating erratically as he waited for some hideous sea monster to show itself. Above, darkened, heavy clouds blanketed the sky, casting a gloomy shadow over the day. There wasn't enough light to cut through the blackness beneath.

The linesman knocked on his helmet; the heavy thudding caused Ryan's heart to leap into his throat. "Give two sharp tugs if there is a problem," the linesman said, holding up his fingers for emphasis. "Three if the jobs are done. Nod your head if you understand."

Ryan nodded his head. The linesman gave a quick tug on the safety line, ensuring it rattled his belt. Somebody thrust a picaroon into his hand and closed his fist over it. It was the best tool for removing ice from the screw. He felt more confident with the tool in his hand; the sharp pick would be a weapon if his nightmare came true. The brass frame of the ADS sizzled as it dipped into the frigid Arctic. Inside the suit, the temperature plummeted, sapping the heat from his body. Through the viewing glass, the sliver of daylight vanished as he plunged beneath the surface. He gripped the picaroon as tight as he could manage through the suit's bulky gloved fingers.

It took a moment for his eyes to adjust. His pupils dilated until his eyes were two large drops of tar, giving him a monstrous appearance. With his eyes focused, details filtered into view, appearing like a mirage in the desert. Shards of ice, suspended in the frigid waters, reminded Ryan of the ash falling from the sky in his dream. It was like he was drifting through space, blackness engulfing everything around him. An eerie silence washed over him. He should have heard the groaning of the ship, but instead the silence somehow drowned out all other sounds.

He twisted around, trying to push the remnants of his dream out of his thoughts and focused on his task. The sooner he finished the job, the better. Ryan drifted forward, the hull of the ship emerging like a ghost ship out of the darkness. He made his way aft of the ship, pushing aside loose floating chunks of ice along the way. When he reached the screw, he found ice lodged between the ship and the keel. He continued to work, chipping away at the ice with the picaroon. Each strike boomed like thunder, amplified by the heavy silence sitting on him.

All the heat left his body and his limbs seized up. Numb fingers made the work harder. His teeth chattered, and he drew in a sharp breath, trying to focus on getting the job done. Every strike with the picaroon sent a shock wave of pain running up his forearm. He concentrated on the task at hand, pushing building frustration aside.

Memories of Caroline's soft voice filled his ears. Whispers from his dreams invoked a sense of serenity. Her song filled his head with images of their lovemaking, taking him away from the discomfort of his current surroundings. They made love on the beach, rolling around in the sand as the sun beat down on them. His consciousness drifted away, lured to some foreign shore by her call.

Distracted by his work and the soothing sound of Caroline's singing, he never noticed the flash of light beneath him, like a brilliant star, growing in intensity until it was impossible to ignore, erupted. Ryan stared down at his feet as the light faded, a rush of bubbles racing towards him. Fear gripped his heart, squeezing it tight, his chest filled with pain and his limbs with lead. After a moment of hopelessness, he yanked on his air hose three times, waited a moment, then repeated. The line moved tight for a moment, and he felt himself being dragged along the keel. Bubbles swirled around his helmet, popping as they struck the glass, leaving behind a greasy smear of black- ened blood on his viewing glass. He screamed, hoping his terrified voice would carry to the sailors above, urging them to action.

No matter how hard he kicked his legs, he didn't seem to move any faster. Panic tightened his muscles, and he put all of his effort into tugging on the line, trying to pull himself towards the surface. Suddenly, the line slackened; he could see it drifting into the abyss. He cursed, his heart fluttering in his chest, as an avalanche of bubbles burst around him in a furious rage. A putrid stench flooded his helmet through the airline, gagging him.

Something tugged on the safety line, jerking him downwards into the abyss. He was being reeled in like a fish, dragged deeper into the dark chasm. Unable to turn over, he was forced to watch the dim light get snuffed out, the sheet of ice growing over the hole.

A shrill scream filled his eardrums, piercing them like daggers. The safety line went slack once more, and he found himself suspended in space. Out of the corner of his eye, he could see movement, the inky water swirling around the fluid movements inching towards him.

"Ryan," a familiar voice called out, distant and weak, "why didn't you help me?"

"Caroline?" Ryan cried. "Where are you?"

"Why did you leave me?"

"You're not real!" Ryan yelled.

A dreadful cackle rose around him, encompassing him. Something played with his boots, slapping at the heels. Ryan craned his neck down, trying to glimpse his tormentor. All he could see were wisps of red hair dancing around his boots.

"Caroline, please," Ryan begged, "leave me alone."

her sweet voice whispered in his ear. "I thought you loved me." He could sense her warm breath on his neck, soothing him, lulling him to sleep. "Kiss me."

Caroline's face appeared out of thin air, her sapphire eyes burned, two green flames emitting soft light in the darkness. Delicate fingers caressed Ryan's cheek, her scarlet red lipstick a sharp contrast to her pale complexion. Her face shifted through the glass viewing port. Her breath was warm on his face; the sweet aroma of wine wafted from her lips. He closed his eyes and enjoyed the tenderness of her lips on his own, tasting hints of strawberries and cherries. Her tongue explored his mouth, entwining with his own. His hand reached out, falling upon the smooth contour of her backside.

Her jaw clamped shut. Jagged teeth sliced through his tongue. Blood spurted from the severed flesh; a putrid taste filled his mouth, and bile rose from his stomach, spitting out between sealed lips. A scraping noise thundered inside his helmet. When he opened his eyes, Caroline vanished, replaced by a hideous sea witch. Long, jagged nails clawed into the glass. The grotesque serpent's eye glowed a piercing, sinister red, its green scales riddled with barnacles and gore. Its jaws opened wide, blackened gums lined with razor-sharp teeth lined the expanding black chasm. The creature's jaw unhinged, and its reptilian tongue explored the glass before it took an unfathomable bite.

Ryan opened his mouth to scream.

Ryan lunged from his Adirondack chair, his fingers sinking into the warm, golden sands. A tranquil sea breeze tousled his frail brown hair, filling his nostrils with a refreshing, albeit bitter, scent of deep ocean. Gentle waves rolled over the golden sand, a head of white foam riding the tide before receding with the retreating flood of water. Overhead, the blazing sun burned like a flanker against the blueish-white sky.

"Must have been a bad dream," he mumbled, picking himself up. He brushed off his khaki shorts. The individual specks of sand were a pristine white and fell like snow onto the beach. He eased himself back into his chair, leaning at an extreme angle that contorted his spine but was nonetheless comfortable. His tongue explored the cracked dry skin on his lips. Without having to look, he reached over and grabbed the waiting beer. It was ice cold. He held it in front of his face. Despite the blistering heat, the liquid inside was solid ice.

Puffy clouds hung around the mountain, their bellies caught against the craggy background, ripping open. Ash fell from the sky, blocking out the sun's rays and casting a dismal shadow over the beach. The wind strengthened, hissing through the high grass behind him. Threatening voices ascended from the field. Shadowed forms lurked in the tall grass behind him, slithering towards the edge of the shore. The stalks of grass broke with a sharp snap as the unknown monsters loomed near, closing in on him.

A crashing wave caught Ryan's attention, the rising tide sweeping over the golden sand towards him. Stained by blood, the sea foam oozed towards him. As the wave withdrew, it left a greasy smear of gore along the beach, rolling back towards the ocean.

Strolling along the beach in her satin green dress, Caroline sang a soothing, familiar song. The breeze tugged at the locks of her hair, tossing it across her face in a vale as she approached. Even through the thick locks of flaming hair, he could see her scarlet smile and the intensity of her sapphire eyes. An awkward stagger replaced her usual grace, her left foot dragging through the sand. Her skin was water-logged and full of blackened blemishes.

"Are you alright, Caroline?" Ryan asked, getting up from his chair.

Her head jerked towards the sound of his voice, her lips parting into a demonic smile. She changed direction, heading straight towards him now. No longer singing, her haggard breath rasped, choking on seawater. Her hand raised to brush her hair away from her face. Yellow-stained nails that had grown much too long tangled in the red locks, pulling clumps of hair out. A sinister cackle escaped her throat through a clenched jaw and spurts of saltwater burst past her lips.

"What are you?" Ryan screamed. Fear gripped him, pinning him in place. His knees came unhinged, and he tumbled back into his chair.

Before Ryan could get back to his feet, the sea creature pounced on him, digging its nails into his chest. He bit back a cry of pain, tears pooling in the corner of his eyes. "Get away from me." He stared into the familiar eyes.

This wasn't his Caroline. The sea witch hiding behind Caroline's sapphire eyes belched. "Didn't I tell you I'd never let you go?" the siren hissed.

"I never loved you," Ryan whispered. His voice trembling. "I've always loved Caroline." He found his voice again upon her name.

"Then why do you always come when I call?" the scorned siren cackled.

THE DEVIL IN I

The engine growls, emitting a low rumble I can feel through the cold metal against my thighs. With my arms pinned against my breasts, I lean into my restraints, rattling the chain links off the bare floor. The straps pull the straight jacket into a tight embrace. A trickle of drool runs down my chin, no doubt a side effect of the tranquillizers. I'm helpless to wipe it away. It pools into a wet puddle between my neck and the collar of my vest. From the front of the cab, I listen to the windshield wipers racing across the window, the motor groaning to keep up with the torrential downpour.

Every turn causes the chains to yank tight, tugging me in every direction. Defenceless in this straight jacket, I'm at the mercy of the reckless driver's will. Up front, they're listening to the radio. The smell of coffee wafts back to me, making my nostrils flare and my stomach growl. I haven't had a decent meal in days. After days of eating prison food, I have a wicked case of heartburn. And prison coffee has the consistency of sludge, with the bitter aftertaste of diesel fuel.

An impenetrable fog has settled over the city of St. John's. Another frigid November night when the weather is threatening to turn nasty. For the last twenty minutes, the police wagon wound its course through downtown St. John's. The vehicle shudders as the tires sink into potholes filled with rainwater, spraying slush over the pavement in giant waves. Outside, the wind wails, buckling the aluminum panels of the wagon in and out. It's as if the vehicle is a living creature, the iron bars resembling the monster's ribcage. Red taillights flood the back of the wagon, casting everything in a malevolent shadow. Gleams of silver light catch on the cold, hard steel.

My brain is groggy from all the prescriptions they force-feed me. My vision blurred, as are my memories of Lucas Green. And I have a splitting headache that won't go away. I've been in and out of consciousness over the last few days as I adjust to the medication. Oblivion is my only reprieve from the painful torment. Haunted by disturbing visions of that harrowing night, I've suffered through restless nights ever since that tragic turn of events. The only thing that stops the aching in my head is to push my fingers into my eyes. Stars dance in my vision. The pain floods my eyes but relieves the tension built up inside my head.

It started out as a fun date; it was our third. Lucas was handsome. Spiked, dirty blonde hair, chiselled jawline, piercing blue eyes. And most importantly, that body. Infatuated, it was no wonder things progressed between us so instantly. Then things escalated, spiralling out of control as I observed from outside my body. Helpless to prevent the actions I allowed to set in motion, Deborah appeared. Before I could react, Deborah regained control, filled with rage, taking things too far.

I'm remorseful even though I'm innocent of the crime that landed me in Her Majesty's Penitentiary. And he deserved almost every dreadful thing that happened to him. I can live with everything she did that night, except for his death. Somehow, my twin sister gets away with everything. No matter who I tell, no one believes Deborah killed Lucas. When they found me, his blood was all over me. But it was Deborah, I swear.

"No means no, right, Samantha?" Deborah asks, her tone a harsh rasp. Since we were children, it was like she could read my mind.

Filled with rage and jealousy, I refuse to make eye contact with those reptilian green eyes. "You could confess," I hiss, speaking to her shadow.

"Why?" she snaps back. "It would only complicate things if I did. And you need to stop feeling bad about it. He didn't show any remorse for what he did to you."

"Just a misunderstanding," I lie. "Really," I add.

"You're pathetic and weak," Deborah groans.

"I don't need you messing up my life," I spit back. "You spoil everything. Take things way too far. Every time."

"You need me."

"Not as much as you need me," I counter, sick of her attitude. "You'd only be a shadow without me. Without me, you'd be nobody."

"Without me, you'd be just like our mother," Deborah snarls. "Knocked up and left alone to go mad. Now shut your fucking mouth."

"Don't hate me because Mom never loved you," I spit out the words as if they were venom in my mouth. "You always reminded her of Dad," I continue.

"You and mom, two peas in a fucking pod," Deborah snorts. "Golden hair, rosy cheeks, and intense blue eyes. Like a princess from a fairy tale. And look at you now. You're like a skeleton with skin stretched over it. I guess Rapunzel isn't so beautiful without her beauty rest after all."

"Go to hell, Deb," I snap. I can't help but notice how her darkened features complement her creamy complexion and exotic emerald eyes. No one would ever guess we were twins. Especially not now.

"Later," Deborah says, her tone resolute. Without another word, I hear her stand up.

Squealing brakes compound my headache as the paddy wagon lurches to a halt. Hinges groan as the orderlies toss open their doors.

"I'll see you soon, little sister," Deborah whispers in my ear, her breath warm on my collar. Her hideous laughter fades away. I can hear her climb over the console and plunk down in the passenger seat.

Heavy footfalls approach the double-wide door, gravel crunching beneath their work boots. Each step splashes through the accumulating water. When they open the door, a blast of wintry wind assaults me, peppering me with droplets of icy raindrops with pellets of hail mixed in. Driven by the gusts of wind, the ice shards tear and rip at my skin. Forced to squint, the wagon dips as the orderlies climb up into the back. The springs of the ambulance groan in protest.

"It's time to go, Miss Beaton," a deep voice announces, void of emotion. "Don't give me any trouble. It's been a long night and I don't have any patience left." He thumps the nightstick dangling from his belt, strumming his knuckles off the vicious weapon.

I say nothing as they go about their business. With practiced ease, they unlock my chains in fluid progression. The orderly drapes a second jacket over my wrists, covering up my handcuffed wrists, a modest token of humanity I'm not accustomed to. They lead me outside, my feet dragging behind me. Wind-blown sheets of rain sweep over the asphalt, the gales driving the rainfall across the parking lot, forming ripples in the puddles.

Harsh fall winds propel the rain against the orangish-brown bricks of the Waterford Hospital, pattering against the barred windows with a relentless, methodical rhythm. The grumble of an approaching engine roars, rising above the storm's raucous clamour. Beside me, the orderlies grunt and groan, complaining about their responsibilities. It makes me sick to my stomach to hear them. At least they aren't being accused of a murder they didn't commit.

Standing in front of his squad car, Detective O'Reilly watches me from beneath the brim of his tilted fedora. To protect himself from the seething storm, he holds it against his forehead, pressed between his thumb and forefinger. Tucked between his armpit, a manilla fold stands out in stark contrast to his black rain slicker. With the rain lashing at my back, and the wind whipping the jacket from my hands, I'm exposed. I watch the detective pat his pocket, slide his hand inside, and produce a pack of cigarettes. He cups his hand over the coffin nail and flicks his lighter, igniting a brilliant red spark. I meet his glare with an idle stare. The orderlies drag me towards the stone steps leading to the front door.

A flash of lightning illuminates the sky coupled with resounding thunder. In that instance, with the orderlies distracted by the luminous glow, I twist my head towards O'Reilly. The blustering wind sweeps my golden hair to the side, and I flash a thin white line of teeth behind an ominous snarl. Behind the detective, highlighted by the incandescent light, a pair of green eyes glare at him from the bushes. Those horrible reptilian eyes go unnoticed by everyone except me. Whether it's a hallucination or a deception of the storm, Deborah transforms into a sinister aberration. Her ebony hair stands out as a stark juxtaposition to her pale complexion.

I can see her snickering as she haunts the detective from the shadows.

Buried in the back of the Waterford, they keep the overflow section out of sight from the public eye. Desperately in need of modernization, these corridors echo past inhumanity. Weathered, red-bricked walls border the cells, only broken by the rows of black iron bars. The slippers they gave me are worthless, sapping heat from my body. The floor is damp with condensation from the water trickling down the walls as the rain hammers the bricks outside. All along the seams and cracks, black mould ravages this ancient section of the institution. More insane asylum than medical facility, the Waterford is a depressing reflection of the Newfoundland government's views on mental health.

"This is abominable," Deborah says, shattering the silence. She's just outside my cell, resting her forearms on the wrought iron bars. "I wouldn't let my dog stay in there. This place needs to be condemned."

Water drips excessively from the leaky window, falling to the cement below. A tributary forms, following a worn path towards the center of my cell and into a metal culvert. An appalling, rancid stench of raw sewage rises from the pipe. Thick strands of matted hair, covered in a mouldy residue, have built up in the drainage, leading down into an abyss. Water bubbles up from the pipe as the flood waters gush into the sewers. I can't stand the smell. My stomach twists, knotting itself, as my abdominal muscles clench, forcing bile into the back of my throat.

A weighty silence remains between us. I refuse to acknowledge her. Every time I look at her at her, I want to scream. But I'm too fatigued from the pills the nurse gave me. My sister told me I could trust her, so I let her give me the shot without putting up a fuss. I don't expect to get any sleep until this was all over. That's our plan, anyway.

Deborah breaks the silence. "You know the detective is in Doctor Yarn's office now. I just wanted to let you know he'll be coming to speak with you soon." Not waiting for me to respond, she continues. "They're scouring our records, drudging up the past. They won't believe your story; the records are wrong. Just stick with my plan, and you'll be free."

I perk my head up. Strands of blonde hair tumble over my face, creating a shroud. Deborah leans into the cell, her jet-black hair blending into the iron bars. Long shadows cast her into darkness, splitting her into two separate halves. I can see tears welling in the corner of her emerald eyes. A single tear tracks over her prominent cheekbone. Her delicate features obscure the suffering within.

I sigh. "What do you need me to do?"

"Stay in this cell tonight," Deborah answers, her tone demanding. "And you need to get another shot, just like we talked about."

"How do I do that?"

Deborah cackles. "Convince them you're crazy. Shouldn't be too hard."

I hesitate. "But I'm not crazy. You're real. They think I killed Lucas. I watched you do it. His blood is on your hands. This is your fault."

"But can you prove it?"

"Why are you being such a bitch?" I cry, another side effect of my new prescriptions.

"Haven't I always kept you safe?" Deborah snaps. "Don't you trust me?"

I chortle. "You didn't need to keep me safe. If it wasn't for you, things wouldn't have gotten out of control."

"He was out of control," she spits, her voice a harsh

croak. "I did what I had to do to keep you safe. Don't forget that, ever."

"How can I forget what you did?" I murmur. My eyes burn and tears track down my cheek. I bury my face into my hands, working my fingers through my matted hair, wondering when the next time I'd get a shower. Deep, hitching sobs catch in my chest as I continue. "What you always do."

"Quit your bellyaching. It makes me sick to my stomach hearing you cry like a baby. Listen, the doctor will be here soon. Despite his flaws, he means well. And Nurse Sally will keep you safe. You can trust her with your life. I'm going to go find out what the detective has in store for us." Deborah pauses. "That son of a bitch is up to something. Once you get your shot, you'll sleep. Everything is going to be okay."

When I glance up, Deborah's gone. I lay down on the cold, hard bench and continue to sob. With my back rounded to the iron bars, I tuck my knees into my chest and hug them close. Footsteps echo down the empty hallway. A man and woman are chatting, their words muffled by the storm. I can hear the rats scurrying through the walls. The grind of their claws over the cement is nauseating. Their squeaks and cries are worse. Dampness creeps into my bones, seeping in through the window. I get up and move into the corner of the cell. With my back pressed against the wall, I slide down onto my ass and tuck my knees into my chest. The floor saps the warmth from my body.

A clap of thunder rumbles overhead, sending tremors through the earth, rattling the Waterford's foundation. Three seconds later I see a spark of white light catch in the cold black iron. The storm is alarmingly close now. I can feel the static electricity in the air; the hairs on my arm stand on edge. Deprived of sleep and food, and groggy from the drug cocktail, I fight off exhaustion. Another clap of thunder explodes like artillery fire, followed by a flash of lightning. Scared, I draw in quick breaths. I'm on the verge of hyperventilating. Each breath I take is a gargled hiss, the drugs numbing my tongue, unable to stop the saliva pouring down my throat.

"No, I'll be making my own observations, Sally." Doctor Yarn says. "What I'd like for you to do is send an orderly in with a pitcher of water and some extra blankets."

I size him up through the veil of my hair that has fallen over my face. Yarn still hasn't acknowledged that he's balding, combing his frail white hair over his pate. Glimmers of light reflect on his scalp and off the black rims of his glasses perched at the tip of his too-big nose. His lips are thin, pressed into a weak smile.

"And bring me a record of the prescriptions the penitentiary has been feeding her," he adds. "She looks haggard and stoned."

Sally nods her head, holding a clipboard over her chest to cover up her cleavage, a move I've used occasionally when a boy's gaze lingers too long. Even in my semi-state of consciousness, it's easy to follow his gaze. Sally's uniform is bleach white, the design reminiscent of the traditional candy striper uniform—more driven to incite male fantasy than for the comfort of the nurse expected to wear this ridiculous outfit during her laborious days. His eyes follow as she struts away. Her high-heeled shoes clack off the cement, the strident noise amplified in the hollow corridor.

Once Sally leaves, his gaze shifts to me. A sombre expression crosses his face as he looks in on me with what I can only assume is pity He digs through his pocket, coming up empty-handed. Then he touches his belt, jingling the key fob. It's almost embarrassing to watch him fumble with the keys. After what seems like an eternity, the latch to my cell opens with a solid thud. The hinges screech as the gate swings inward towards me, the shrill sound piercing into my eardrum.

"You're here to ask me questions?" My voice comes out fragile, matching my emaciated appearance. I nod my head up and down, "To evaluate me?"

Yarn took a step towards me, pieces of crumbled brick crunching beneath his feet. "I'm here to help you, nothing more," he says, tapping his pen against the clipboard. "Whatever it takes to make sure you get better."

I suppress a fit of laughter rising in my stomach. How many times has he used that line? And how many times did anyone leave this hell hole cured? The government did not equip this facility to handle the health and well-being of the mentally ill. This disgrace of a mental institution conjures up images of antiquated sanitoriums, a monument to the misguided past.

"You can't help me…" My voice trails off. Why can't Deborah be here for this?

"I will do everything in my powers to make sure you get the help you need," he answers, sounding sincere. His eyes examine me. What could he be staring at? I look awful in this grey jumpsuit.

I fix my gaze on Doctor Yarn. "I'm not the one who needs help. You're looking for my sister Deborah. But you can't help her either. Besides, she's not with us right now. I want her to come back."

"Well," Yarn pauses, "shall we start by talking about her? Would that be okay?"

When I open my jaw, a low, groaning croak escapes my larynx. My tongue lolls around inside my mouth as if something was pushing it aside to make room. "Why?" My voice takes on a shrill rasp, making me sound like my sister. "You're just like the rest of them."

Deborah's voice rises from behind me."He won't believe you."

Yarn's eyes dart up, scanning the room, a perplexed expression on his face. "I won't judge." His voice cracks. He pauses, taking a moment to steady his voice before he continues. "I'm only here to listen…" another lengthy pause, "…to you."

"They all judge you, Samantha," Deborah spits.

I turn my head towards the barred window. "You're back. Thanks for coming."

Yarn scribbles his pen across the paper, the clipboard rattling nervously as he jots down a note. He shifts on his feet, fidgeting. Miraculously, he steps deeper into my cell. I can tell he's trying to get a good look out my window. A booming clap of thunder sends him jumping backwards. When the flash of lightning strikes, his eyes grow wide with fear and his jaw hangs open, a silent scream caught in his throat. His Adam's apple bobs up and down as he swallows.

A whistling wind screams into the cell, knocking the window as another burst of lightning illuminates the room. Despite the bright light, mysterious shadows creep and crawl around the chamber. As the light diminishes, a glacial chill floods the room. A stiff breeze rushes past, tossing my hair around. Thunder grumbles overhead. The fluorescent light flickers and hums as the power surges. When the next flash of lightning strikes, I can see Deborah's elongated shadow fall across the cell and flood into the corridor. I wave my hand to the waning shadow, knowing my sister is still looking after me.

Yarn stammers, peering over his shoulder, his entire body shuddering. He closes his eyes and takes a deep breath, exhaling slowly. "Why don't you tell me about what happened the night of Lucas Green's death?" he asks, tapping his pen against the clipboard, just one of his many nervous ticks. There's something about the way he asks his question. He studies me with his eyes, taking in everything and processing it. But he wants out of my cell.

My lips don't move. "He wanted to hurt her," Deborah's harsh voice hisses.

Slack-jawed, Yarn glares over his shoulder. He can't see her, but I can.

"Did you mean Lucas tried to harm you?" Yarn asks. He thumbs through the papers on his clipboard. The manilla folder that Detective O'Reilly brought is fixed beneath the medical records; he didn't bother to open it. With an insidious grin, he steps closer. "Or did he try to hurt your sister?"

Deborah laughs at his statement, but I ignore her. "Please just go away," I beg Deborah, pointing back towards the window. When I turn around, a flash of lightning tears the sky in half. I've pissed her off.

Not realizing who I was speaking to, Yarn answers, "I can't do that. If you want me to help you, we need to discuss all the things in your file." The electricity surges in the room, casting the room in wavering light. On the wall, Deborah's shadow dances around the brick, moving with an eerie grace, flittering in and out of existence. "Did Lucas try to..."

"Yes," I answer, cutting him off. I'm so sick of that question. It's the only thing that people believe. How many times have they asked that question over the last several days? More than I'm willing to count. Deborah laughs at me. She whispers something, her voice drowned out by the driving wind and precipitation.

"And how did that make you feel?"

"I was afraid." My voice quivers. With considerable

effort, I push away the images that are seeking to rush back into my mind's eye.

"So, you fought back?" Yarn asks, tapping his pen against the clipboard.

"I fought back," Deborah answers for me in a snarling hiss.

"Deborah doesn't let anyone get away with anything. Even when I beg her to leave me alone, she just takes control of the situation."

"You mean," Yarn pauses, staring vacantly at his paperwork, "Deborah takes control of you?"

"No," I roar. The electricity surges in sync with my pulse. "What I mean is," I growl, "my sister attacked Lucas when she witnessed him trying to hurt me."

"Your sister's always around whenever you're in trouble?" Yarn asked, his tone incredulous. Yarn pulls the manilla folder out, laying it on top of his papers. He furrows his brow, pinching the bridge of his nose as if it hurts him to look at the content. "Let's start at the beginning Samantha," he sighs, "maybe it will help me understand you better."

I glance over at Deborah just in time to see her eyes roll, her long lashes batting. She shakes her head. A revolting smile creeps over her face.

"Alright, let's get this over with," I say to both of them. But he doesn't understand it yet. Deborah remains quiet for a change.

"Did your mother ever talk to you about your biological father?"

"Rarely," I answer. "It came up a few times when I was younger."

"And you weren't curious about him?" Yarn asks. He taps his pen against the paper, waiting for a response.

"I am, but I gave up asking when I was five because I realized how much it saddened her." I feel a tear well in the corner of my eye.

"What did she tell you about him?"

"Not much really. Basically, they met at a party, spent enough time together to fall in love, then he disappeared, breaking her heart."

"Did your mother tell you she was pregnant with twins?"

"Yes." That was a lie. "And that the doctors told her she'd lost one. It was a miracle when Deborah came out alive."

Yarn stares at me, concentrating, wrinkles creasing his forehead. "Then," he stammers, "why aren't there records of Deborah? Not a single picture?"

"Because she detested me. I'm a reminder of the sorrow our father caused," Deborah explains, choking back tears. "I had my father's eyes, Samantha has hers."

Yarn nods, his pen scratching across the page. Before turning the page, he licks his fingers, his dry tongue scraping over his index and middle finger. His jowls shake, the folds of skin draped over his Adam's apple. "And your mother remarried after?"

"Right away," Deborah answers for me. Yarn still thinks that I'm the one talking to him. This time he doesn't search the cell.

"It wasn't proper for a young woman to raise a child alone, embarrassing," I add.

"Then your brother was born a few months after they got married." Yarn's eyes search for the answer within the folder.

"Four months after," I recall. "She fit into her wedding dress without showing."

"Your brother died young." Yarn lifts a page up. "Sudden infant death syndrome is what the coroner wrote on the death certificate."

"Deborah smothered his face with a pillow." I watch the shame distort Deborah's pretty face, turning it sour.

"Why would she do that?" Yarn asks. "He was only a

few months old when it happened."

"He was stealing all the attention," I retort, wiping a tear away from the corner of my eye. "Deborah couldn't stand it. She wanted to scare him, but it went too far."

Deborah refuses to establish eye contact with me, staring out into the storm. A gust of wind batters the Waterford with a barrage of hail. A crack of thunder rocks, tears, and booms. The lights flicker as the electricity surges through the lines. The weather always fluctuates with Deborah's moods, manifesting the dismal abyss that is her soul.

Yarn offers the typical explanation. "Are you certain it wasn't an accident? While your brother passed from asphyxiation, the medical examiner found the fibres from the bed sheet in his throat. They determined you couldn't have done it. Your mother swore you couldn't reach him from the floor and were too small to crawl into the crib. I'm sure you feel guilty about it because you couldn't help him, so you created a story to help you cope with this needless tragedy."

Not bothering to respond, I sit here, absorbing the information. I perceive what question is coming next, so I answer it for him, "Deborah shot him with a pistol."

"You mean your stepfather?"

I nod.

"Now, why would she do that?"

"Because he thought if he killed me," I allow my eyes to wander over to Yarn, "he could stop her. He believed what you suspect. You both jumped to the same conclusion. The same one as everyone else." I peer at him through glazed eyes and continue, growing sick of the same old song and dance.

"And what conclusion would that be?" Yarn asks, his tone curious.

"That I have split personality disorder. My mom

thought the devil possessed me. That's why she tried to save me by performing an exorcism on me."

Yarn flipped through the manilla folder, dropping his pen to the cement floor. It rolled towards the drain. "The Vatican denied your mother's request. I remember O'Reilly telling me. I can't find it in here." Agitated now, his words blend together.

A sadistic smile crosses Deborah's face, darkening the lines on her face. "Oh, she tried anyway. Both of them paid for it. Hell, who knows, maybe it would have worked if there was a demon living within Samantha. But I'm not the devil. I'm real. Just like you."

"Wait a minute," Yarn stammers, his eyes darting back and forth. "Who tried to perform the exorcism? And what happened to them?"

"Two priests from the mainland showed up and performed a series of sadistic rituals to rid Samantha of the demon." Deborah bursts into a fit of cackling laughter. "When they left, I followed them out and made them pay for what they did to my sister," Deborah explains. "And my mother."

"Can you tell me their names?" Yarn asks. "And what did they do to your mother?"

"Easton and Sharp," Deborah spits out their names like they were poison in her mouth. Yarn's pen races across the page as he records their names. "They took advantage of my mother, knowing she was desperate. They took her money after performing a fake exorcism."

"Listen, Samantha," Yarn shivers, his voice faltering, eyes wide, "I don't understand what's happening to you. But you're very sick, and I suspect you need help. I'm going to make a phone call and make sure you stay here with us at the Waterford." He was already edging towards the hallway, his hands groping for the iron bars.

When he turns to leave, Deborah slithers past me, her shadowy form as swift as a summer's breeze, and as frigid as an Arctic blast. She reaches out, her fingers curling around his wrist. Yarn stops dead in his tracks and draws a hitching breath. He spins around, his eyes bulging with fear. He stares at Deborah, then his gaze wanders over to me. Then he raises his arm, examining a blackened smear sullying the cuff of his dress shirt. He stares up at the ceiling, searching for something.

"How did you do that?" he stammers.

A boisterous grumble of thunder rocks the floor. The power dies, casting the room into complete blackness. The temperature plummets as a wintry chill settles over the cell.

"Samantha…" Yarn's voice trails off. Flashes of lightning cracked. The vivid cluster of lights snake through the horizon, casting the cell in silvery light. A scream escapes Yarn's throat, and he tumbles backwards, his back slamming hard against the iron bars.

Deborah stands beside me, a shadowy replica of my gaunt frame. Blackness swirls and pulsates around her, illusions of movement dancing on the walls. A dark mist billows from my mouth, puddling into a sinister aberration. A stiff breeze sweeps it across the floor. The light vanishes as another clap of thunder roars outside. From the shadows, a pair of reptilian green eyes peer out from within the entombed darkness. The light filaments flicker and buzz as electricity labours to make its way back. Water-stained bulbs emit a pale yellow glow.

"Deborah!" I cry out. "He's trying to help. He just doesn't understand."

Deborah's gargled voice speaks from within the shadows. "No, he's just like the rest of them."

Her shadowed figure lurches forward. Before she can

reach Doctor Yarn, I grab my sister by her ankle.

"Let go, silly girl. I need to protect you," she snarls.

Yarn fumbles his way out of my cell. He trips over his own feet and falls hard on his backside. His head snaps back, and the back of his skull smacks the cement hard. I grip Deborah's foot, her legs pumping, working to throw my grasp. Yarn's survival instincts take over, and he drags himself away from the cell. Desperate, he starts kicking at the door. It slams shut with a raucous clatter. Deborah throws herself against the bars, and the gate jerks open. Yarn drives his foot into the door. His legs buckle, his backside scraping over the cement floor. Yarn pumps his legs straight. Deborah screams out in a fit of madness as the gate crashes shut once.

"Help me," Yarn screams in terror, his shrill voice piercing through the darkness like a scalpel.

"What's the matter?" Sally demands, standing over Yarn and gawking down at him with a confused, frightened expression. "What are you doing lying on the floor?"

Yarn twists his neck, staring up at her, then back towards me. I watch his face twist and writhe as he tries to piece together the last thirty seconds.

"Where did Deborah go?" he asks. Finally, he believes me.

"You caught a break, Doctor," Sally says, unimpressed. "The subject stayed put in her cell."

"How did you know to come down here?" Yarn stammers.

"I watched you exit the cell and lay down on the security camera." Sally thrusts the key into the lock and turns the bolt. It falls into place with a heavy thunk.

"How? The power's gone out," the words tumble out of Yarn's mouth.

"What are you talking about? The power never went out," Sally says, bending down to pick up the clipboard.

A frown cuts wrinkles across her face as she glares at the manilla folder. "You're not well, Doctor. Maybe you should head back to your office for a break?"

"No, we have to observe Samantha..."

"I'm sorry," Sally cuts him off, lowering her head.

Yarn swings his head down the corridor, towards the approaching footsteps. Two orderlies stand beside Detective O'Reilly.

"We need to have a chat, Doctor," O'Reilly says. "It's time for you to come with me in my car down to the station."

Yarn fumbles his way to his feet, clutching the bars to steady himself. "What's all this about?"

Detective O'Reilly waves a warrant at the doctor. "We have some questions concerning the relationship you have with your patients."

"That's a fake document," Deborah says.

"What?" Yarn barks. "This is preposterous."

"Why did you have the cameras disabled in this part of the building doctor?" O'Reilly asks, an unlit cigarette dangling from the corner of his mouth.

"What in God's name are you talking about?" Yarn half screeches.

The orderlies step forward, but O'Reilly holds them back with the wave of a hand. Hidden behind them are two more police officers. A pair of stainless steel handcuffs dangle from one officer's hands, clattering as he strode forward.

"Doctor Yarn," O'Reilly sounds high and mighty, his chest puffed out, "you are under arrest for suspicion of assault."

A police officer grabs Yarn by the shoulder, twists him around, and slaps the cuffs over his wrists. Once they lock his hands behind his back, the officer grabs a fistful of Yarn's shirt, guiding him down the hallway out of sight.

"You can't do this to me," Yarn screams as they drag him from view.

I remain in the corner, pretending to be oblivious to everything taking place just outside my cell. The only person who ever believed me is snatched away when I need him the most. No one notices as Deborah's shadow slithers up the wall and slips outside through a crack in the window.

Deborah speaks to me from outside. "I'll be back. Remember what I told you, the detective switched out your dose of amobarbital with a fatal dose of potassium chloride. You know what to do." The wind steals her voice, and she vanishes with it.

Once more, I find myself alone.

An orderly with a nameplate reading "BRAKE" steps into the room. This is the orderly Deborah warned me about. I can hear his heart flutter inside his chest, beating the rapid cadence of fear. Beads of perspiration drip down his face, his complexion pale and clammy. As he reaches out to take the syringe off the tray, his hand trembles, knocking the tray off the cart. His Adam's apple bounces up and down as he swallows anxiously. He bows down to pick up the scattered contents of the tray.

"Are you going to be alright, Aaron?" Sally asks as she rubs an alcohol swab over my shoulder, preparing to give me the fatal injection. Not willing to take any chances, Sally has two orderlies holding me in place. My heart thumps in my chest with anticipation. My mouth is dry, and I try to speak but my tongue cannot form the words. Instead, a trickle of saliva drips in thick ropes from the corner of my mouth.

"Yeah," Aaron stutters, "just rattled by everything that

took place tonight."

Eying him suspiciously, Sally asks, "What took you so long to offer these accusations about Doctor Yarn, anyway? And why tonight?" She grabs a ball of cotton, presses it against my shoulder, and holds her hand out for the syringe.

"Thank you," I rasp.

"Of course, my dear," Sally answers with a motherly affection.

I roll my tongue around in my mouth, drawing in moisture. "Not you." I stare vacantly at Aaron, lifting my arm to point a finger. "Him." I allow the vague outline of a smile to surface despite the waves of panic crashing hard over me. "You released me from this torture." I revel in watching Aaron sweat, his mouth twisting in terror.

"Just doing my job," he mumbles, holding up the syringe as if it were a trophy.

"No, honey," Sally interrupts, "I'll be giving you the dose. He's only holding it for me." Sally holds out her hand, her fingers outstretched unknowingly for the mortal dose.

Aaron breathes a sigh of relief. He removes the plastic tip before handing the syringe to Sally. I roll my tongue around in my mouth, dispersing what moisture remains around. With my head turned towards the window, I can see Deborah glaring at me, waiting impatiently. She doesn't expect me to follow through with her plan. Sally pinches the flesh of my shoulder. Her nails dig into my flesh, releasing an exquisite stream of endorphins.

"Don't be frightened," Deborah whispers into my ear, "we got them now."

My mouth shifts open into a gaping smile. "I'll miss you."

Sally jabs the needle into the muscle, depressing the

plunger. The icy liquid drains into my veins. With each beat, the lethal dose creeps toward my heart. Outside, Deborah howls. The others stare out the window, thinking it's the wind. The orderlies ease me towards my bunk where I slouch deeply. Sally glances down at me for a moment. Her tender smile is reminiscent of my own mother's and tears well in the corner of my eye. Before she leaves, she straightens out her skirt.

"Aaron, can you get her settled into the bed please?" She looks down at me for the last time. "I want her straps secured, so she doesn't fall."

The effects of the potassium chloride are already working; I'm lethargic, serene. My heartbeat slows to a methodical rhythm, my pulse all but non-existent. As Sally walks away, the rhythm of her high heels pounds into my skull like nails driven into a coffin. Aaron shuffles into view, working the straps as instructed. He yanks them too tight, cutting off the circulation in my wrists and ankles. But soon, that won't matter. When I try to speak, the fluids building on my chest muffle my words, the sound of my voice a distorted rasp.

"What are you trying to say?" Aaron asks, leaning forward, his breath hot against my neck. His nose scrunches, repulsed by my vile body odour.

"Thank you for setting me free," I croak. My insides are dying, my breath reeking of rot and decay.

"You're getting what you deserved," he whispers into my ear as he wrenches the wrist strip along the wall tight. The bones in my wrist snap.

A rattling laugh escapes my lungs. The fluids building in my chest gargle the supernatural echo. "I didn't kill your cousin."

Aaron's eyes grow wide with fear as his face flushes with blood. "How did you know?" No one at the Waterford knew about that. How?"

"Deborah knew." My lips curl into a merciless smirk. "And now that I will not be here to hold her back, she's free to do what she wants."

"What are you doing in there, Aaron?" Sally calls out, poking her head into my cell. "We have lots of work to do tonight, and I'd like to get out of this section of the building now."

With the final strap secured, Aaron bolts up straight. Carried by a fear-induced sense of urgency, he turns to leave. Before he gets far, I reach out, snatching a handful of his pants.

"You'll meet her tonight after she's done with that detective." My words fade into oblivion with me.

When I awake, the world is pitch black. Wherever I am, it's freezing. Muffled voices speak nearby. My head is spinning, and my body aches all over. I want to sit up, but lactic acid floods my muscles, rendering them useless. The rhythm of my heart thumps inside my skull, pounding to get out. I realize my eyes are closed, but when I try to open them, I can't, they're stuck together. So are my lips. I push my tongue against my lips; strands of thread prevent it from pushing my mouth open.

Footsteps approach, the conversation becomes clearer.

"It's a shame what happened to her," Yarn's familiar voice drones. "I don't get it, she was healthy."

"Well," a stranger's voice answers, "that's why we are here. An autopsy will determine what happened."

"Thanks for waiting for me," Yarn replies. "That corrupt detective had something to do with my incarceration, I know he did. There's no way Aaron Brake came up with those lies by himself."

"I'm still shocked no one knew he was Lucas's cousin.

He should have never been allowed near this woman."

A moment of silence passes between them.

Yarn shatters the dead air. "Let's just get this over with."

The boisterous clamour of a zipper tearing open bores into my skull. An intense orange light shines against my eyelids. Metal instruments clang off a cold, stainless steel countertop. I feel the sharpened edge of scissor blades prod into my mouth, cutting the threads. My tongue slips into the back of my throat, gagging me until the doctor lifts my head up.

"What drugs were you feeding her?" the stranger asks. "Her breath is foul. They must have rotted her guts."

Next, the doctor removes the stitches from my eyes with surgical precision. "That's creepy," Yarn says. "It's like she's watching us with those reptilian eyes."

I can sense the fluids draining from my muscles.

"Is she breathing?" Yarn asks with a great deal of concern.

"Just a build-up of gasses releasing," the coroner responds, his voice lacking any emotion. "I left my damn cart in room two, I'll be right back." His footsteps fade away, the sounds fade into the hallway.

I can hear Yarn pacing back and forth. Finding enough strength, I sit up. "Where is 'O'Reilly?" I ask, my voice a dry rasp.

Yarn stumbles backwards, tumbling over his feet and collapsing to the floor. "Sam... Samantha," he sputters.

I swing my legs over the edge of the autopsy table. My hands cradle my jaw, and I crack my neck, the vertebrate popping loudly. "Samantha is dead," I state. With my feet planted on the floor, I stand up. "Now tell me," I snarl, "where is the bastard who tried to kill me?"

"Deborah?" Yarn cries.

"Nice to finally meet you, Doctor." I grin at him. "And if you want to live, you're going to tell me where O'Reilly's family lives."

THE HITCHHIKER

The car bounced up and down on the old woods trail. Emma made her finest attempt to avoid the potholes and exposed rocks, but years of neglect had left this old dirt track in appalling shape. Dave was having a marvelous time, rejoicing because she'd insisted that her father's brand-new car could handle the ride while they left Dave's Jeep back at the gas station. Emma cursed under her breath with every loud rattle from the deep holes disguised under the pools of water that filled them up. An air freshener swayed back and forth, the string holding it from the rearview mirror spinning the tree in circles as it wrapped around one way then the next. Emma was wearing her worn jean jacket over a white sundress covered in yellow sunflowers. Her dad wouldn't have let her leave with Dave in such a short dress, but she yearned for his attention. The dress' delicate fabric rested about halfway down the bronzed skin of her thigh.

"Maybe next time you should listen to me," Dave mocked her, employing his best impersonation of their high school gym teacher, the only class in school they both took.

Emma worked faithfully in all her advanced courses. Her father insisted that she belonged in them, even though she doubted her own abilities. Dave was the school's star athlete, and that was his ticket to a free university scholarship. She envied him. Every night, she toiled with homework just to earn a chance to apply for a few small grants.

Emma pretended to punch Dave's broad shoulder, acting as if she had hurt her fist to flirt with him. "Shut up, blockhead." They'd been best friends since before Emma could remember. Their parents spent a lot of time together, which meant they had no choice but to get to know each other. "This little machine is just getting warmed up." Emma ran her hand through her strawberry blond curls and bit her fist as a worrying bang rattled the car.

Dave grinned, the dimples in his cheeks added a soft edge to his rugged jawline. He kept his jet-black hair short, matching sideburns trimmed into a narrow strip of hair that stopped to meet the onset of his jaw. "I think you should start saving up your money."

"You think I broke something?" Emma's father was hardworking, but it didn't result in him having a lot of money. The last car they had was the only other car Emma had ever known. It had taken her father years to save up the cash for a new car and he would yell at her if she broke it the first time she'd taken it out for a spin.

Dave placed his hand on her knee. "I think you need to buy your own vehicle, so you don't have to worry about it." His skin rough with calluses, but it sent a quiver up Emma's spine.

Emma could feel her face flush red, the freckles on her face lost for now. She wanted to say something, but she couldn't think of anything that wouldn't embarrass her. Dave took his hand back and didn't seem to notice Emma's reaction. If he did, he was doing an exemplary job of suppressing it. He rolled down the window and stuck his arm out, strumming his palm of the passenger door to the beat of the techno music. He reached over and turned up the volume. The speakers on the doors rattled with the boom of the bass. Emma looked up at the sun. It was resting on top of the tree line, getting ready to disappear for another day. The thick trees that lined both borders of the road were thinning out. Emma could see the extensive stretches of verdant fields taking their place, which meant the highway was nearby. It would be a relief to get these wheels back on the asphalt after this rocky trail.

Obscured by the bushes, a celestial glow caught Emma's attention. A woman, swathed in an elegant white dress, held out a hand, gesturing for Emma to stop. She held up her hand, veiling her face.

"Do you see that?" she asked.

"See what?" Dave replied, mystified.

"Look." Emma pointed towards the woman. "There. Moving through the bushes by the side of the trail." She looked at Dave with indignation in her eyes. How could he not recognize it?

"Is there an animal or something?" Dave stared out the window, confused. "I see nothing except bushes."

When Emma looked back, the vision had disappeared. Embarrassed, she thought of something to tell him that wouldn't make her sound frantic. "Yeah, I thought I saw a big bunny." Dave nodded his head in agreement, a low grunt escaping his lips. They drove down the old dirt road in silence for the next twenty minutes, neither of them speaking up.

As Emma eased the car up a modest slope, she rose out of her seat at the sight of the familiar fishing hole. Water spewed out of an enormous round metal culvert, feeding into a deep pool on the side of the road. Large white waves rippled at the base of the waterfall, but the surface remained calm. The water was as mysterious as the midnight sky.

"Well, we are just about there now, just one more turn than I guess I'll take you back to the gas terminal." Emma wanted him to suggest catching a movie or grabbing something to eat.

"It's an hour drive back to work, don't sound so glum." Dave turned at stared at Emma. "If you want maybe we could grab a slice of pizza or something."

Emma stared into Dave's deep olive eyes a little too long, but she didn't care. "Yeah, that sounds like fun." She worked not to let her excitement show too much, but she could tell by the expression on Dave's face he had recognized the elation in her voice.

Dave snapped his head forward as the car made the turn. "Hey, slow down." He pointed ahead to a tall man standing at the turnoff. He wore a weathered fedora tugged down in the front to shield the sunlight from his eyes. Long coils of silvery hair concealed his face. The choker on his black trench coat fluttered with the breeze, encompassing the sides of his neck, his exposed chest on display. Gray curls of hair poked out from underneath his grimy white undershirt. Mud-covered jeans blended into his soiled work boots.

Emma eased off the gas a little. The car's momentum kept it rolling at a brisk pace. "You recognize this guy?"

"No, but he's an old man in the heart of nowhere." Dave seemed eager to help the stranger. A concerned tone had hastened his typically calm demeanor.

As the car pulled up closer to the man, he pushed aside a clump of hair from his face and peered in. Emma could only see the white of his eyes. Her heart vaulted into her throat, thrashing with fear. She tramped on the gas peddle, and the tires spun out in the dirt. The car lurched out of control and nearly side swiped the stranger, who jumped out of the way just in time to avoid a collision.

"Jesus, Emma." Dave raised his voice. "What are you doing?"

"The guy gives me the creeps," Emma said in defiance.

Dave glanced over his shoulder, trying to spot the man. "You should at least go back and apologize to the poor guy. You almost ran him over."

"No way," Emma said. Her heart was still pumping, racing faster than ever before. "Did you see his eyes?" She checked for traffic and once the car's tires touched the pavement, she put the gas pedal to the floor and observed the odometer speed up to 100 km/h.

"What are you talking about?" Dave sounded confused. "He never even looked at us."

Emma glimpsed the old man in the rearview mirror as he stood up. His hat had slipped from his head, and he was dusting it off by beating it against his leg.

"I saw him glaring at me with pure white eyes," Emma said. She glanced down at the odometer and was driving well over the speed limit, but she wanted as much distance as possible between the car and that guy.

"Slow down." Dave placed his hand against the dashboard, bracing himself as the car sped around a curve. "Your parents will freak out if you get a ticket." Emma looked up in the rearview mirror, refusing to slow down until the stranger was out of sight. "Emma!" He raised his voice this time.

Emma checked all her mirrors once more to make sure the old man was out of view. She double-checked just to be positive he was gone before she eased her foot off the peddle. The car eased down to the speed limit after a few tense moments. The car approached another turn before her heartbeat returned to a steady pace.

"I can't believe you wanted me to pick that man up,"

Emma said.

"Just forget about it." Dave sounded like a child pouting. "There's nothing we can do about it now."

Long dark shadows crept across the road. The tree branches appeared to be reaching out to capture the car. The orange tinge of the sun had sunk behind the distant mountains, and the sky was turning a dingy blue. It would be black before they reached the gas station.

"Are you serious?" Dave continued to plead his case. "What if he needed help? He could be out there all night in the middle of nowhere?"

Emma defended her opinion. "If he got all the way out there, then he can find his way back."

"His car may have broken down," Dave replied without hesitation, "and he was trying to hitchhike back to get help."

"If you're so confident you can go back and get him after I drop you off."

Emma regretted snapping back at Dave. She didn't want to be so confrontational. The words slipped from her tongue without notice and they sat in silence for what seemed like an eternity. They both stared out of the window. Emma wanted to apologize, but she didn't want to let him believe he was right. She worried he would try to persuade her to drive back to get the stranger.

She turned the headlights on, casting a subdued white light over the highway ahead of the car. The side of the street was illuminated just enough to keep the shadows at bay. The road straightened out for a long stretch and Emma frowned. Ominous clouds approached them from just beyond the mountains. A lightning bolt split through the pitch-black sky and a crack of thunder exploded, rumbling somewhere far away.

Dave broke the silence. "I think I left my windows

rolled down in the truck."

Emma looked over at Dave, who continued staring straight ahead, a vacant expression on his face. "Your truck is overdue for a wash," she quipped, hoping he'd smile. His lips didn't even crack.

Dave turned his head towards Emma with his best attempt at an evil smirk on his face. "I should roll down my window." He hovered his finger over the button for a moment before opening the window a crack then closed it before Emma said anything.

"You are a dolt." Emma peered at Dave with the meanest stare in her repertoire. "I should go back and drop you off with your friend back there." She studied Dave's facial features, trying to gage his reaction. He looked agitated with his eyebrows raised and his eyes opened wide. "What's wrong?"

Dave didn't say a word, he just pointed his finger ahead. Emma looked ahead at the road. A tall shadowy figure wearing a fedora stood at the base of the hill. His elbow was tucked tight against his body and his arm was stuck out at a ninety-degree angle, his fist in a ball and his thumb sticking up.

"It can't be," she said.

His features were still too dark to distinguish, but the ghostly figure struck a remarkable resemblance to the man on the old dirt road.

Dave leaned forward, squinting his eyes, struggling to get a better look at the man on the highway. "I guess it is."

Emma's heartrate climbed. "That's not possible." As the light from the car reached the figure, his white straggly hair draped down from under his hat and concealed his face. He tied his black trench coat shut, and it hung down around his boots, hiding his legs from view. "It's just can't be the same guy, that's not possible."

"These people have an odd sense of fashion," Dave joked then discovered Emma wasn't in the mood.

Emma pressed down on the gas pedal a little heavier now. She didn't want to slow down when she scaled the slope. Something deep down inside of her gut wouldn't let the man get close enough to reach out and touch the car, so she steered the car away from the man standing at the side of the trail. As the car rushed past the hitch-hiker, a gust of wind sent his hair whipping behind him. Emma was sure she glimpsed a pair of flaming white eyes glaring back at her as she looked over her shoulders. The haunting portrait of those devilish eyes burned into her brain. No matter which way she looked, she felt them staring back at her.

"Did you see his eyes?" she asked.

"No, I didn't..." Dave hesitated, "and it wasn't the same dude. We're just getting carried away after a good scare. Our imaginations are getting the better of us." Dave's voice was reassuring. He reached out and put his hand on the steering wheel. "Steady now. The car is swerving back and forth."

Emma had been trying to get the piercing white lights to go away and hadn't been paying attention to the road. She let Dave keep the car steady as she tried to blink her eyelids, each time hoping that the ghastly image would vanish.

"I don't think I can keep going," she said.

Dave patted Emma on the back, trying to reassure her that everything would be okay. "Do you want me to drive?"

Emma didn't want to drive, but she didn't want to pull over. "No, it's okay. Thanks," she said, suppressing her high-pitched tone to sound brave.

She concentrated on the road and steadied the car as it crested the hill. She refused to look up in the rearview mirror, anxious that the man would appear from the dark recesses of the woods.

"There's no way that was the same guy," Dave said. "It's just not possible."

Emma's grandmother told ghost stories about an evil spirit that had tormented her on the highway. Her mother, long deceased, was slain by a horrific automobile accident. But her grandmother said it because the spirit was after her family. Her grandmother gave up driving after the sun went down and would never travel the highway alone. Emma had always assumed she was telling tall tales. Was it possible she had been speaking the truth?

"Do you believe in evil spirits?" Emma inquired.

"Do you mean like ghosts and goblins?" Dave paused, waiting for an answer from Emma. But she didn't respond, humiliated by his question. "I can't say that I do. I used to be afraid of the dark, but that was only when I was young. Do you believe in them?"

"I never used to until now," Emma responded with a harsh snap to her voice. After what they had just seen, she needed an explanation. "I have a terrible feeling in my gut." Emma's stomach twisted and turned with anxiety. With every curve and turn in the road, she expected to see the hitchhiker again standing there, waiting for her.

Dave placed his hand back on her knee. "Hey, we'll be back at the gas station before we know it."

In the distance, another hill came into view. Emma kept scanning back and forth, expecting to see the man standing in the same spot. Even with the light illuminating the hill, she couldn't spot any signs of him. Her heart beat a little slower now. She felt a surge of relief wash over her. She had driven this road almost every day during summer break and would not miss it after tonight. She looked over at Dave and was glad to see him relax as he couldn't locate the hitchhiker either.

"Yeah, it's not much further from here," she said.

"I think it's two hills after this one." Dave leaned back in his seat. "I honestly thought it was the same guy for a second. I guess I let my imagination run wild there."

"Me too. It's probably my fault." Emma felt she'd been the reason for the panic. "So, movie's on me tonight."

When Emma looked over at Dave, she was disheartened by the fear plastered on his face.

"Are you trying to scare me or something? I said I'm sorry."

Dave didn't respond. He just stared blankly at the horizon. Emma looked around, trying to spot the cause of his distracted gaze. Pushing up the ridge, the engine worked hard to maintain its speed as it clambered up the highway. Emma scanned the sides of the road but saw nothing in her view.

"What's wrong, Dave?"

His eyes were wide open and his eyebrows were raised. "You didn't get gas before we left, did you?"

Emma glanced down at the gauge. A thin red line rested just under the empty line on the dashboard.

"Goddamnit." She smacked her hand off the steering wheel. "Do we have enough gas to get back to the station?"

"We might..." Dave's voice fluttered. "If we let it coast down the hills, we should be fine."

With the sun vanished now, and the stars twinkling against the night sky, the moonlight dimmed, obscured by the impending clouds. A strong flash of lightning lit up the sky for a moment before the resounding rumble of thunder scared it away. Suddenly, the clouds burst open with rain just as the car reached the top of the hill. Lifting her foot off the gas pedal, Emma let the car coast down the hill, picking up as much momentum as possible to help her up the next hill. As the car headed down the hill, the headlights pointed towards the valley and the crest of the next hill was just a few hundred meters away. But would she have enough speed to reach the top if she didn't use her brakes anymore? It helped that the rain hadn't gathered on the pavement yet.

"It's the next hill I'm concerned about, and even if we don't make it, we are close enough to walk the rest of the way now." Emma tried to sound chipper, but she didn't want to get out in this horrible weather.

She strained her eyes as the car raced towards the bottom, almost catching up with the headlights as they charged down into the valley. Intensified shadows swirled at the edge of her vision. The downpour intensified as the car's wipers swooshed back and forth, clearing the rain that beat against the windows.

"Emma, you need to drive faster!" Dave shouted as he gripped the dashboard and tensed up.

Emma looked around the base of the hill and noticed nothing in the car's headlights, but about halfway up the slope, she discovered the shadowy figure standing at the top of the roadway. Emma slammed the pedal to the floor. With reckless abandon, the car sped towards the bottom of the hill. She peered at the odometer, trying to convince herself they were moving too fast for the hitchhiker to try anything. Before she realized it, the car was going over 160 km/h, but she refused to ease back, pushing the car to its limits. The man's hair was soaked to the side of his face, but his white piercing eyes leered back at Emma.

"Dave," she said.

"What the hell is going on?" Dave's voice came out

shaky, corrupted by hysteria.

Emma wanted to close her eyes, but her brain forced her to watch. Even in the pouring rain, the man's trench coat was open now. A mysterious stain soiled his white tunic. The car started pushing up the hill, the engine blaring as it reached its limits. Now, as the hitchhiker approached, vivid details that she hadn't noticed before horrified her. He wasn't holding up his thumb; he was holding a knife in his fist. The light gleamed on the blade, and a thin sliver of bright light reflected at Emma. He was holding it up between his white glowing eyes, which burned into Emma's brain. She swerved the car just as the man lunged onto the highway. Her heart thrashed around in her chest, beating against her rib cage and stifling her breath. Desperate, she pressed her feet so hard against the pedal that her leg hurt. The car reached the top the hill and careened down the other side.

"How did he do that?" Dave peered over his shoulder through the rearview window. "There's no fucking way that's possible."

Emma was on the verge of breaking down, her voice choking in her throat. "That's not a man."

"What are you saying?" Dave sounded astonished.

Emma watched the bottom of the hill light up as the car raced towards down the highway.

"I'm saying it's an evil spirit." Emma challenged Dave to disagree. Her muscles were so tense it hurt. She looked at her bone-white knuckles and was afraid her fingers would break.

"Emma, there's no such fucking thing. We just need to get to the gas station and call the cops." Dave was looking at his phone. "My phone has no signal out here." He threw it against the dashboard, and it ricocheted into the back seat. "This is bullshit." The anger masked the fear in his trembling voice.

Emma frantically searched for any signs of the hitch-hiker. The wipers were working overtime to keep the window clear long enough for her to get a good view of the road ahead. Water splashed over the pavement as the car swerved, the tires catching in an enormous puddle that had formed in the ruts as the highway flattened out. Without reason, the car jolted forward. the seatbelt dug sharply into E'ma's shoulder, and her neck throbbed with pain from the whiplash.

"Damnit," Emma swore as the car lost most of its momentum. She kept the gas pedal to the floor, but the flash flooding prevented the car from speeding up. The car's engine sputtered. Terrified, Emma stared down at the gas gauge and forced back tears. Running on fumes now, the motor made loud knocking sounds as it struggled to suck in enough gas to keep it running. The car sputtered up the hillside. Thankfully, the hitchhiker was nowhere in sight. They slowed to a crawl as it climbed the short ridge. She leaned over the wheel to get a better view of the road. The car crested the hill as the engine died, tires ambling over the pavement. Lights from the gas station filled her heart with hope, shining like a lighthouse beacon leading them to safety. A giant white and blue sign at the edge of the parking lot shined brighter than the sun. Emma's heart leapt into her throat as a blood curtailing scream ripped through the silence. The sound of heavy footsteps slapping off the wet pavement drew her attention.

"Fucking move, you piece of shit." Tears streamed down her cheek. She pressed hard on the gas pedal. The car rolled down the slope, building momentum. The hitch-hiker was racing down the highway after them, wielding the blade around violently.

Dave threw the passenger door open and got out to

push the car.

"What the fuck are you doing?" Emma begged Dave to get back in the car. He dug his shoulder into the car and groaned as he churned his legs, the car picking up speed much faster now.

The hitchhiker's hat flew off his head as he raced towards the car. The blemish on his shirt looked like thick blood. His trench coat flapping behind him, his mouth wide open with his jagged teeth exposed. His piercing scream grew louder with anticipation as he swung his blade, narrowly missing Dave's back. He slashed the blade at Dave again, and this time the steel blade bit into the flesh on Dave's back. With a jerky motion, Dave jumped back in the car, but the hitchhiker grabbed hold of the door before he slammed it shut. With the car rolling down the hill faster than the hitchhiker could move his legs, he took one last swipe at Dave before the car put distance between the man. A resounding bang startled Emma as the hitchhiker dug his blade into the trunk, the blade cutting through the aluminum with ease. Emma looked over her shoulder, expecting to discover the man hanging on to the back of the car, but he was nowhere in sight. The car sped down the hill and was moving much too fast to make the turn into the gas station parking lot, but Emma tried anyway. As she cut the wheel, the tires dug into the gravel and Emma struggled to keep her grasp on the wheel. The car took a sharp left turn and nearly drove into the ditch. Emma slammed on the brakes just in time. The car screeched to a halt.

"That was too...." Dave began, his voice snatched away by a blustering whistle.

A loud, metallic screech ruptured Emma's eardrums as the door flew off the hinges. A pair of hands gripped Dave by the shoulders, yanking him fiercely. His body caught in the seatbelt. Bones snapped and crunched as his body crumpled into a decrepit position. His eyes bulged out of the sockets. Panic twisted the features of his face. Their eyes caught in a deadly gaze as bloody tears flowed from his eyes. Without warning, the hands snatched him from the seat and tossed him like a rag doll against the bare pavement.

Emma's lungs burned as she shrieked relentlessly. She tossed open the door and sprinted towards the lights of the gas station. The hitchhiker's footfalls dogged her the entire way until she reached the light. An eerie silence swept over her like a blanket. Too afraid to turn her head, she dashed for the door. She gripped the metal handle and yanked with all of her might, nearly tearing her shoulder out of its socket.

"No way!" she screeched. "There's no way you're closed." Deep sobs escaped her throat.

She tugged at the door again, but it wouldn't budge. A woman wearing a white dress walked towards the door from the shadows inside. Another figure wearing faded blue jeans followed behind.

"Help me." Her pleas choked her throat. "You have to help me."

It was the woman she had seen at the side of the road, holding her mother's hand. Her mom's eyes spilled with sadness, tears streaming down her cheeks. She wasn't holding the woman's hand; she was being dragged towards the door.

"Mom!" Emma screamed, banging her fists against the glass. "What's happening?"

The ethereal vision of her mother opened her mouth to warn her daughter. Instead, malevolent shadows spewed out, covering the door and coating them in darkness. A smile reflected back at Emma in the glass. Warm blood trickled down Emma's belly. She looked down to observe the hitchhiker's blade protruding from her guts. A length of intestine spilled through the wound, dangling down her thigh as the blade was ripped out. She dropped to her knees, trying to hold her organs inside her stomach. Wetness seeped out between her fingers as the blade plunged down, in between her collarbone and neck.

In a desperate bid to escape, Emma dropped down on her knees. The knife slid out of the flesh with a sickening, sucking noise. Warmth traveled down the nape of her neck and over her chest. The man cackled a gargled, curdling rasp. Droplets of blood stained the pavement below her as a length of pinkish-gray intestine trailed behind her. Somehow, she managed to get to her feet and stumbled away from the hitchhiker. Her legs floated beneath her, the tips of her sneakers scuffing along the road. Heavy footsteps lumbered behind her, the shrill laughter gaining on her. Reflective yellow paint stared up at her as she tripped over her own feet. She collapsed to the road, managing to brace her fall with an outstretched hand, the rough surface shredding strips of flesh off her palm.

She cried out in agony, but her voice fell on death ears, drifting through the surrounding forest. Her hand, already sticky with blood, fumbled across the road as she braced herself, urging herself to get up. When she turned her head, the hitchhiker was nowhere to be found.

Emma reached out towards the vacant building. "Mom..." As she drifted into oblivion, she heard the maniacal laughter once more. A sweeping darkness covered her like a dreadful blanket. She could feel the weight of it pressing down on her eyelids.

MUMMERS: CELEBRATE ENDINGS

Ice clattered off the side of Travis's glass as he mixed his drink with his index finger. Slumped into the leather recliner, he stared absentmindedly into the opaque amber liquid. When he gazed up from his rum, he caught his sister staring at him. "What?" Travis snapped, his voice far harsher than intended.

"Are you going to be a lump for the rest of your life?" Anna asked in a falsetto of concern. When her brother didn't answer her, she continued. "You didn't even love Sally. I think you're more upset that she dumped you before you could pull the trigger yourself."

Travis' lips curled into a grimace as he sipped his drink. "I'm more upset that I've got to spend New Year's Eve with you guys," he said, pointing into the kitchen at their parents. "I can't believe that this is how I'm being forced to ring in the new year."

Anna's gaze wandered over to the window, watching the snowflakes float by, and said, "What's keeping you?"

"The town of Crooked Creek doesn't have a lot to offer," Travis answered. "I've grown far beyond what this dump offers."

"Seems that you can't escape getting dumped," Anna said as a grin crossed her face, bringing out the dimples in her cheeks; a chortle of laughter rocked her entire body.

At a loss for words, Travis drained his drink in two giant gulps and stood up; the ice clanked around the empty glass. He made his way towards the kitchen, staggering around the coffee table, and bumping his leg off the jagged corner. But he felt nothing, his body blissfully numb from the alcohol. "Would you like me to get you a drink?" he asked before leaving the room.

"I'm only seventeen," Anna called out.

Travis stopped dead in his tracks and shook his head. "Is that a yes or a no?"

"That's a big fat no," Travis's mom yelled out from the kitchen.

Travis heard his father's response, barely audible, float in from the kitchen.

"Linda, it's New Year's Eve. Let her have a glass of wine or something."

"I'm not having Anna turn into a party animal. You introduced Travis to the drink and now he's flunked out of university."

Travis's grip tightened around the glass, feeling the first splintering cracks forming against his palm. He wanted to hurl the empty glass into the kitchen sink with all of his might. But that would only add fuel to his mother's assessment. Instead, he took a moment to compose himself before heading into the kitchen. When he felt he had his emotions under control, he stepped into the kitchen.

"Jesus Christ, Linda," his father cursed when he saw Travis standing there.

"If you want to take pity on your son, go right ahead, George." Linda stood up, pushing the chair across the worn hardwood floor. "But you gotta realize that you helped him make his bed." She made her way across the kitchen towards Travis, her floral dress billowing behind her.

George pounded his fist against the table. "Damnit,

Linda, that's far enough."

Linda crashed against the counter as if mortally wounded by her husband's outburst, her fingernails scratching at the stainless steel sink as she braced herself against a fall. With a sour scowl on her face, his mother looked aged far beyond her years. George reached out, placing his hand just below her elbow to steady her. His gaunt frame was a stark contrast to his wife's robust figure. With a swift jab, she swatted George's arm away.

"Mom," Travis sighed, reaching out for his mother's hand.

Yanking her hand back, she refused to make eye contact. A whimpering grunt escaped her throat. "I'm just upset that you failed out of school and wasted all of our money." Flushed with anger, beads of sweat rolled down her face.

"Now, Linda," George said, his voice filled with calm. "You're going to get yourself all worked up. And there's nothing we can do about any of this tonight." Out of nervous habit, George licked at his lips. "Why don't you head back into the living room with your sister?" He snapped his fingers to get Travis' attention. "Don't mind your mother, son. She's just all worked up about last night, is all. I'll get her pills, then we can all head outside for the fireworks."

"What happened last night?"

"Some fellers decked out as mummers stopped by," George began, worked up and speaking a mile-a-minute, his words slurring together. "When we told them no, they started hammering on the door and hollering at us."

"Did you call the cops?"

"Christ no," George spat.

"Why not?" Travis asked. "Is there something wrong with you?"

"Now what's that mean?" It was George's turn to raise his voice.

"You heard about what happened to those two couples on Halloween?"

George nodded his head in approval but didn't offer a response.

"Well, are you brave or fucking stupid?"

Angry, George pushed himself up from the table, the chair skidding across the floor. He stomped over to the door and got himself dressed for outside, his youthful pride enduring with him.

A lump formed in Travis' throat, choking off the apology that he needed to offer. But he simply turned away and wandered back into the living room. Outside, the wind howled against the house; the old foundation groaned in protest as the gathering storm grew in intensity. Wind-driven snow pelted the windows with every gust, drowning out the sound of his sister's voice.

"I said," Anna raised her voice, snapping her fingers. "Did you fail out of university?"

Travis found his way to the recliner, slumping into the familiar leather, keeping his eyes glued to the window to avoid his sister's questioning stare. Defeated, he let out a long sigh, wishing he had made himself another drink.

"What are you going to do?" she asked.

"I don't know," Travis said, his voice a mile away. "Try taking an easier degree, I guess. Maybe business or something."

"School isn't for everyone," Anna said.

After a pregnant pause, Travis found the courage to meet his sister's eyes. When he saw the genuine concern in her eyes for him, he rubbed his hand across his face to stifle a sniffle, dropping his eyes back to the floor.

Anna stood up from her chair and made her way

behind Travis. "It's not the end of the world," she said, stroking his back.

"Kids," George called out from the kitchen. "Time for fireworks in ten minutes." The back door was open, allowing a frigid gust of wind to rip through the old home before George closed it shut behind him.

Saved by his father's timely interruption, Travis wiped a tear away from the corner of his eye. "We should get ready to head outside. You know he will not wait for us."

Anna nodded her head in agreement. "We'll talk about this later?"

"Promise," Travis answered. They went to the porch, grabbed their winter clothes, and got dressed slowly, pulling on scarves, gloves, and toques to combat the crisp winter air that awaited them outside.

George's footsteps crunched through the snow as he paced back and forth across the patio. The sound of the shovel scraping across the frozen boards rumbled through the entire house. Travis dreaded heading out in the cold. He just wanted to put his head on the pillow and sleep. But he realized that this tradition meant a lot to his father. And right now, he owed his father at least this much.

When he stepped outside, the crisp night air assaulted him, stealing his first breath and filling his lungs with ice-cold daggers. He tucked his hands into his jacket pocket, dipping his chin under his collar to protect his face. Above, stars littered a pitch-black sky. A pregnant moon cast a dull yellow glow over the snow-clad backyard, everything it touched tainted by a dull haze. The trees along the edge of his parents' property cast a looming shadow over the edge of the property, acting as a border between civilization and the wild. After growing up at the edge of the woods in Crooked Creek, Travis had grown familiar with the forest in the daytime, but at night, the landscape became unfamiliar and spooky.

George trudged through the snow towards the tree line, the box of fireworks squeezed against his hip. Alongside the shed, a giant stump jutted out of the snow, the axe handle protruding through the dusting of snow from this morning. At the edge of the shadows, he passed the stump, bent down to pick up a bucket from behind, and headed back towards the light, setting the bucket down in the middle of the lawn. Using his hands, he scooped snow into the bucket, filling it. He tore open the box of fireworks and started transplanting them into the bucket.

When he finished, he took out a barbecue lighter and lit the first one. The wick fizzled with a low, reddish-yellow glare before igniting. A hissing whiz echoed in the quiet night sky until it reached its crescendo, ending with a clapping pop. The night lit up with a dazzling glitz of green and red, the glittering debris defying gravity, drifting back to earth at its own pace before dying, never reaching the snow.

"Travis?" Anna pleaded, her voice hesitant as she tugged at his jacket. "Do you see that?"

"Yeah, this night isn't so bad after all."

"Not that," Anna said, jerking Travis's arm with a demanding yank. "Over there, by the shed."

Travis scanned the area as another firework rocketed high into the night sky. For a moment, the darkness consumed the shed, cutting it in half. A brilliant explosion of purple and white lit up the yard. Hidden in the shadow, a looming figure lurked amongst the trees, moving towards the shed.

"Please tell me you saw that too," Anna said, hysteria slithering into her voice.

"I don't know what I saw," Travis answered as the light died, the darkness sweeping over the yard again. "It could have been some bed sheets blown off the line from the summer flapping in the wind." Travis wanted to believe that.

"Dad," Anna called out, trying to get his attention, but the sharp whistle of another firecracker drowned her call out.

This time, as the light brightened the edge of the lawn, the figure appeared next to the shed. "Hey, buddy!" Travis yelled.

Nearly level with the shed's eave, the figure lumbered forward, draped in multi-coloured scarves that distorted the behemoth's abnormal size. Overhead, a firework exploded, sending a twinkling shimmer of sporadic light across the snow-clad lawn. A straw-woven potato sack covered the man's face with two inverted triangular eyeholes carved into the fabric, a smirking smile, drawn in red paint, slashed across the sack.

Oblivious to the stranger behind him, George lit another firework. A dazzling sparkle of light erupted from the wick before a sizzling whistle rocketed into the air. Sparkes of red and green exploded, casting the man's shadow dancing across the lawn, obscuring his movements. The crackling pops of the pyrotechnics drowned Travis's warning cries out. Lurching through the shadows, the ominous figure stalked George, moving in sporadic bursts, freezing every time the sky lit up.

Before Travis could make his way down the stairs, a thundering crash from inside the house froze him in his steps. Anna jumped in surprise, coiling towards the sound with a distraught expression plastered on her face. Travis called out to his mother, and silence answered him from within. Anna took a hesitant step towards the door, her shaky hand reaching out for the handle.

Travis fell back towards the stairs, his hand reaching

out for the railing, using them to haul himself down the stairs faster than his legs could carry him. As he reached the lawn, a sparkling dazzle of brilliant white lit up the night sky. The mummer silhouetted George, an axe raised high above his head, the sparkling light gleaming off the sharpened iron. George smiled at his son, never recognizing the horror distorting Travis's entire face.

"Dad..."

The mummer wedged the blade between George's shoulder and neck, driving the iron with enough force to splinter his collarbone and lodge it deep into the flesh. A gout of blood erupted from the blow, sending a cascading spray of blood across the snow. The mummer gripped the axe tightly, holding George up with ease until the blade slid out of the vicious wound. George collapsed to the ground in a lifeless heap, falling on top of his legs with a sickening crack.

Behind Travis, Anna let out a blood-curdling scream. The stranger in front of Travis began to trudge through the snow towards him, the head of the axe dragging through the snow, leaving behind a snaking trail of gore. If Travis ran down the stairs now, he could beat the stranger to the gate along the side of the house and make a break for it, but he couldn't leave Anna behind.

"Christ," Travis grumbled to himself, forcing himself to turn away from the stairs. "What's happening, Anna?" he called out to his sister, but there was no response. The mummers' footsteps were slow and methodical, the snow crunching loudly beneath each stomp. There wasn't much time for Travis to reconsider his next movement. "If you're in there, you'd better answer me."

With his grasp tightening on the railing, Travis's foot hovered over the steps, ready to flee at the last moment. Just as he made up his mind to leave, his sister's muffled cry rang out, drawing him back towards the back door. He rushed across the patio, the frozen boards creaking against his meagre weight. When he threw open the door, he found Anna standing back on to him. She stumbled backward toward him, blocking his view into the kitchen.

"Anna?"

A jarring shriek escaped her lungs as she spun around to face her brother. Hitching sobs rocked her shoulders, and she leaned into him for comfort. When she leaned her head on his shoulder, the tears spilling from her eyes dripped over his jacket in a torrent.

"Mom's..." Anna tried to say something, but her voice faded away.

Outside, the mummer lumbered up the staircase. The wooden frame rattled against the house as he made his way up. Travis grabbed the bolt hanging from the chain and tried to slide it into place as Anna tugged at his elbow, making it difficult to line the bolt up.

"Travis...mom."

"Not now, Anna." Travis raised his voice, beads of sweat rolling down his forehead as he struggled to lock the door. Somehow, he managed to slide the rusted bolt into place just as the doorknob turned. The chain rattled as the door swung inward until the chain caught. A frigid gust of cold air ripped into the porch, the chain shuddering as the mummer outside tested its durability.

Travis tried to back away from the back door, but Anna was resisting, her hands grasped on the door frame and her feet planted firmly against the floor.

"What's wrong with you?" Travis asked, his voice filled with confusion. The door jerked closed, rattling the entire house.

THUMP THUMP THUMP THUMP THUMP THUMP

"Any mummer's 'loud in?!"

"Go away," Travis yelled at the door. He turned back towards his sister, grabbing her by the shoulders and giving her a good shake. "We need to get out of here."

The strength in Anna's legs gave out, forcing Travis to catch her before she fell into him. "Don't make me go back in there," Anna said, her voice timid.

Travis spun Anna around so that she was facing the kitchen and he was watching the door as it jerked back and forth, the chain link clattering off the metal door. "Just bury your face in my back. I'll guide us out."

With a weak nod, Anna agreed. As Travis turned around, he felt her hands wrap around his waist as she pulled herself tight against his back. He had to drag her forward with him, the toes of her shoes dragging against the worn hardwood floor. When he entered the kitchen, he found his mother at the kitchen table. Her head was against the table, her hair fanned out around her, the white hair dyed blood red by the oozing puddle that had pooled around her. Someone had bashed the back of her head in. Fragments of skull tore through the flesh, the bone-white bits a stark contrast to the blackened ooze gushing from the savage wound.

Bile rushed up Travis's throat, the acidic liquid burning his esophagus on the way up. He raised a hand to cover his mouth. The yellowish-brown liquid spewed out of his pursed lips and sprayed between his fingers, splattering over the floor. Anna's high-pitched scream pierced his eardrum and the door pounded against the frame as the mummer opened and closed it, his maniacal laughter coming in sporadic bursts.

THUMP THUMP THUMP THUMP

"Let... me ... in."

"Go away," Travis yelled. "I called the cops and they're on the way."

He stumbled through the kitchen, his boots slipping in the oily slick of blood and cranial fluids as he passed by his mother's chair. His hand reached out, grasping the counter to keep himself from falling down. Anna pressed her face into Travis's back, the bone of her nose digging in between his shoulder blades, her gasping moans muffled by his jacket. When they reached the living room, Travis broke into a sprint toward the front door, finding it wide open. A wisp of snow had blown into the house, coating the floor and furniture in a thin layer of white.

"Come on," Travis urged his sister, grabbing her by the wrist and hauling her towards the front door.

Before they reached it, a figure stepped from the shadows, blocking the way. Travis halted in his tracks. Anna slammed into his back, nearly toppling them both over. Dressed in a gray sweater that had toy boats knitted into the fabric going around the chest mimicking a child's sweater, the figure ambled into the house. A black pillowcase was draped over their head, the eyes cut in thin slants and rimmed in red, matching the lips of the gaping mouth drawn onto the case. They had drawn gnarled teeth onto the fabric, which stood out in sharp contrast to the black pillowcase.

"Fuck it," Travis said, deciding to run through the mummer in front of him because they weren't as big as the stalker at the back door and he liked his odds here better.

As he took his first step toward the mummer blocking their way, the mummer pulled a knife out from behind their back and waved it across their face. The eight-inch blade caught the harsh light from the porch light, a gleam of white racing up and down as it swayed back and forth. Travis stopped dead in his tracks.

Anna poked her head out from behind Travis and

screamed at the mummer to get lost. The mummer pointed the tip of the blade towards them and tilted their head.

"Any mummers 'loud in?" a woman's voice asked. A shrill fit of cackling laughter erupted from behind the pillowcase.

Suddenly, the thudding at the back door ceased and an eerie silence fell over the house. Footsteps echoed from somewhere inside the house. A stiff wind whistled into the house, tufts of snow blustered around the mummer and swept across the welcome mat. A grinding metallic screech rang out, and the bolt clanked against the back door as it swung open, the breeze tearing through the house now, the curtains billowing.

Heavy footsteps violated the sanctity of the house, thudding against the hardwood. The female mummer in front of them stepped into the house, brandishing the knife in front of her face, forcing them to back peddle toward the sofa.

"Sit," the female mummer demanded.

Travis's heel stubbed the sofa, and he fell into the cushion unceremoniously. Anna sat beside him with far more control and grace. Her legs trembled, her knee knocking against his. Two mummers wandered into the living room from the kitchen, seemingly admiring the photographs on the wall. The largest mummer dragged the axe behind him, the head thrumming off the floor as he went. He took his place behind the female mummer and stared over her shoulder at them.

"Last night, we asked your mother permission to come in," the female mummer said. The two behind her remained silent, their gender unknown. Both figures towered over the female mummer. "All we wanted was to sing a song, dance, and play a little game. But she wouldn't let us."

"So?" Travis snapped.

The female mummer snapped her finger. Without hesitation, the largest mummer raised the axe over his head, the iron head busting through the ceiling, sending a shower of dust sprinkling over their pillowcases. He drove the axe down into Travis's leg, the edge slicing through the flesh with ease and the impact shattering his femur. Travis rolled off the couch and wailed. Blood spurted from his leg, the arterial spray coating the female mummers' yellow rubber boots.

"I wasn't asking you a question." She knelt down in front of Travis, pinning the point of the blade underneath his chin. A bead of blood trickled from the wound as the stainless steel pierced the flesh at the nape of his neck. "Stop the crying. No one is coming to help you."

"Help!" Travis screamed at the top of his lungs.

The woman dragged the knife across his throat, opening a jagged smile that spewed blood over the floor. Travis tried to say something to his sister, but the only sound that came out was a gargling muffle as his voice drowned in the fluids filling his lungs. With his dying breath, Travis lunged forward, his fingers grasping at the pillowcase on the woman's head. It slipped over the back of her head, her hands reaching up to clutch the fabric to her face before he could yank it off. For a moment, Travis held the end of the fabric, his head tilted up at her to glimpse her face. But before he could reveal her identity, he collapsed to the floor, his life essence spilled over the living room floor.

"Why are you doing this?" Anna asked, sobbing.

"Because you were home." The other mummer said, his voice deep and booming. He stepped in front of the female mummer and reached over, grabbing the knife out of her hand. "Now it's my turn to have a little fun."

Anna bolted between his legs, her hands slipping through the blood oozing from her brother's throat. The large mummer reached down to grab her, but she rolled to the side and into the female mummer's legs, sending her toppling over into the coffee table, crashing through the glass top. She cried out in agony as red blotches dotted her tattered clothing in an instant.

Desperate, Anna kicked her leg behind her, the heel of her boot connecting with the man's shin. He howled in pain, hopping on one leg. And before the biggest mummer could lunge toward her again, she got to her feet and dashed for the door. The fresh air of freedom filled her lungs for a moment. Before she reached the front door, she glimpsed the outside world. The night sky lit up with fireworks firing from all angles, the brilliant colours captured against the sodden gray clouds hanging low in the sky.

As the fresh air kissed Anna's face, she heard a powerful grunt behind her. She made it two more steps before something hard struck her in the back of the head. Her vision blurred, and the world around her spun out of control. She fell forward, her hands bracing her fall, but the ice buildup on the walkway tore the flesh from her hands in large stripes. Beside her, the axe lay on the walkway within her grasp. She reached out for the worn wooden handle covered in deep red stains and flecks of gore. With every ounce of strength remaining in her body, she dragged the axe toward her, the iron scrapping off the ice. Before she could pick it up, a boot stomped on her wrist, snapping the bones with ease.

The mummer reached down, covering Anna's mouth with his mammoth hand, her dying screams muffled by the faux leather glove. He locked her in a bear hug, squeezing the breath from her lungs in a rush of soundless air that passed between her lips. Anna tried to move, but the man overpowered her, dragging her back inside with ease. He slammed the door behind him to keep her dying screams from being heard over the celebratory fireworks ringing in the New Year.

ACKNOWLEDGMENTS

As always, I wouldn't have been able to write these stories without the support of my wife, Leah. Thank you for allowing me to type away on my computer as the kids roam free throughout the house. And for taking the time to read my stories, which I know aren't your cup of tea. Thank you.

Thank you to the entire team over at Engen Books for your unwavering support of my work. Without everyone pulling together to make these stories a book, they would just be words left on a Word document on my computer. Sometimes I wonder if that's where they should be kept, but for another year, the Engen team makes this work.

Thanks to my family and friends for your support and for promoting my books to everyone you know. Every little bit counts and means the world to me.

And as always, thank you to the readers for buying this book. I wouldn't be doing this without you.

ABOUT THE AUTHOR

Paul Carberry is a huge proponent of the horror genre and its place in literature. He has two children, daughter Dana and son Rick, with his wife Leah.

Previously, Paul has published six novels with Engen Books: the four-novel *Zombies on the Rock* series, *Carcharodon*, *The Last of the Dragons* and *The Cottage Across the Lake*.

The Gray Chapter collects his numerous short stories featured in publication in anthologies such as *From the Rock* and *Terror Nova*, including The Light of Cabot Tower, Into the Forest, and Halloween Mummers.